WITHDRAWN

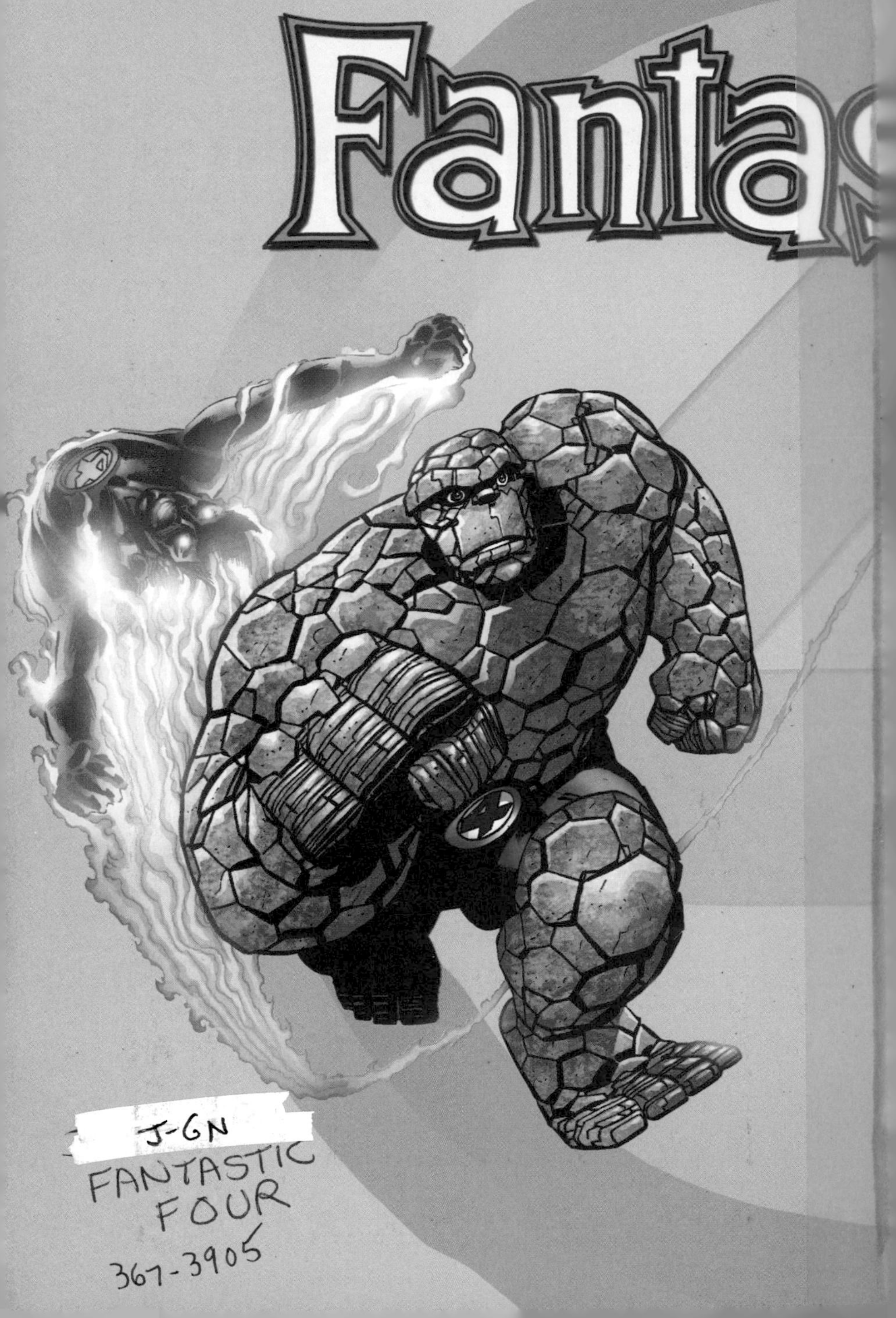
Fantas

STIC FOUR

FANTASTIC VOYAGES

Writer:
Jeff Parker
Pencils:
Manuel Garcia

Inks: **Scott Koblish**
Colors: **Sotocolor's A. Crossley**
Letters: **Dave Sharpe**
Covers: **Juan Santacruz, Carlo Pagulayan, Jeffrey Huet, Raul Fernandez & Chris Sotomayor**
Assistant Editor: **Nathan Cosby**
Editor: **Mark Paniccia**
Consulting Editor: **MacKenzie Cadenhead**

Assistant Editor: **Michael Short**
Senior Editor, Special Projects: **Jeff Youngquist**
Vice President of Sales: **David Gabriel**
Book Designer: **Jerron Quality Color**
Vice President of Creative: **Tom Marvelli**

Editor in Chief: **Joe Quesada**
Publisher: **Dan Buckley**

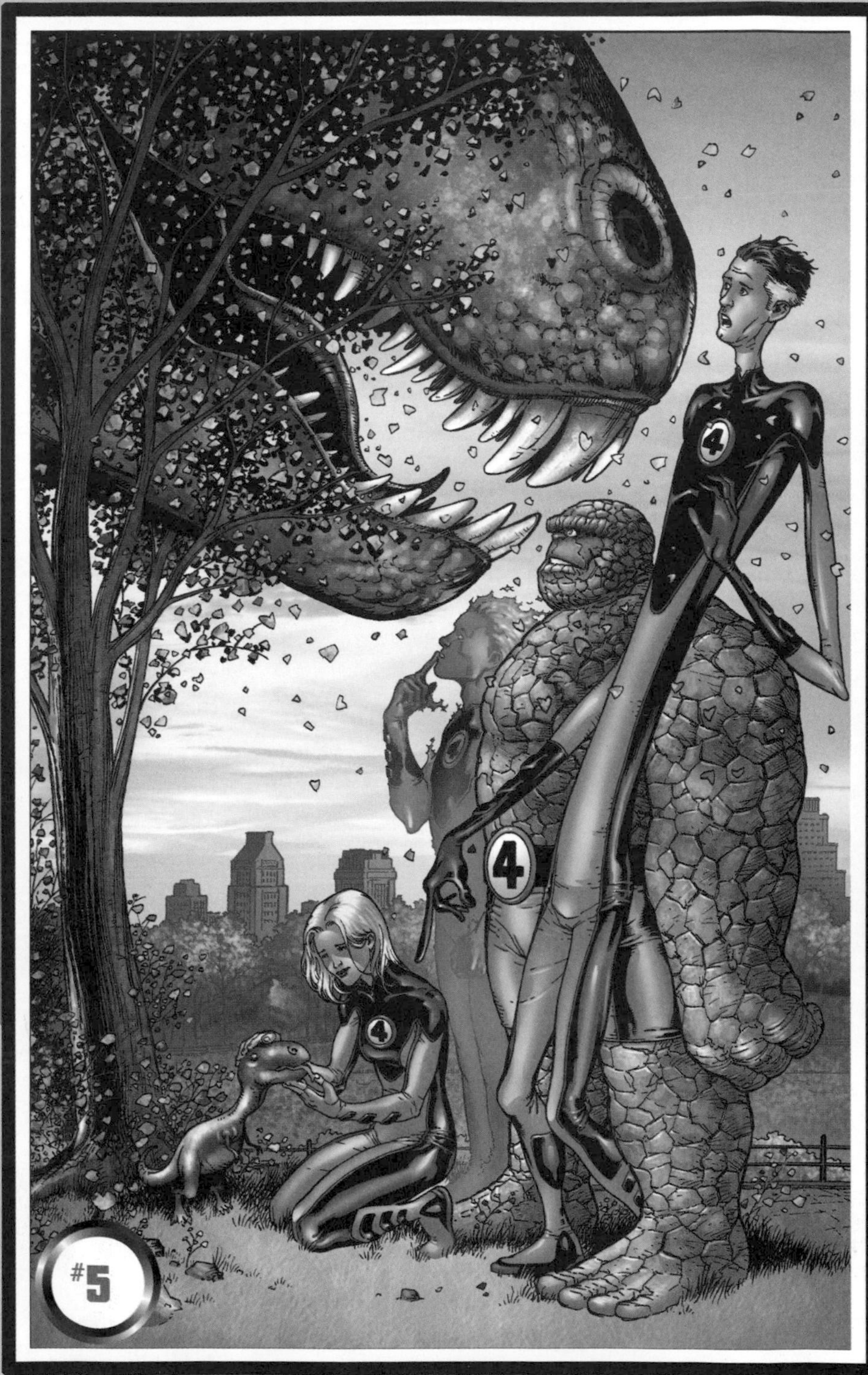
#5

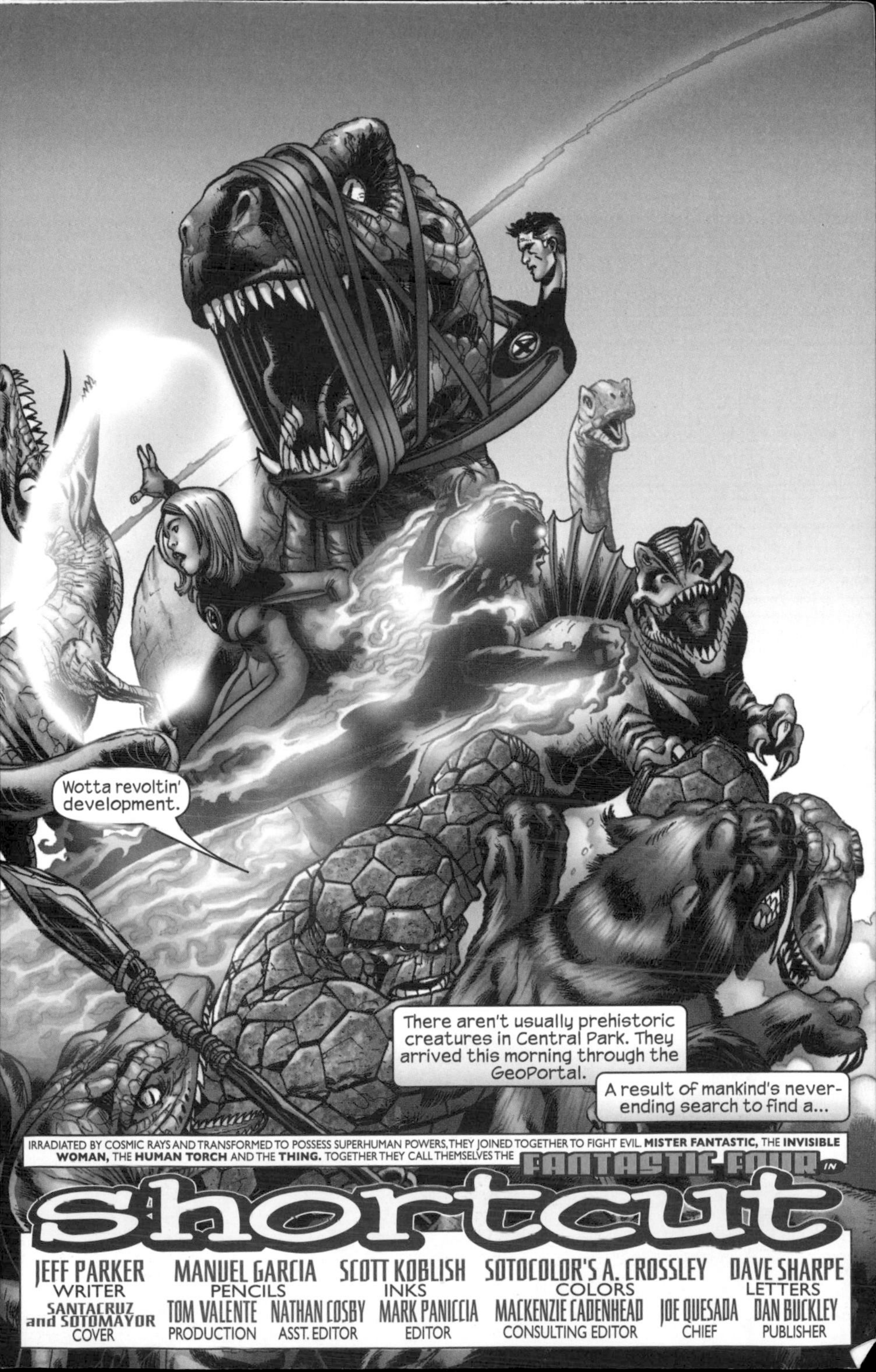

Wotta revoltin' development.
There aren't usually prehistoric creatures in Central Park. They arrived this morning through the GeoPortal.
A result of mankind's never-ending search to find a...
IRRADIATED BY COSMIC RAYS AND TRANSFORMED TO POSSESS SUPERHUMAN POWERS, THEY JOINED TOGETHER TO FIGHT EVIL. MISTER FANTASTIC, THE INVISIBLE WOMAN, THE HUMAN TORCH AND THE THING. TOGETHER THEY CALL THEMSELVES THE FANTASTIC FOUR IN
shortcut
JEFF PARKER WRITER
MANUEL GARCIA PENCILS
SCOTT KOBLISH INKS
SOTOCOLOR'S A. CROSSLEY COLORS
DAVE SHARPE LETTERS
SANTACRUZ and SOTOMAYOR COVER
TOM VALENTE PRODUCTION
NATHAN COSBY ASST. EDITOR
MARK PANICCIA EDITOR
MACKENZIE CADENHEAD CONSULTING EDITOR
JOE QUESADA CHIEF
DAN BUCKLEY PUBLISHER

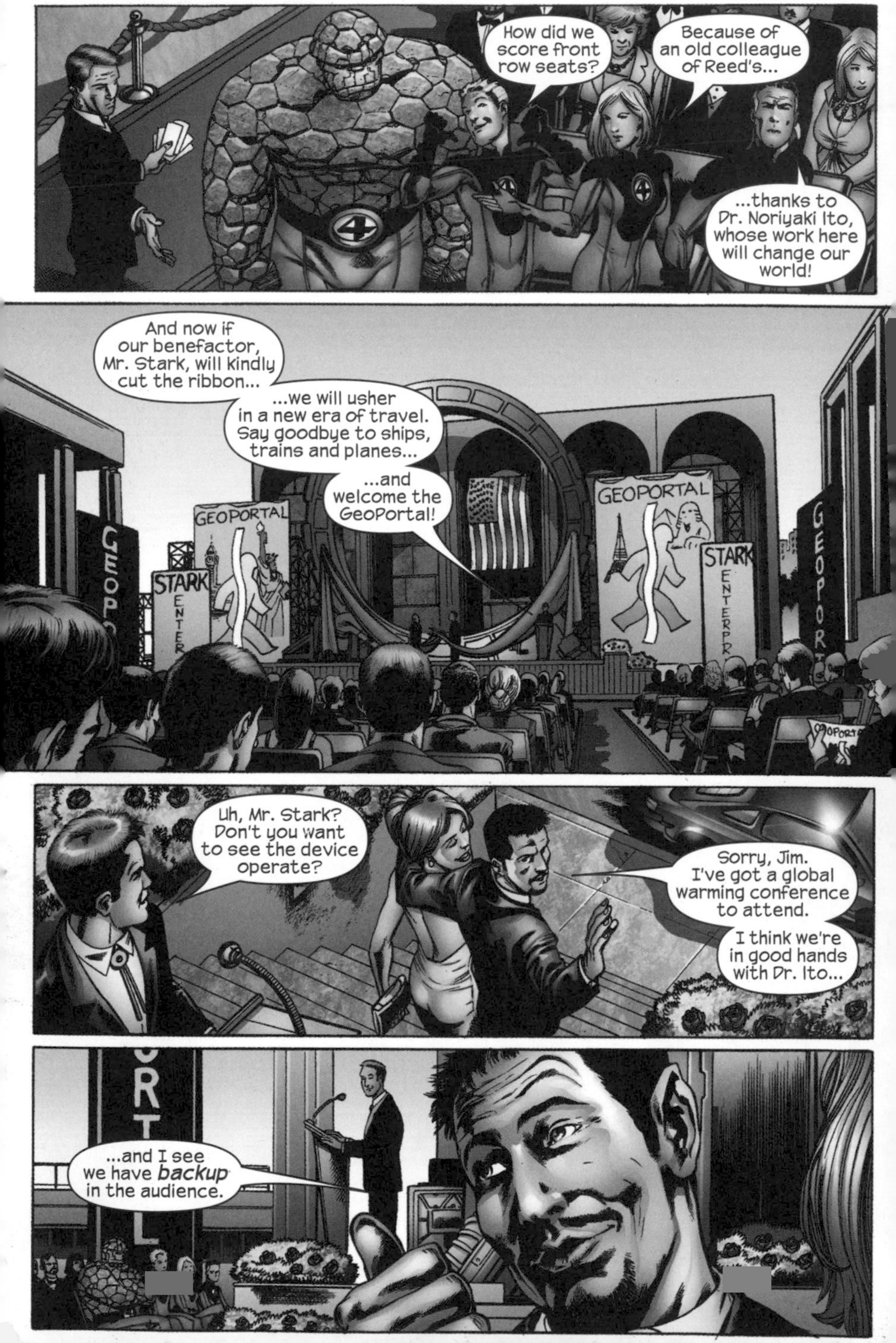
How did we score front row seats?
Because of an old colleague of Reed's...
...thanks to Dr. Noriyaki Ito, whose work here will change our world!
And now if our benefactor, Mr. Stark, will kindly cut the ribbon...
...we will usher in a new era of travel. Say goodbye to ships, trains and planes...
...and welcome the GeoPortal!
GEOPORTAL
STARK ENTER
GEOPORTAL
STARK ENTERPR
Uh, Mr. Stark? Don't you want to see the device operate?
Sorry, Jim. I've got a global warming conference to attend.
I think we're in good hands with Dr. Ito...
...and I see we have *backup* in the audience.

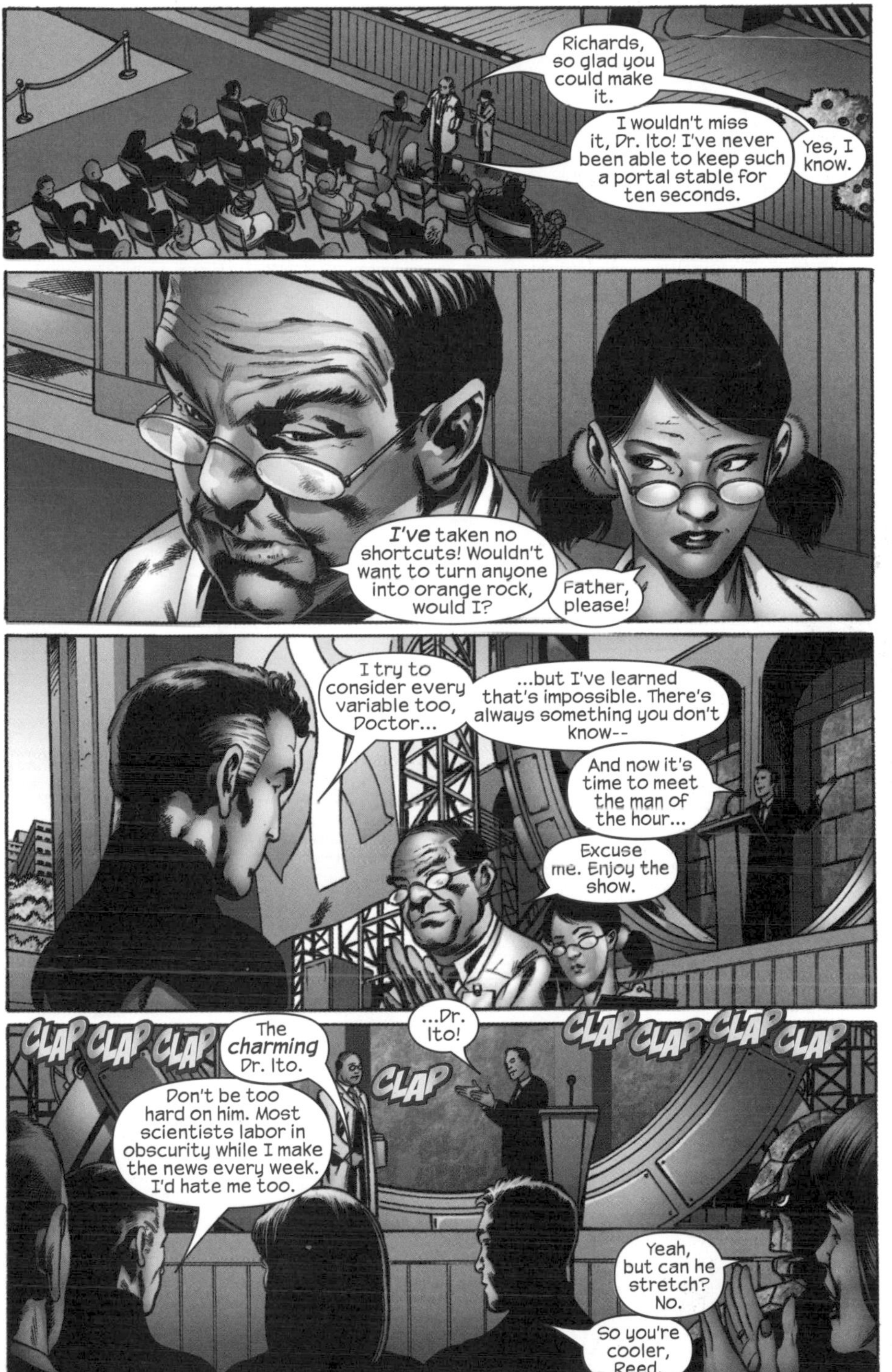
Richards, so glad you could make it.
I wouldn't miss it, Dr. Ito! I've never been able to keep such a portal stable for ten seconds.
Yes, I know.
I've taken no shortcuts! Wouldn't want to turn anyone into orange rock, would I?
Father, please!
I try to consider every variable too, Doctor...
...but I've learned that's impossible. There's always something you don't know--
And now it's time to meet the man of the hour...
Excuse me. Enjoy the show.
CLAP CLAP CLAP
The *charming* Dr. Ito.
...Dr. Ito!
CLAP
CLAP CLAP CLAP CLAP
Don't be too hard on him. Most scientists labor in obscurity while I make the news every week. I'd hate me too.
Yeah, but can he stretch? No.
So you're cooler, Reed.

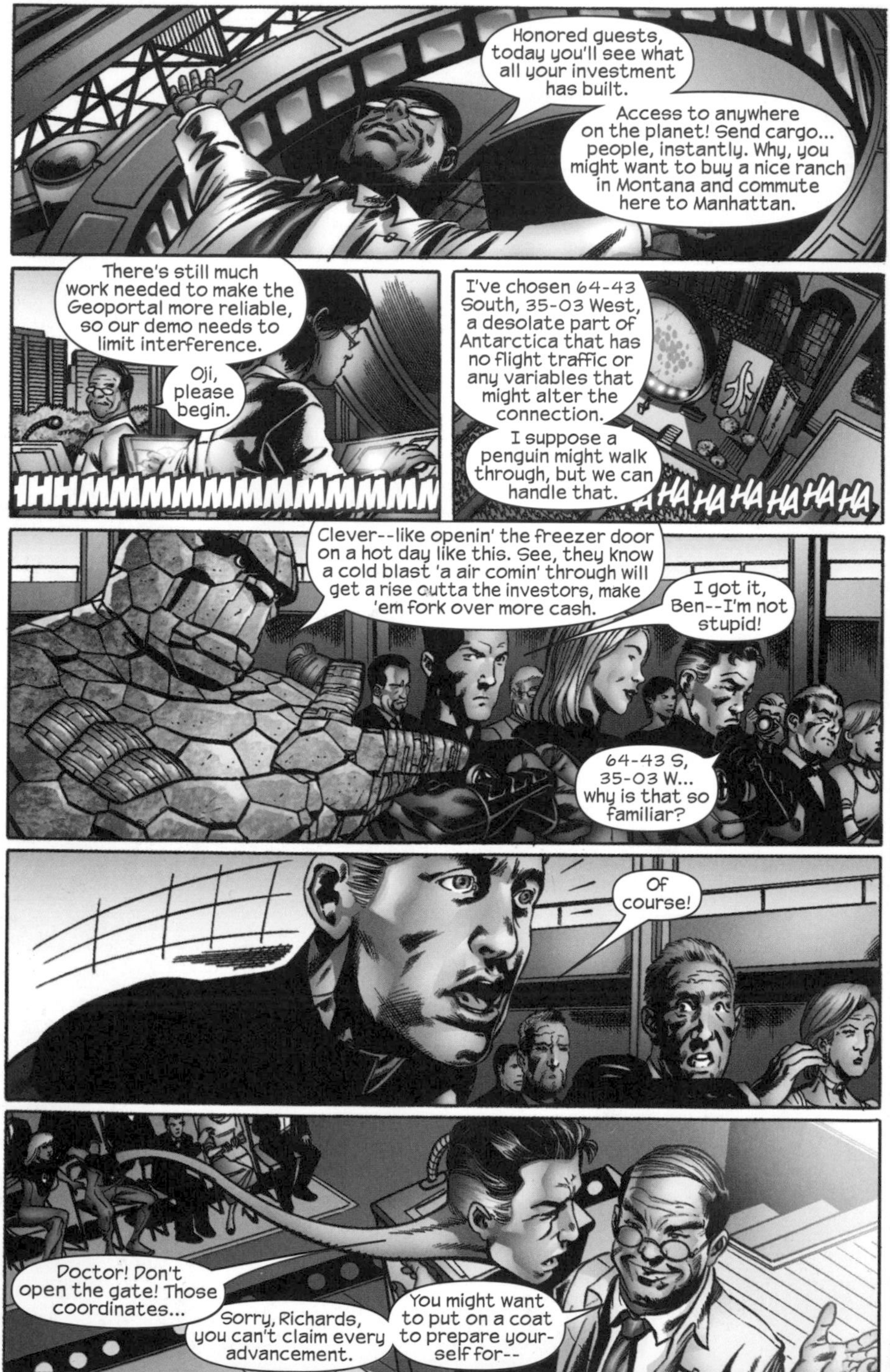
Honored guests, today you'll see what all your investment has built.
Access to anywhere on the planet! Send cargo... people, instantly. Why, you might want to buy a nice ranch in Montana and commute here to Manhattan.
There's still much work needed to make the Geoportal more reliable, so our demo needs to limit interference.
Oji, please begin.
HHMMMMMMMMMMMMMN
I've chosen 64-43 South, 35-03 West, a desolate part of Antarctica that has no flight traffic or any variables that might alter the connection.
I suppose a penguin might walk through, but we can handle that.
HA HA HA HA HA HA HA
Clever--like openin' the freezer door on a hot day like this. See, they know a cold blast 'a air comin' through will get a rise outta the investors, make 'em fork over more cash.
I got it, Ben--I'm not stupid!
64-43 S, 35-03 W... why is that so familiar?
Of course!
Doctor! Don't open the gate! Those coordinates...
Sorry, Richards, you can't claim every advancement.
You might want to put on a coat to prepare your-self for--

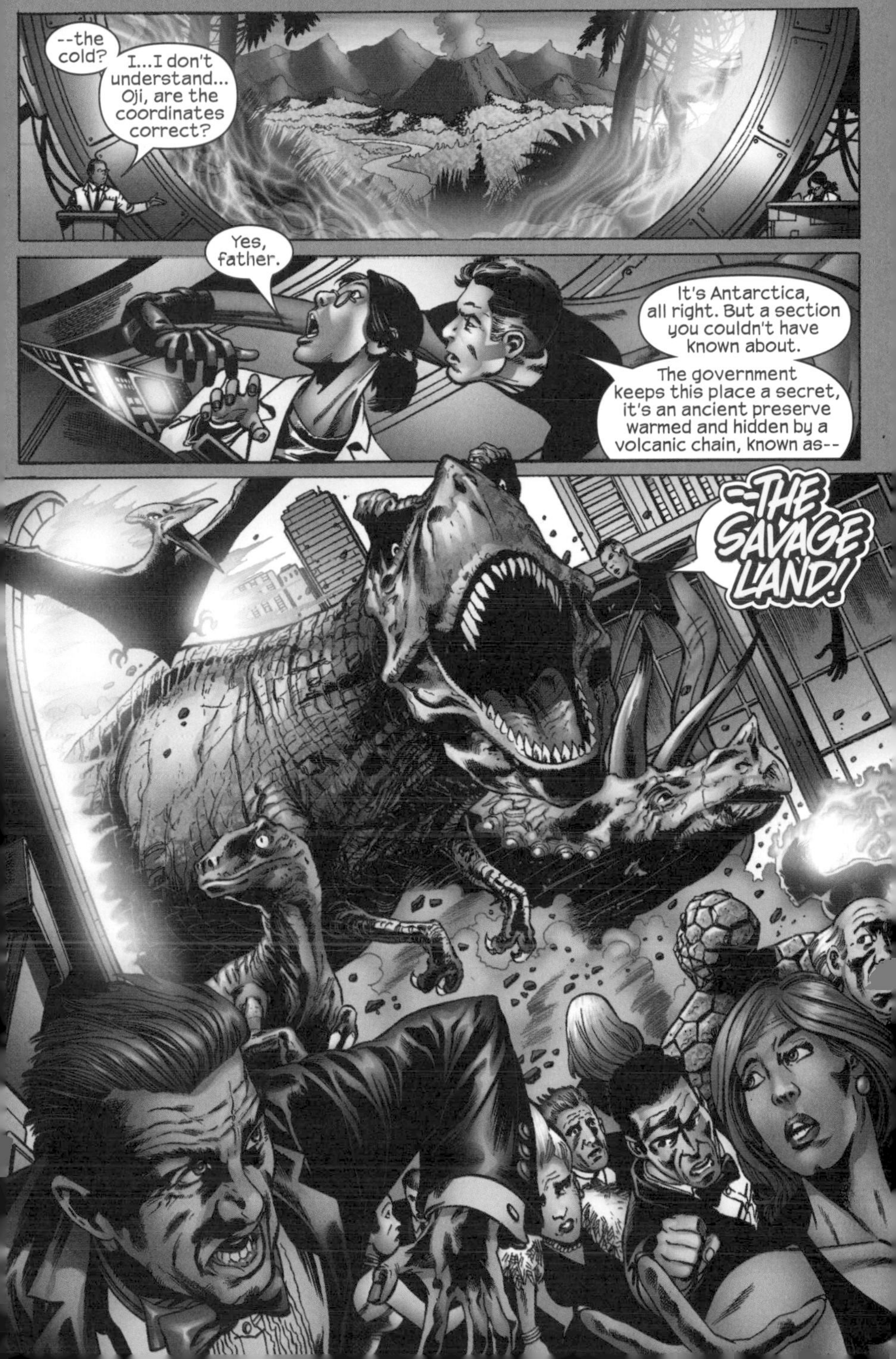
--the cold?
I...I don't understand... Oji, are the coordinates correct?
Yes, father.
It's Antarctica, all right. But a section you couldn't have known about.
The government keeps this place a secret, it's an ancient preserve warmed and hidden by a volcanic chain, known as--
--THE SAVAGE LAND!

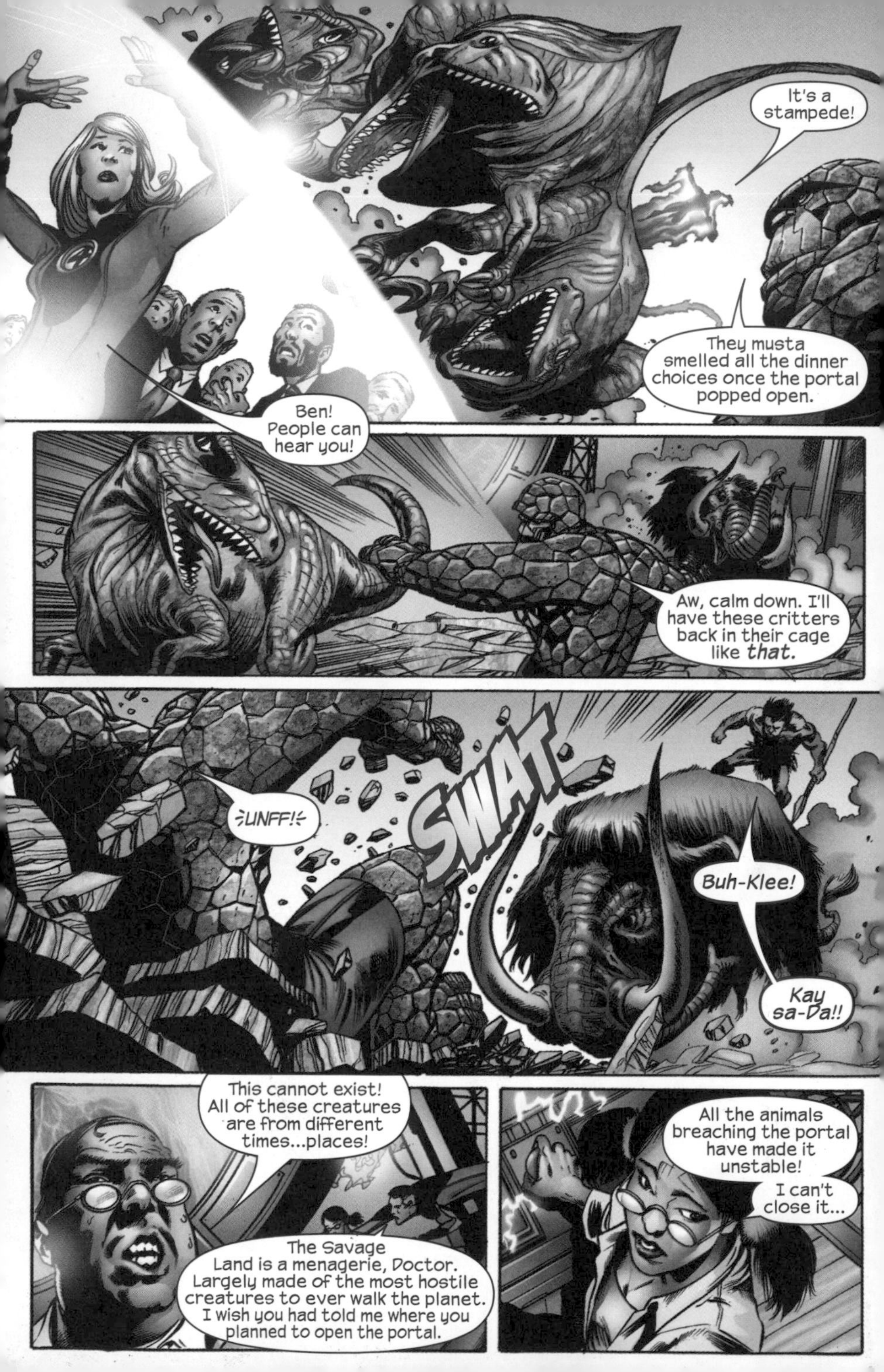

It's a stampede!
They musta smelled all the dinner choices once the portal popped open.
Ben! People can hear you!
Aw, calm down. I'll have these critters back in their cage like *that.*
UNFF!
SWAT
Buh-Klee!
Kay sa-Da!!
This cannot exist! All of these creatures are from different times...places!
The Savage Land is a menagerie, Doctor. Largely made of the most hostile creatures to ever walk the planet. I wish you had told me where you planned to open the portal.
All the animals breaching the portal have made it unstable!
I can't close it...

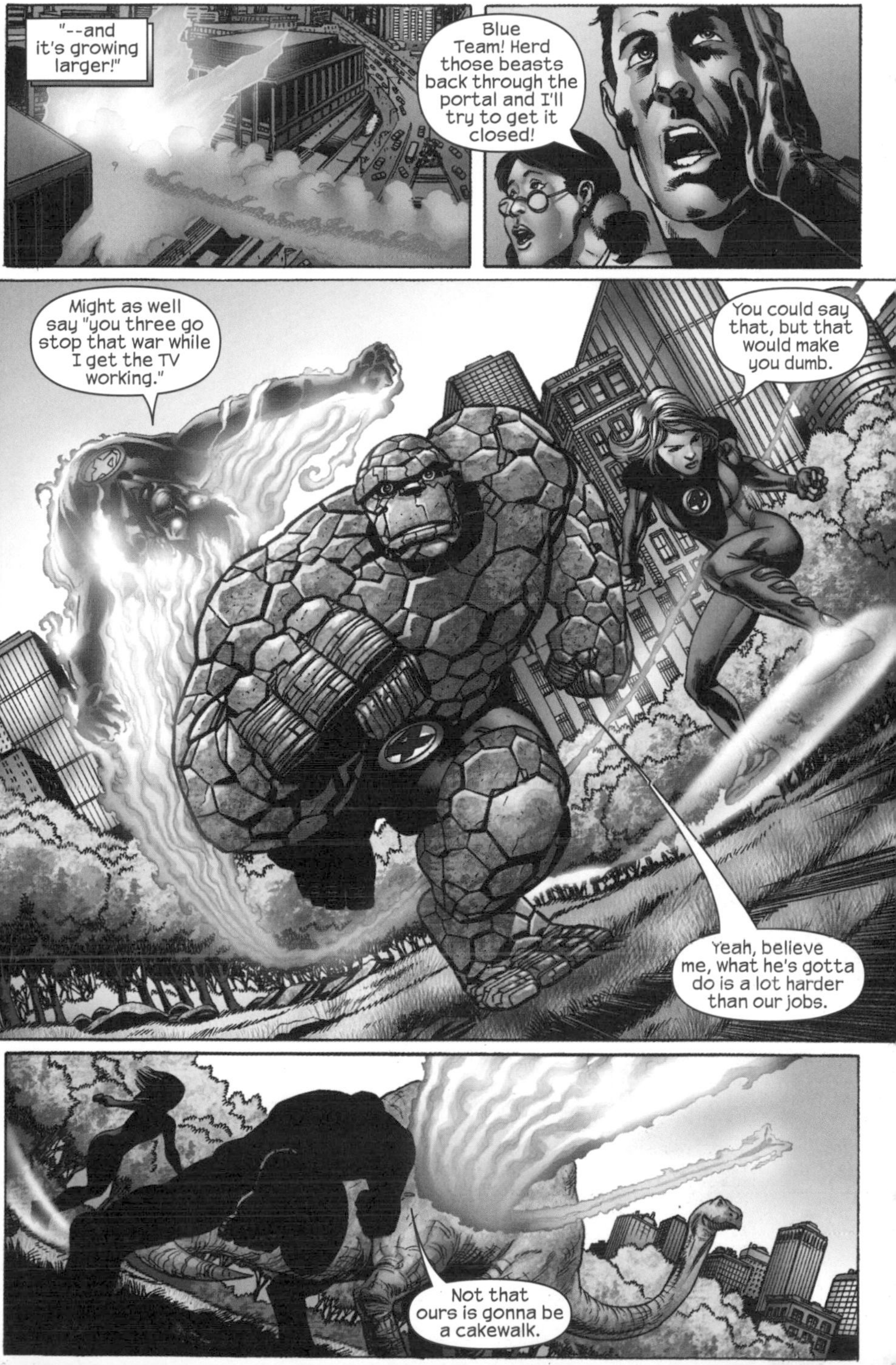
"--and it's growing larger!"
Blue Team! Herd those beasts back through the portal and I'll try to get it closed!
Might as well say "you three go stop that war while I get the TV working."
You could say that, but that would make you dumb.
Yeah, believe me, what he's gotta do is a lot harder than our jobs.
Not that ours is gonna be a cakewalk.

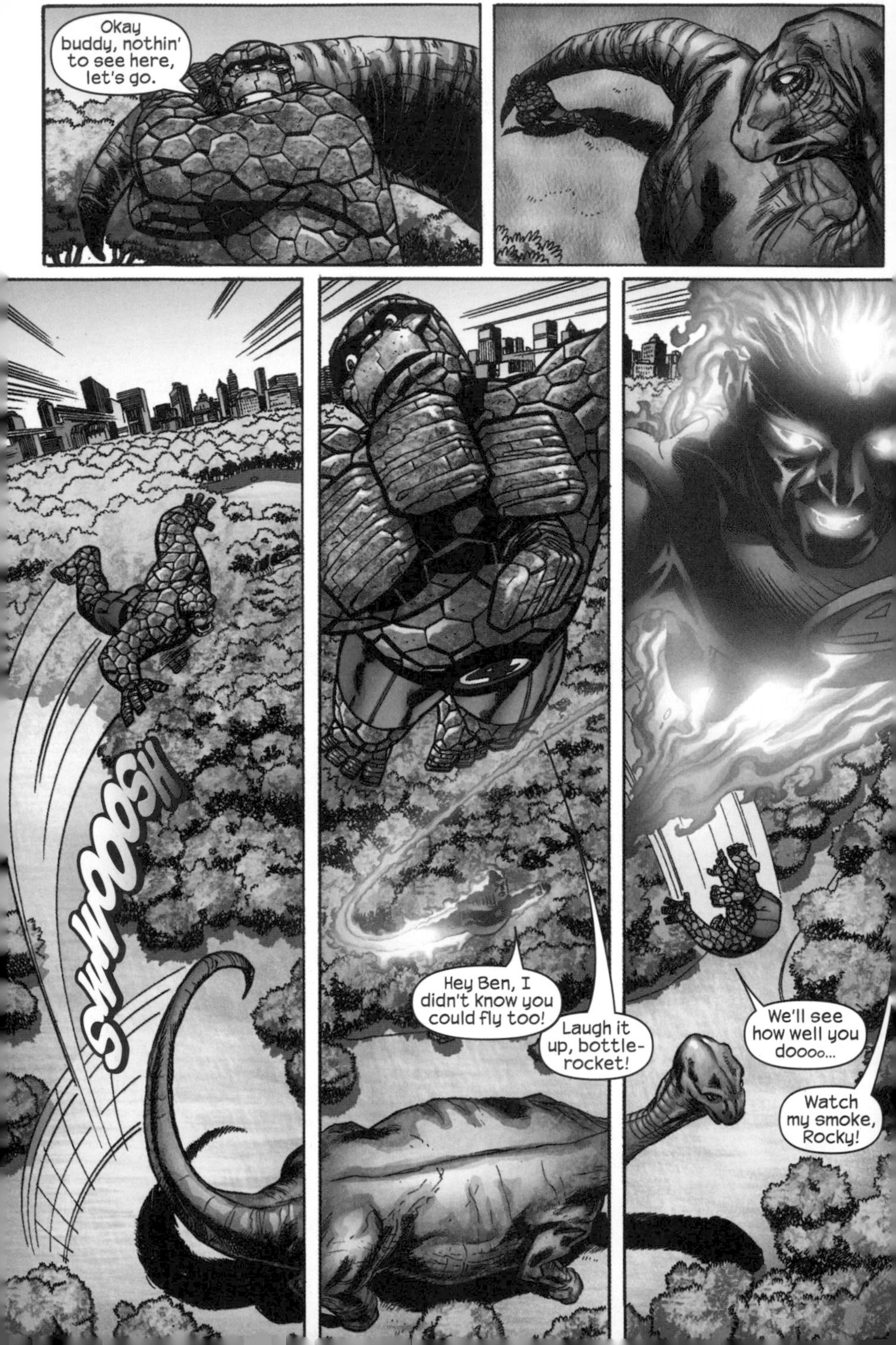
Okay buddy, nothin' to see here, let's go.
SWHOOOSH
Hey Ben, I didn't know you could fly too!
Laugh it up, bottle-rocket!
We'll see how well you doooo...
Watch my smoke, Rocky!

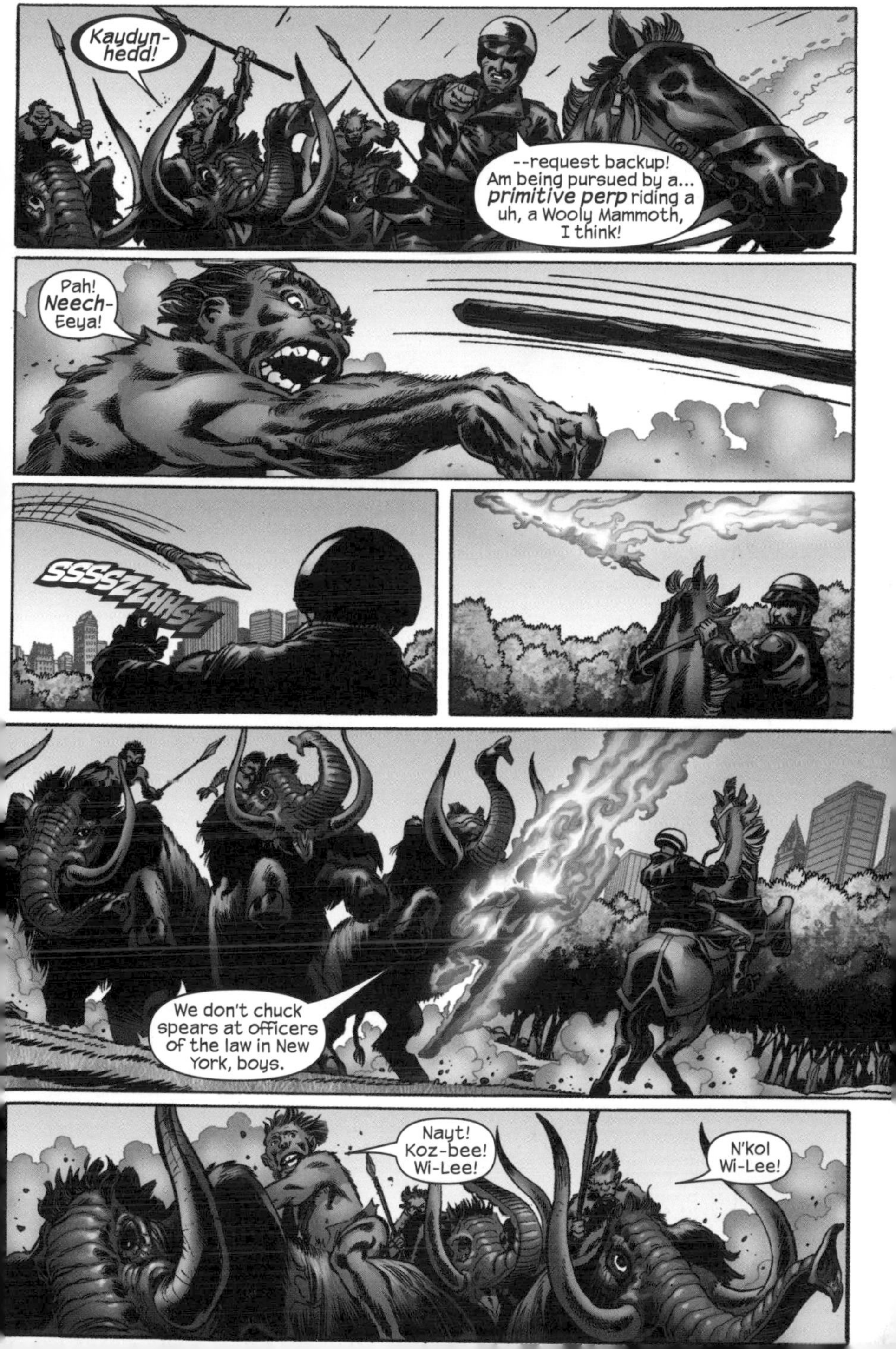
Kaydyn-hedd!
--request backup! Am being pursued by a... primitive perp riding a uh, a Wooly Mammoth, I think!
Pah! Neech-Eeya!
SSSSZZHHSZ
We don't chuck spears at officers of the law in New York, boys.
Nayt! Koz-bee! Wi-Lee!
N'kol Wi-Lee!

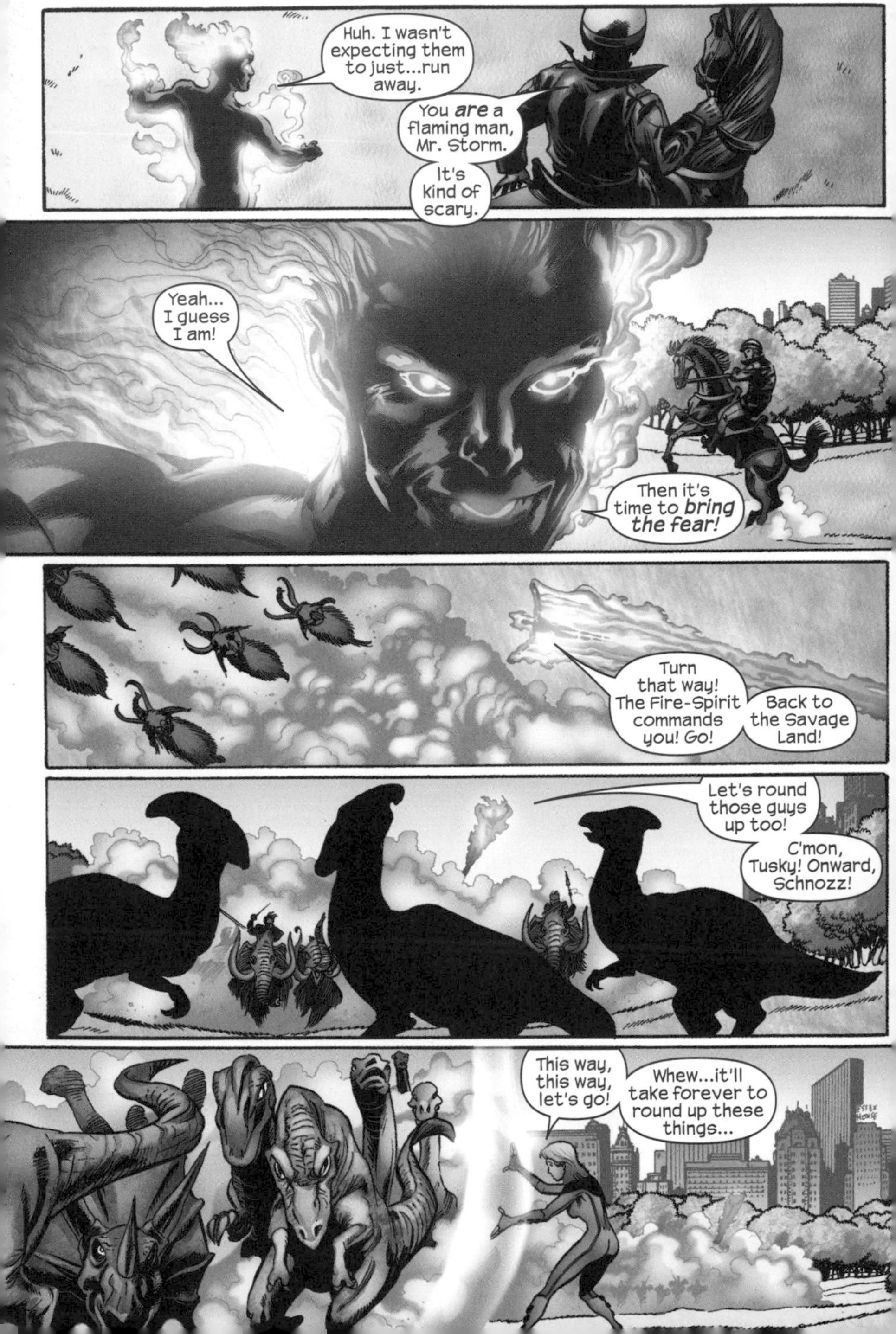
Huh. I wasn't expecting them to just...run away.
You **are** a flaming man, Mr. Storm.
It's kind of scary.
Yeah... I guess I am!
Then it's time to ***bring the fear!***
Turn that way! The Fire-Spirit commands you! Go!
Back to the Savage Land!
Let's round those guys up too!
C'mon, Tusky! Onward, Schnozz!
This way, this way, let's go!
Whew...it'll take forever to round up these things...

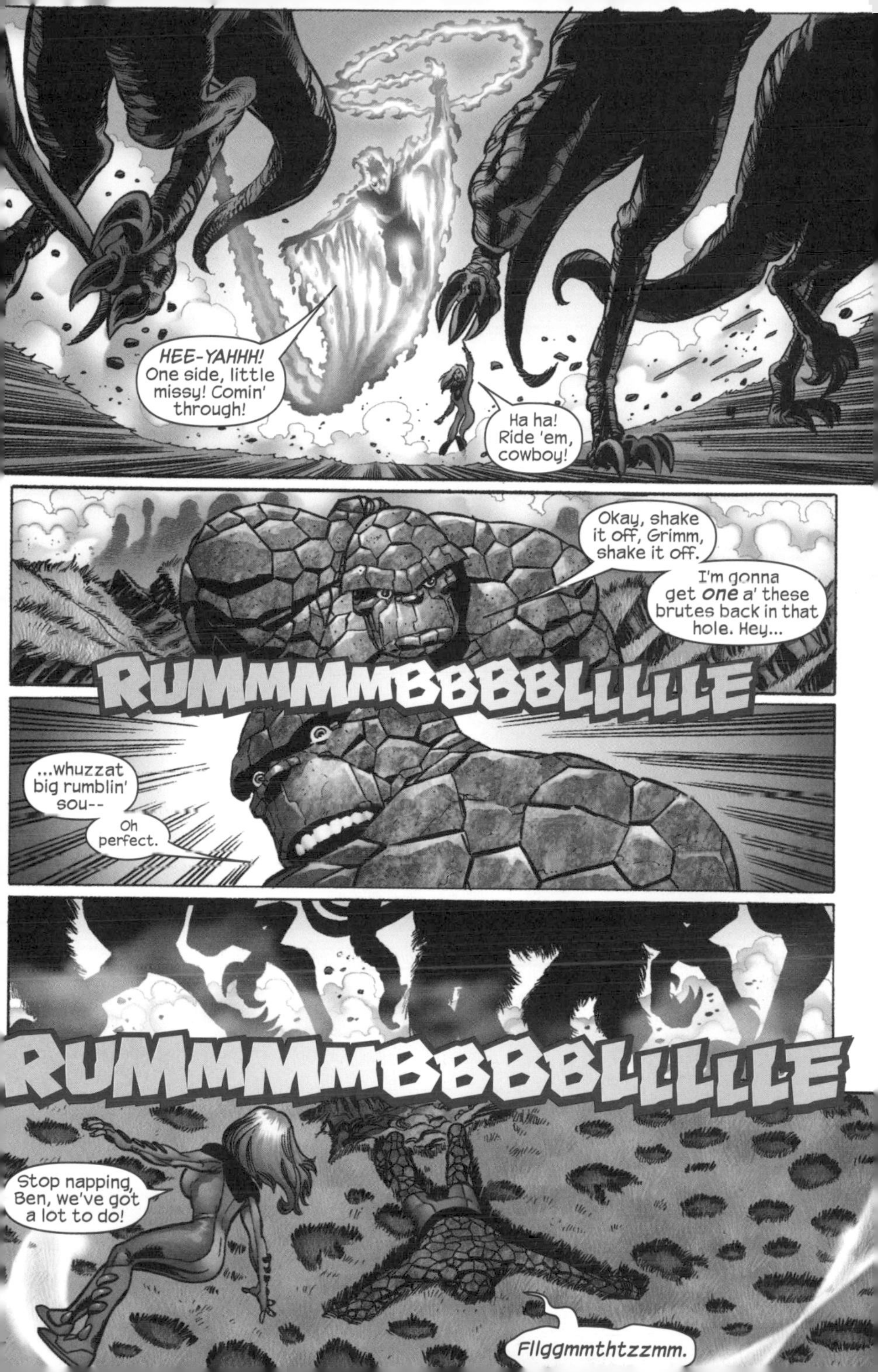
HEE-YAHHH! One side, little missy! Comin' through!
Ha ha! Ride 'em, cowboy!
Okay, shake it off, Grimm, shake it off.
I'm gonna get *one* a' these brutes back in that hole. Hey...
RUMMMMMBBBBLLLLLE
...whuzzat big rumblin' sou--
Oh perfect.
RUMMMMMBBBBLLLLLE
Stop napping, Ben, we've got a lot to do!
Fllggmmthtzzmm.

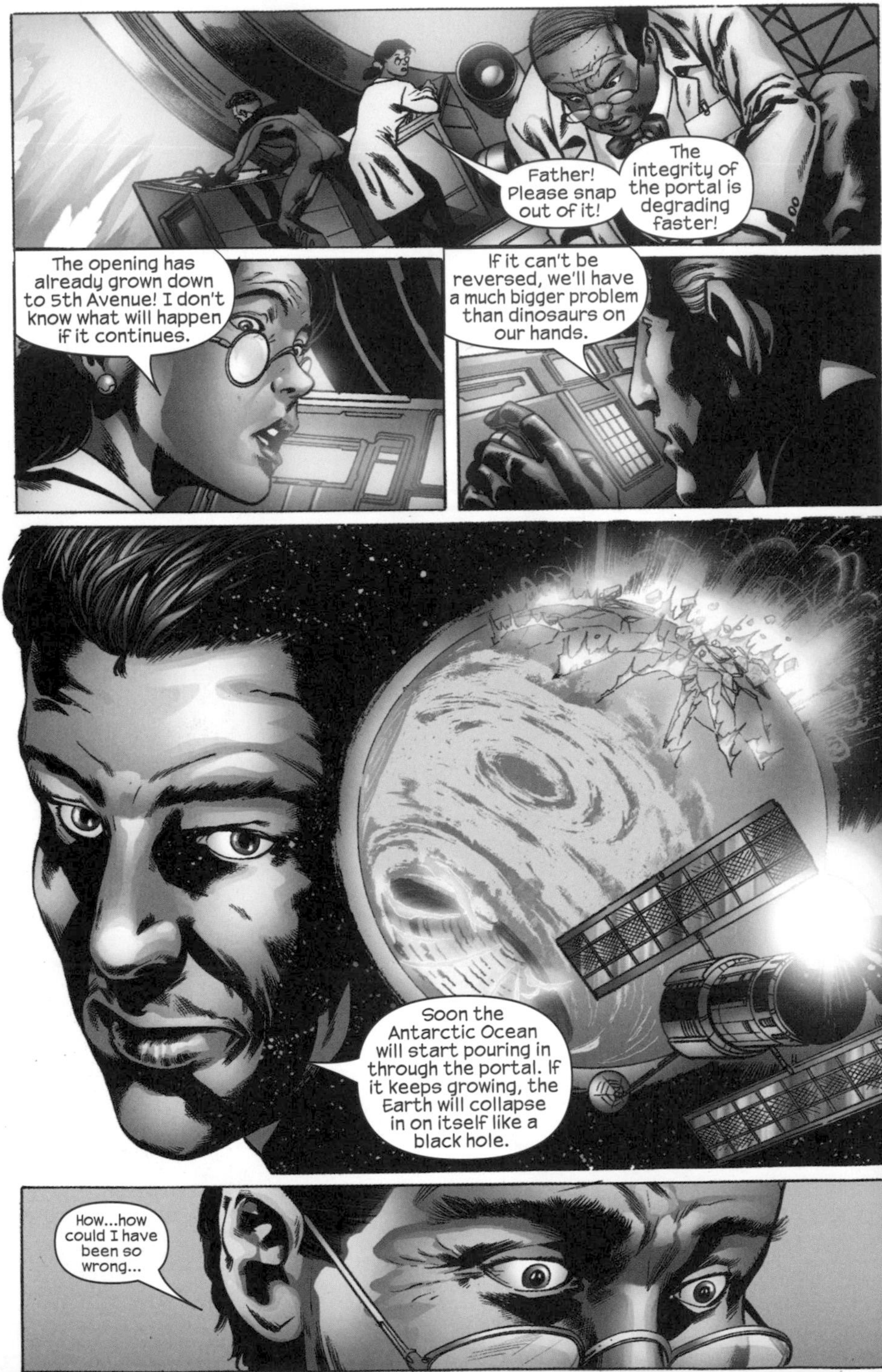
Father! Please snap out of it!
The integrity of the portal is degrading faster!
The opening has already grown down to 5th Avenue! I don't know what will happen if it continues.
If it can't be reversed, we'll have a much bigger problem than dinosaurs on our hands.
Soon the Antarctic Ocean will start pouring in through the portal. If it keeps growing, the Earth will collapse in on itself like a black hole.
How...how could I have been so wrong...

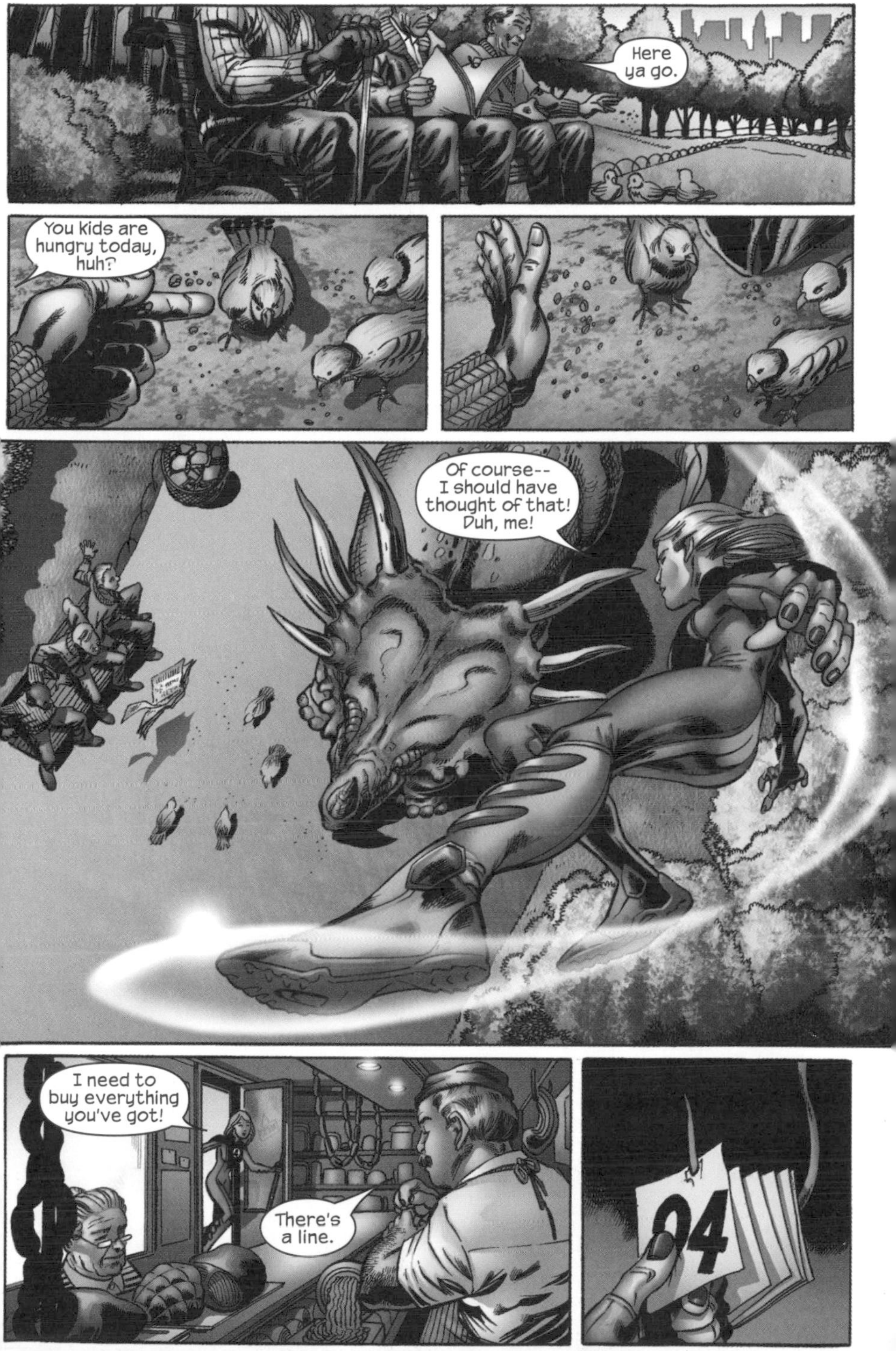
Here ya go.
You kids are hungry today, huh?
Of course-- I should have thought of that! Duh, me!
I need to buy everything you've got!
There's a line.
04

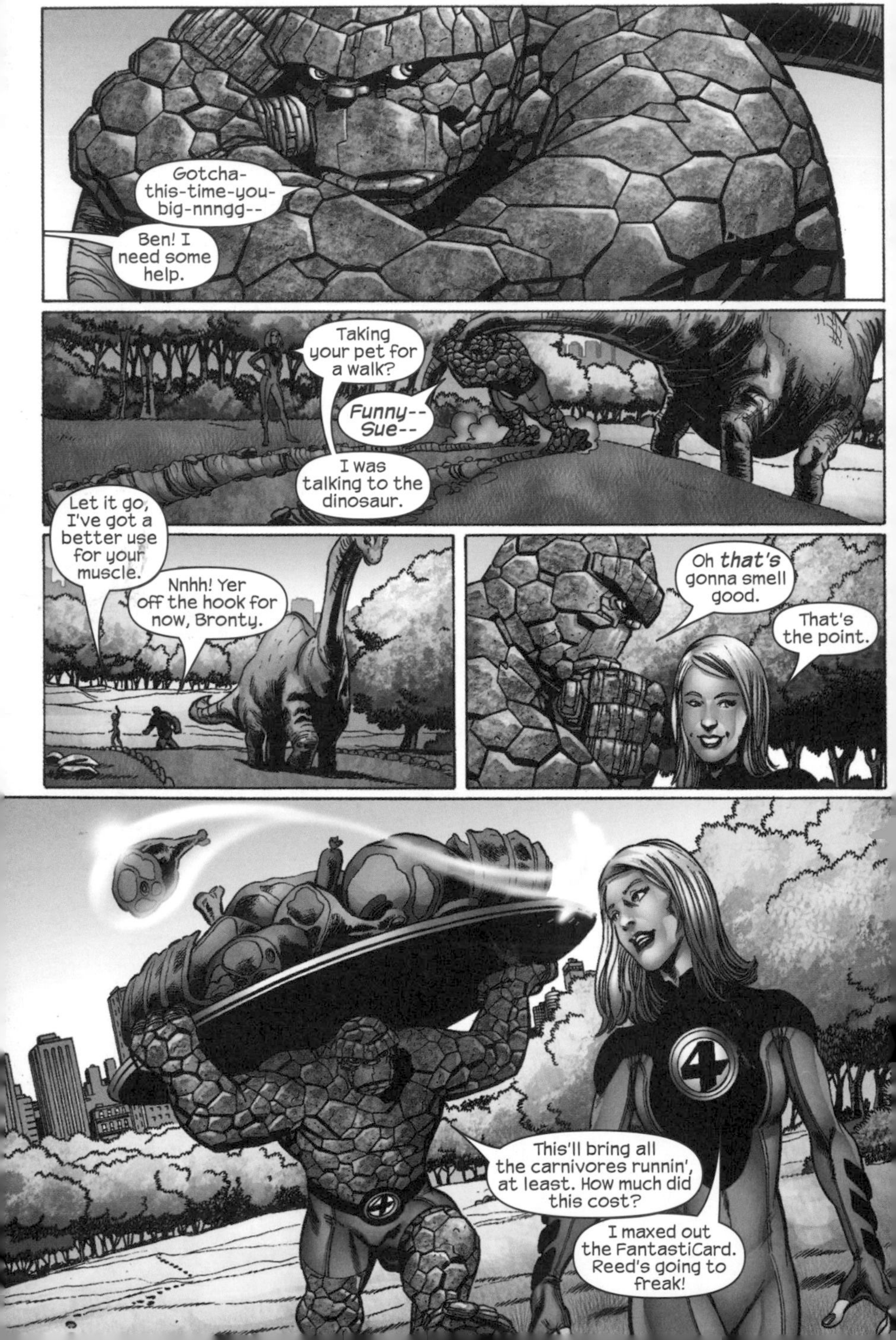
Gotcha-this-time-you-big-nnngg--
Ben! I need some help.
Taking your pet for a walk?
Funny-- Sue--
I was talking to the dinosaur.
Let it go, I've got a better use for your muscle.
Nnhh! Yer off the hook for now, Bronty.
Oh that's gonna smell good.
That's the point.
This'll bring all the carnivores runnin', at least. How much did this cost?
I maxed out the FantastiCard. Reed's going to freak!

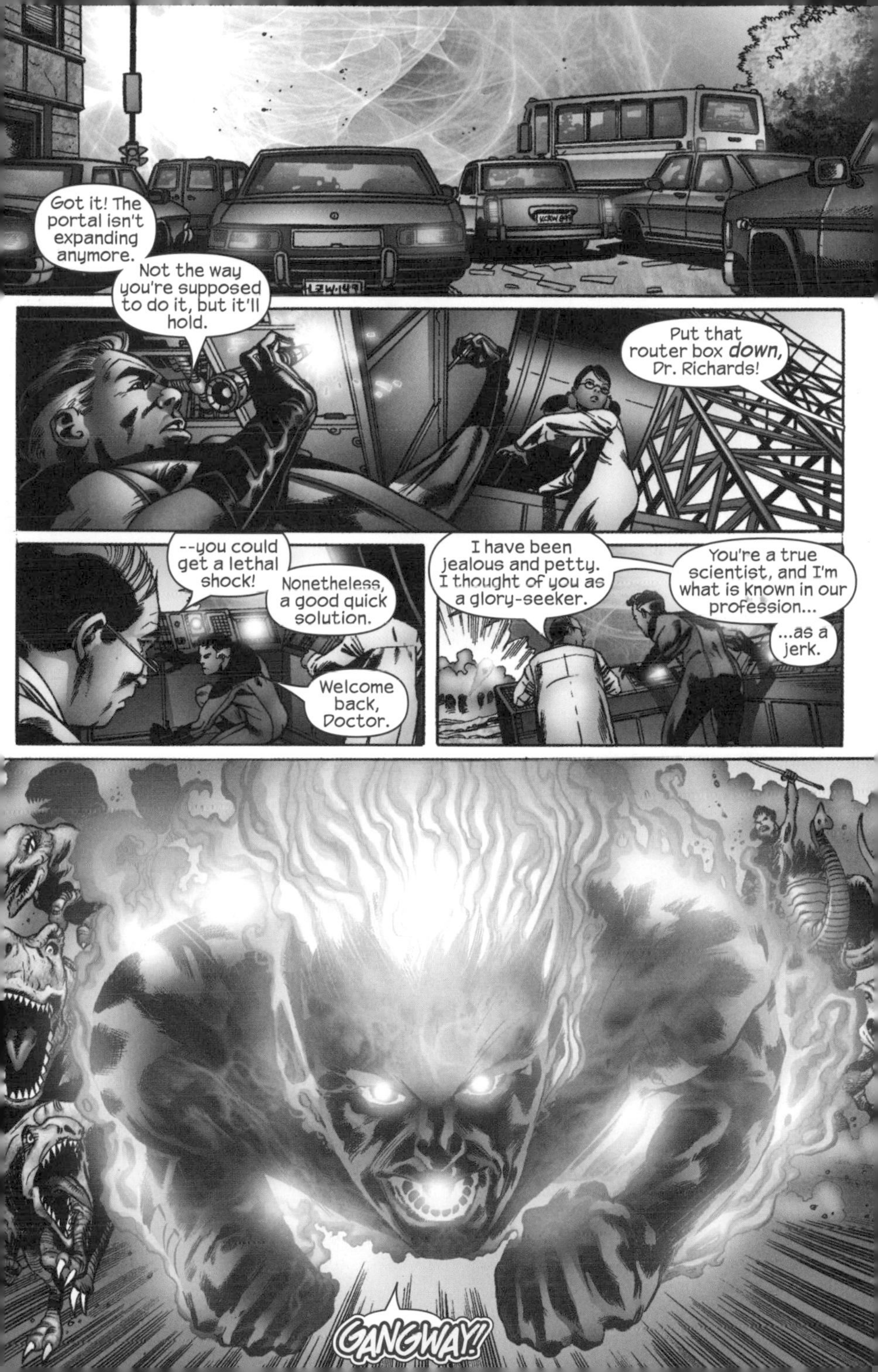
Got it! The portal isn't expanding anymore.
Not the way you're supposed to do it, but it'll hold.
Put that router box *down,* Dr. Richards!
--you could get a lethal shock!
Nonetheless, a good quick solution.
Welcome back, Doctor.
I have been jealous and petty. I thought of you as a glory-seeker.
You're a true scientist, and I'm what is known in our profession...
...as a jerk.
GANGWAY!

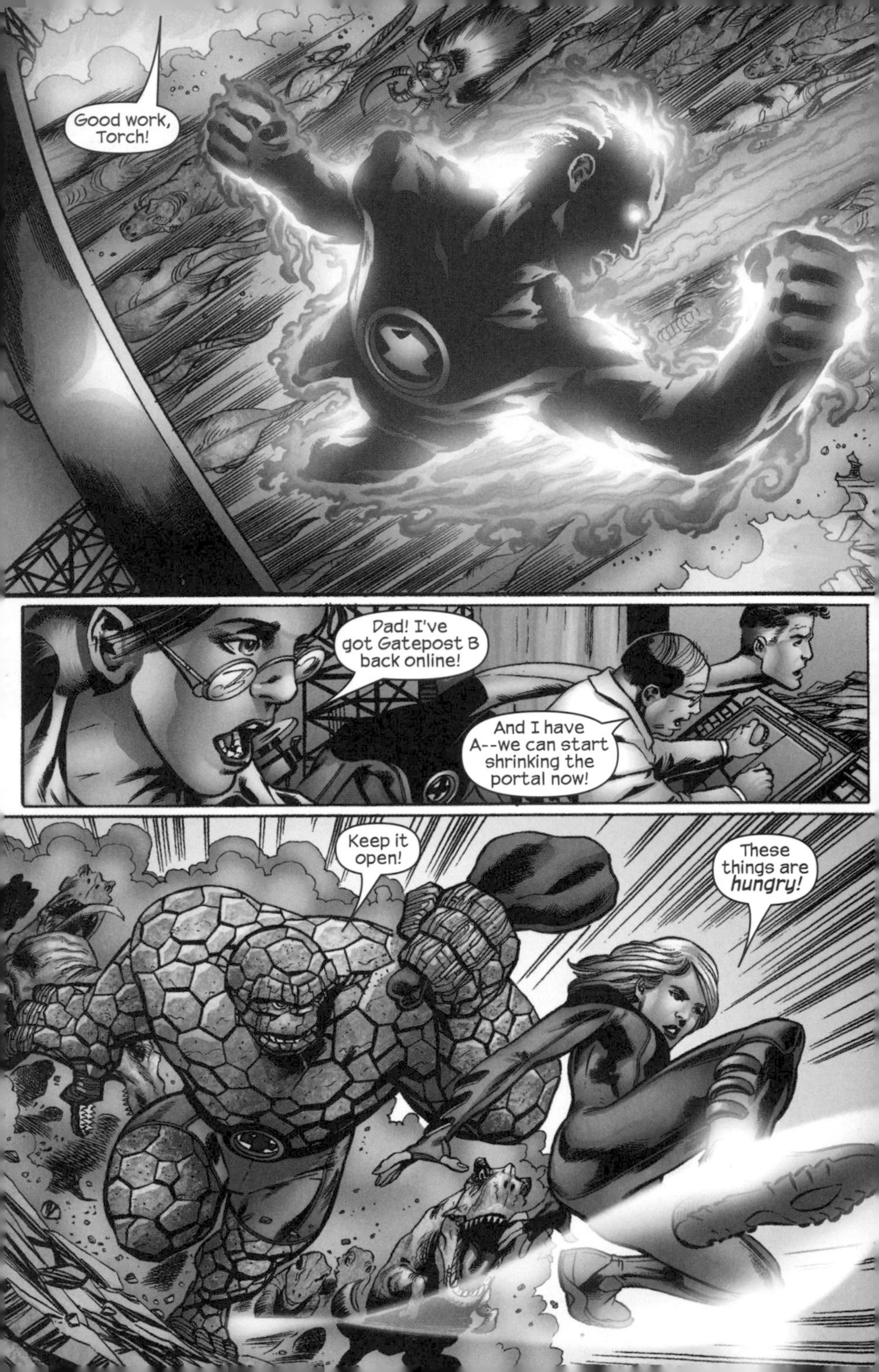

Good work, Torch!
Dad! I've got Gatepost B back online!
And I have A--we can start shrinking the portal now!
Keep it open!
These things are *hungry!*

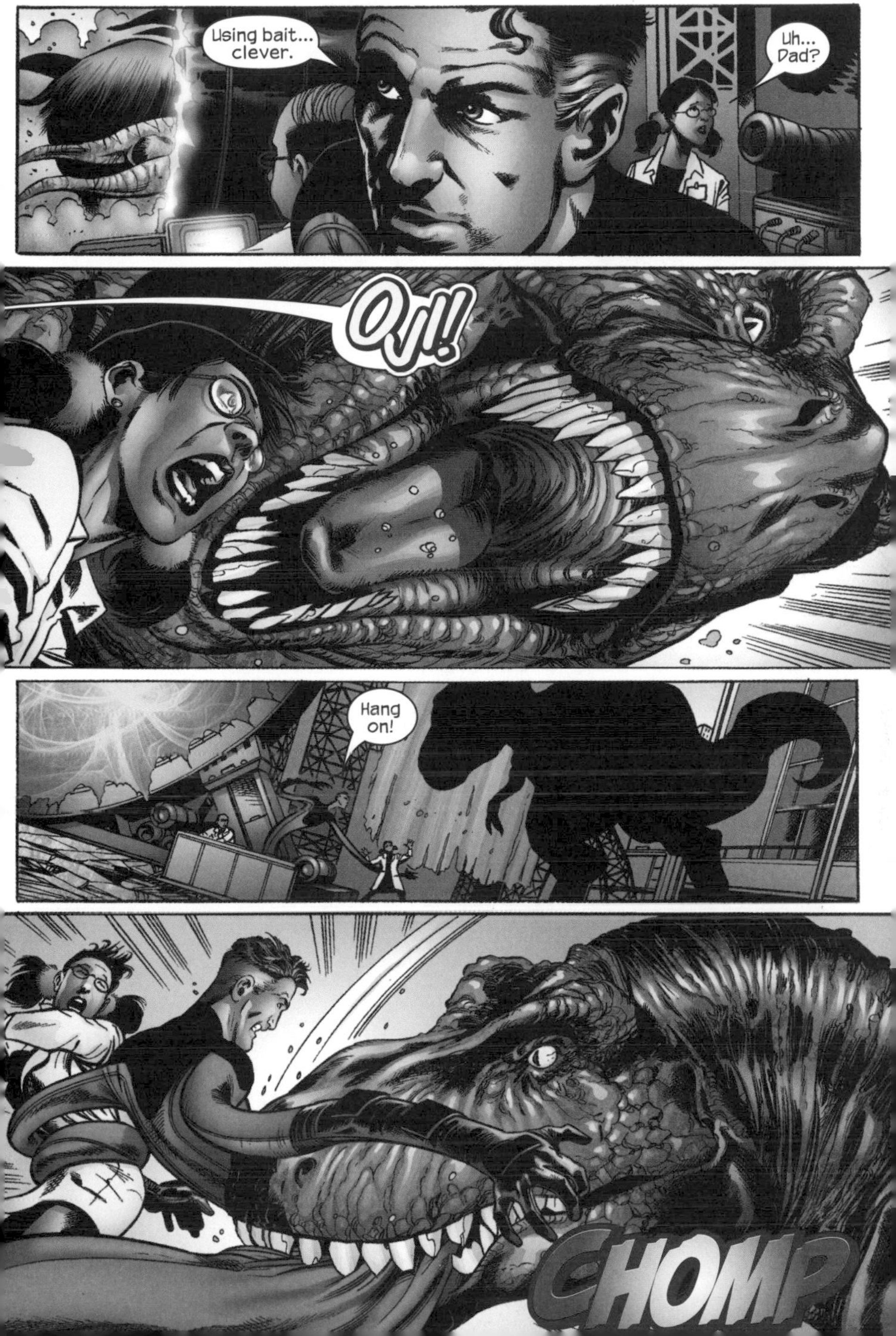
Using bait... clever.
Uh... Dad?
OW!!
Hang on!
CHOMP

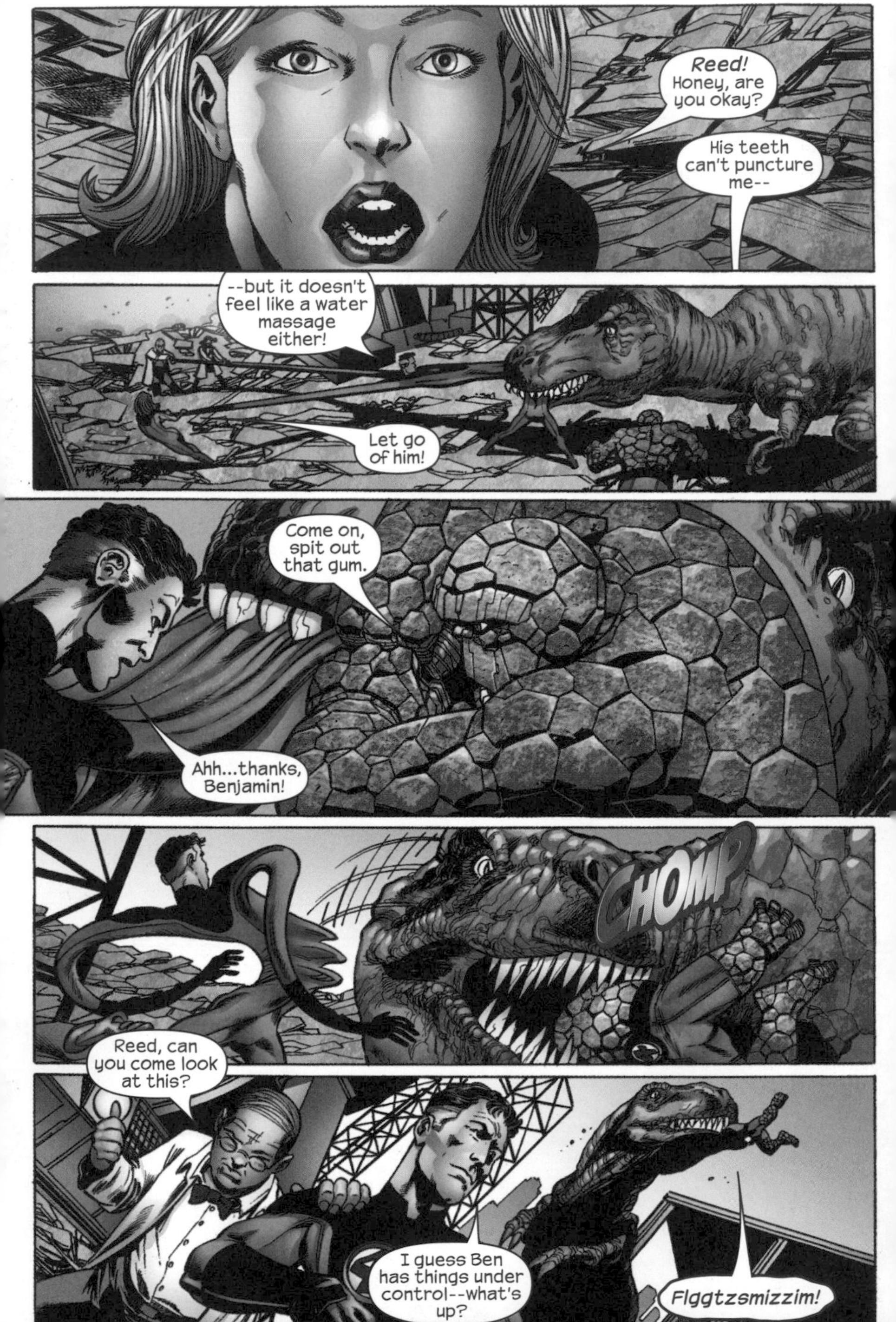
Reed! Honey, are you okay?
His teeth can't puncture me--
--but it doesn't feel like a water massage either!
Let go of him!
Come on, spit out that gum.
Ahh...thanks, Benjamin!
CHOMP
Reed, can you come look at this?
I guess Ben has things under control--what's up?
Flggtzsmizzim!

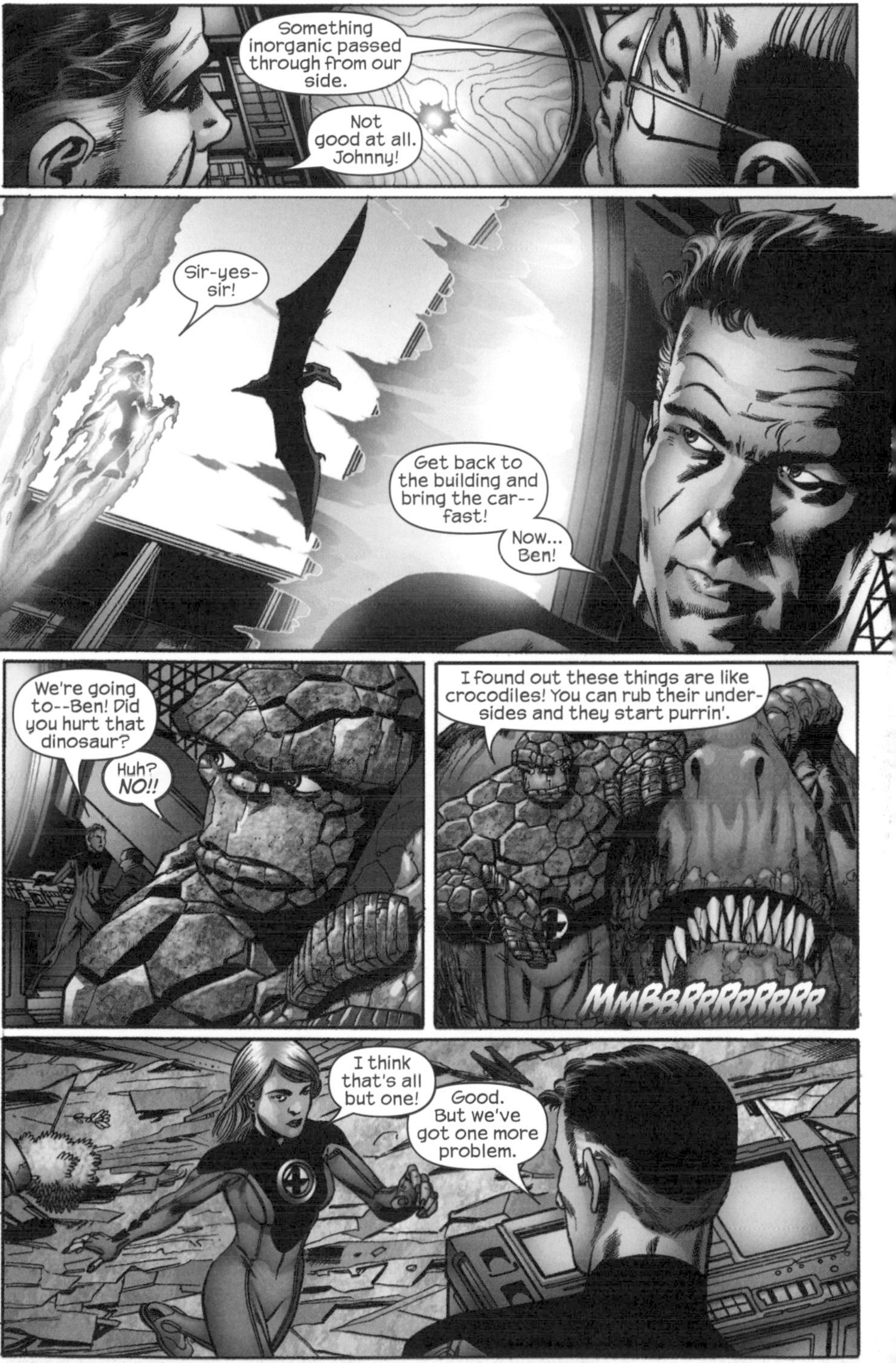
Something inorganic passed through from our side.
Not good at all. Johnny!
Sir-yes-sir!
Get back to the building and bring the car--fast!
Now... Ben!
We're going to--Ben! Did you hurt that dinosaur?
Huh? NO!!
I found out these things are like crocodiles! You can rub their undersides and they start purrin'.
MMBBRRRRRRRR
I think that's all but one!
Good. But we've got one more problem.

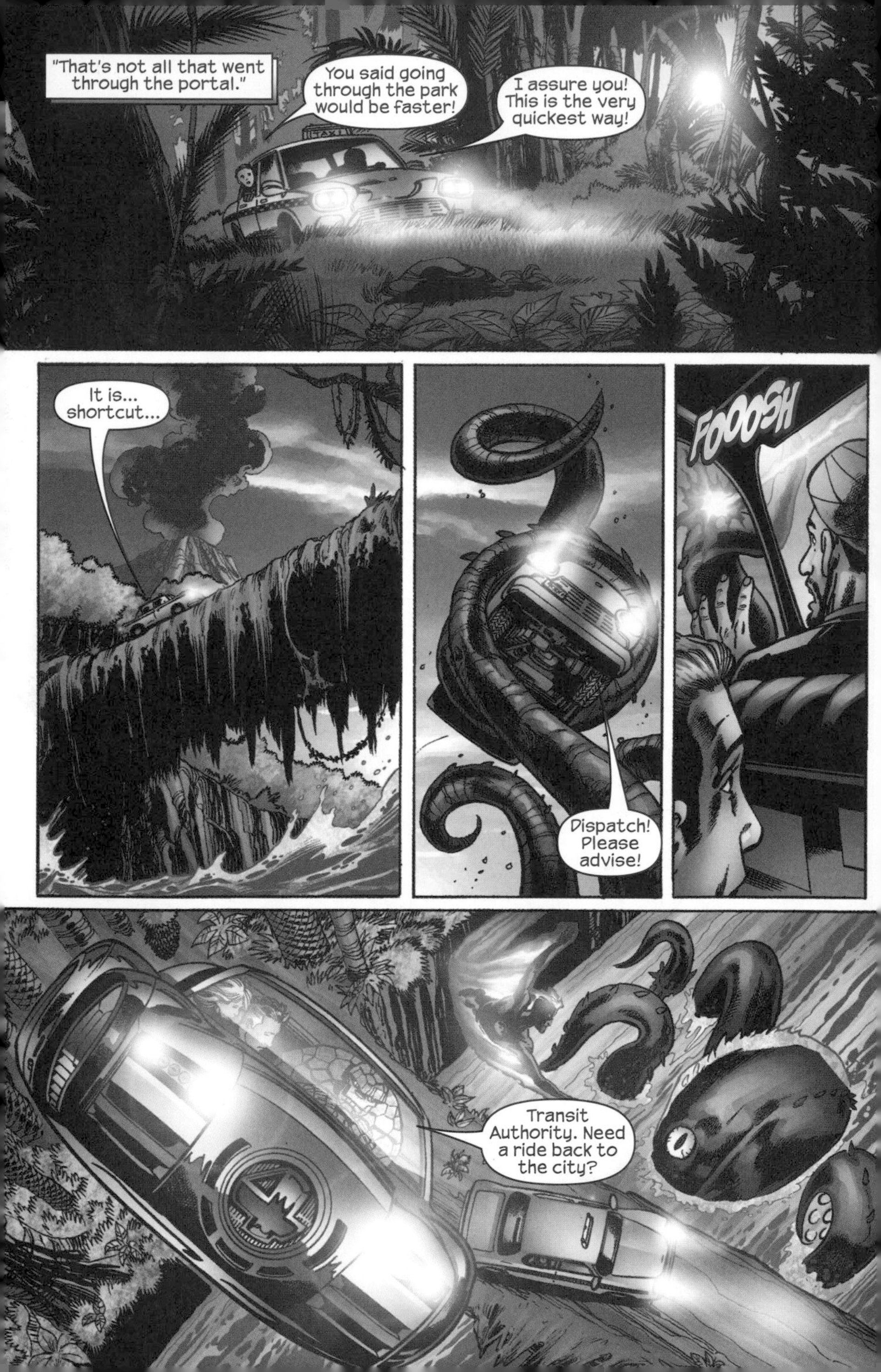
"That's not all that went through the portal."
You said going through the park would be faster!
I assure you! This is the very quickest way!
It is... shortcut...
Dispatch! Please advise!
FOOOSH
Transit Authority. Need a ride back to the city?

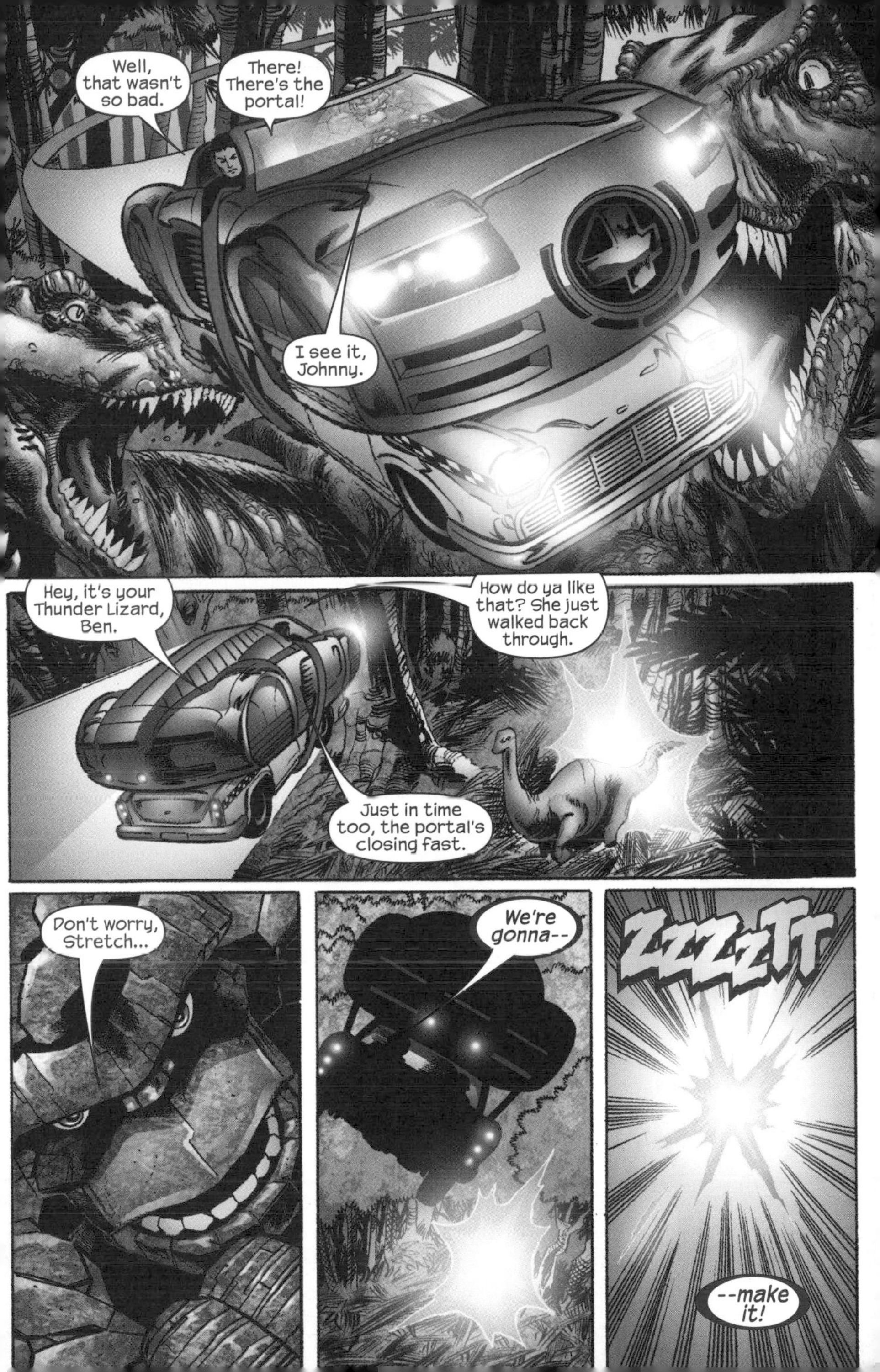
Well, that wasn't so bad.
There! There's the portal!
I see it, Johnny.
Hey, it's your Thunder Lizard, Ben.
How do ya like that? She just walked back through.
Just in time too, the portal's closing fast.
Don't worry, Stretch...
We're gonna--
ZZZZTT
--make it!

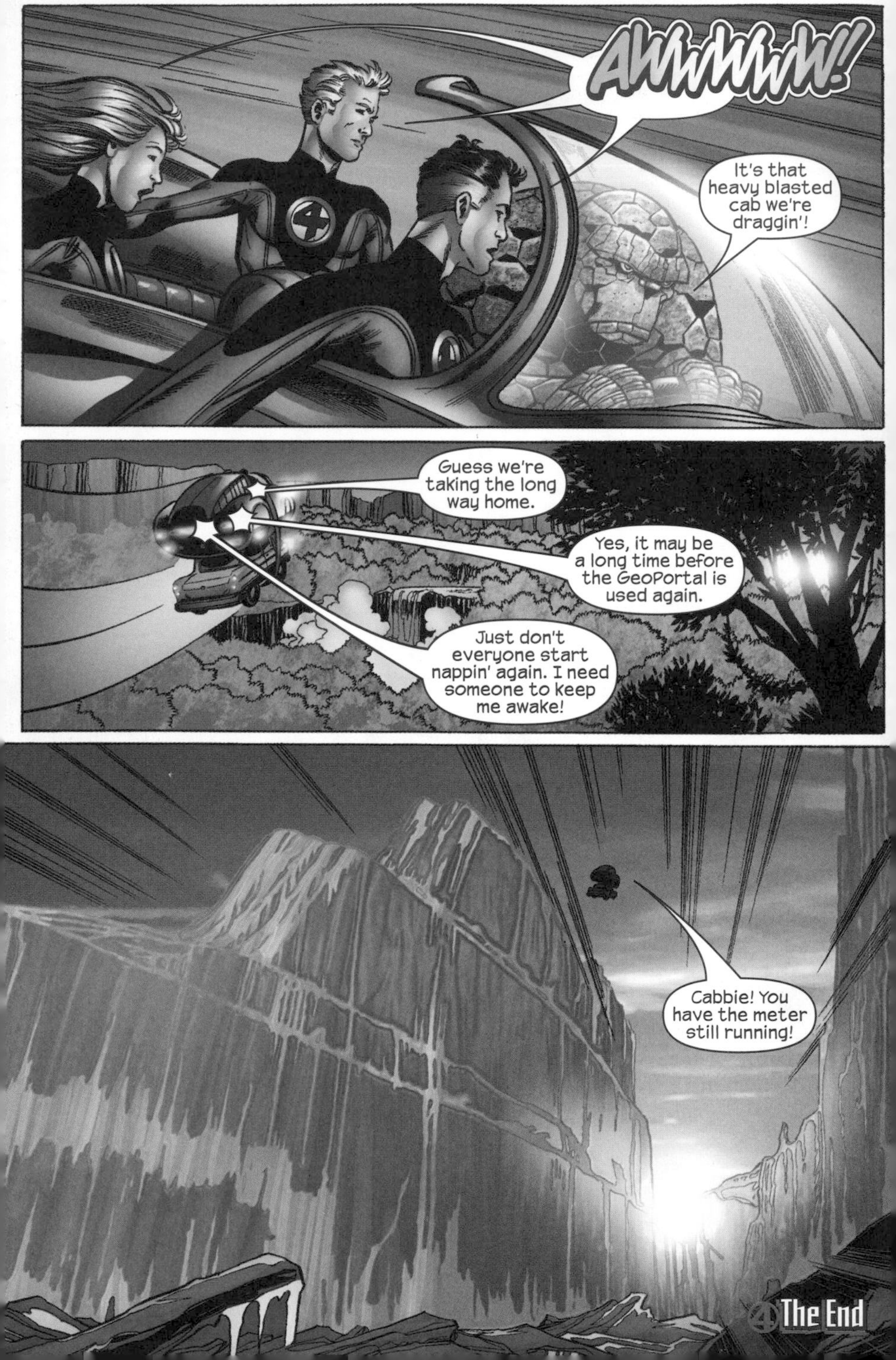
AWWWWWW!!
It's that heavy blasted cab we're draggin'!
Guess we're taking the long way home.
Yes, it may be a long time before the GeoPortal is used again.
Just don't everyone start nappin' again. I need someone to keep me awake!
Cabbie! You have the meter still running!
The End

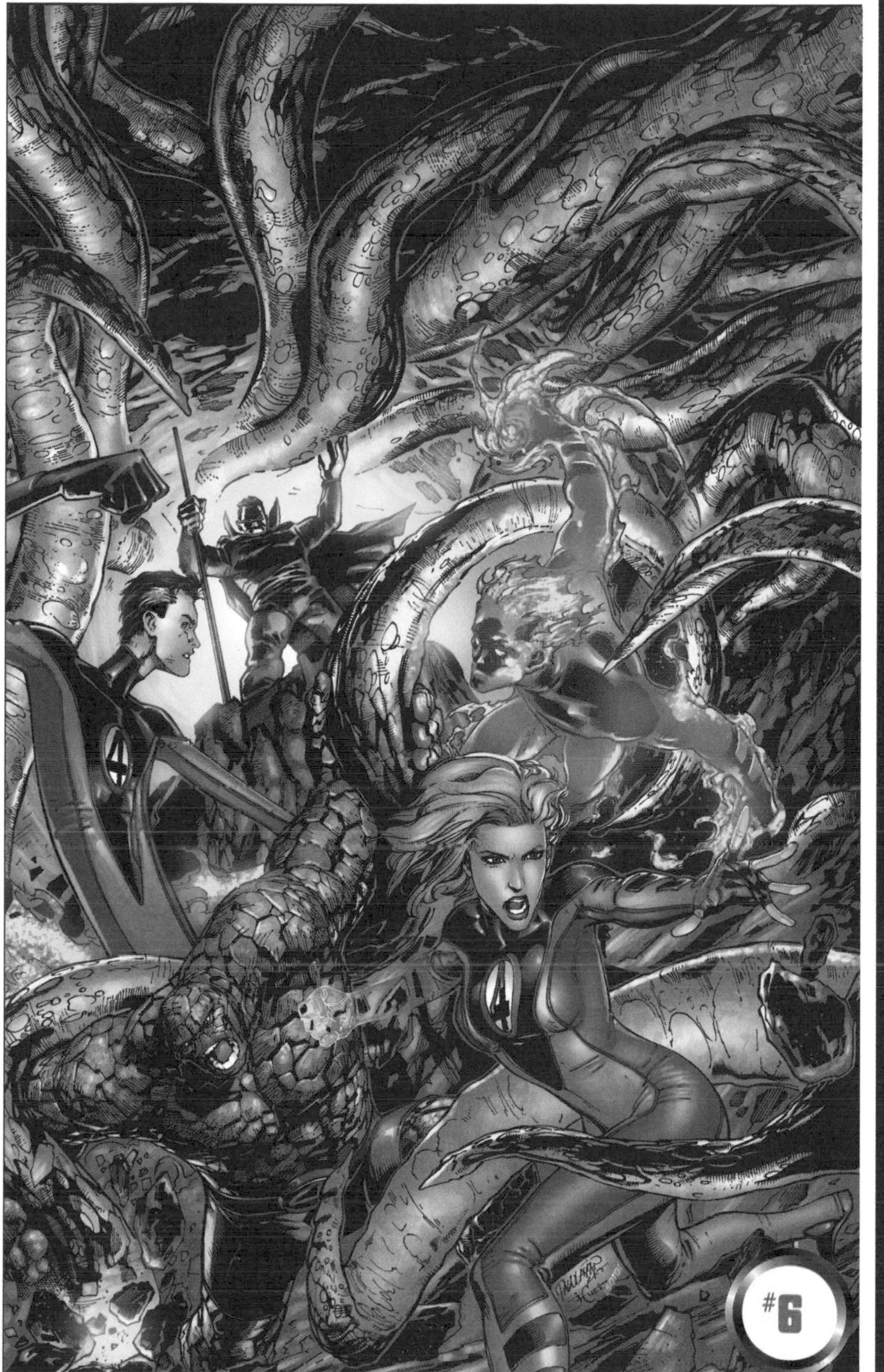
#6

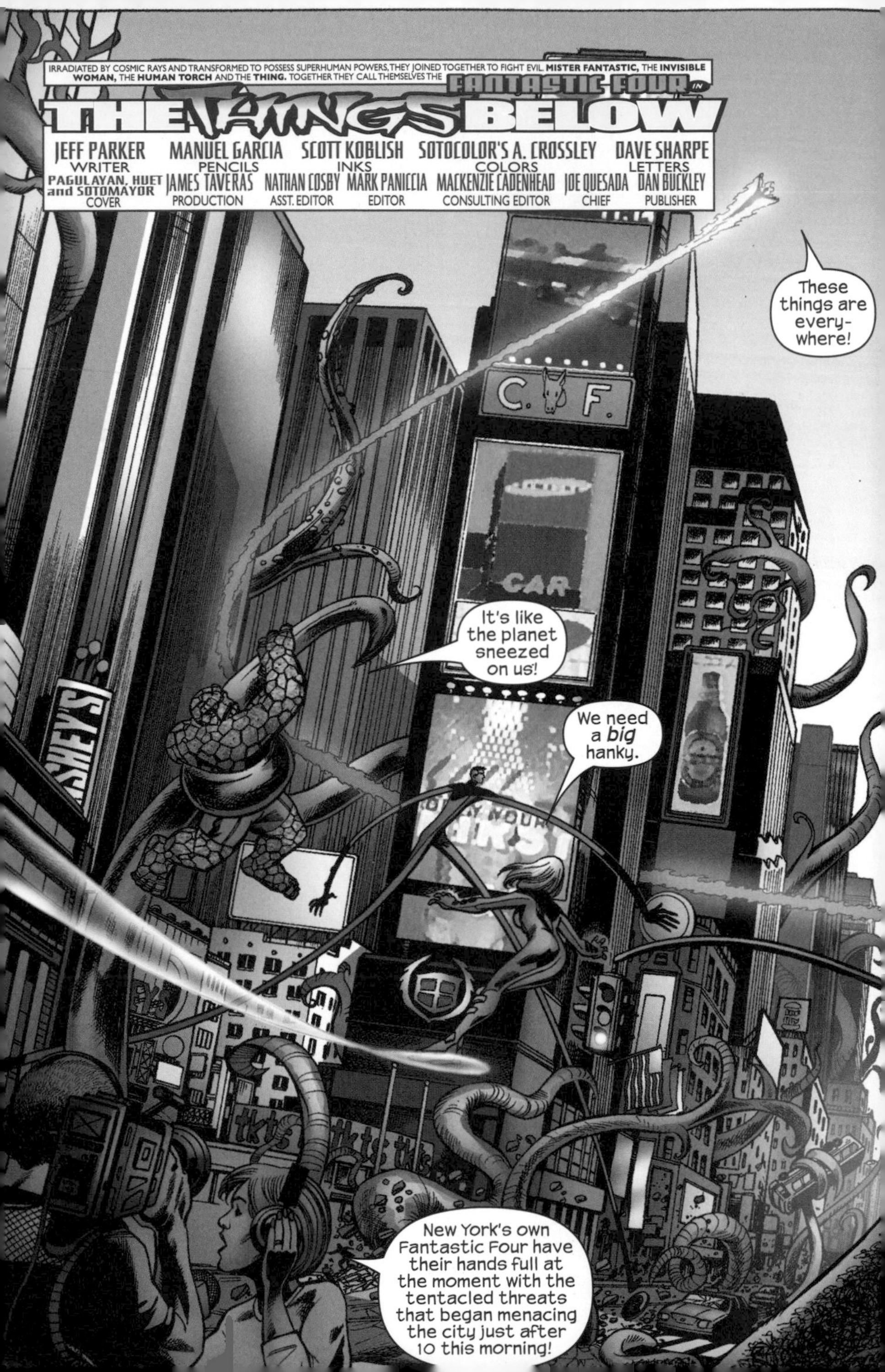
IRRADIATED BY COSMIC RAYS AND TRANSFORMED TO POSSESS SUPERHUMAN POWERS, THEY JOINED TOGETHER TO FIGHT EVIL. **MISTER FANTASTIC**, THE **INVISIBLE WOMAN**, THE **HUMAN TORCH** AND THE **THING**. TOGETHER THEY CALL THEMSELVES THE FANTASTIC FOUR IN
THE THINGS BELOW
JEFF PARKER WRITER
MANUEL GARCIA PENCILS
SCOTT KOBLISH INKS
SOTOCOLOR'S A. CROSSLEY COLORS
DAVE SHARPE LETTERS
PAGULAYAN, HUET and SOTOMAYOR COVER
JAMES TAVERAS PRODUCTION
NATHAN COSBY ASST. EDITOR
MARK PANICCIA EDITOR
MACKENZIE CADENHEAD CONSULTING EDITOR
JOE QUESADA CHIEF
DAN BUCKLEY PUBLISHER
These things are every-where!
It's like the planet sneezed on us!
We need a *big* hanky.
New York's own Fantastic Four have their hands full at the moment with the tentacled threats that began menacing the city just after 10 this morning!

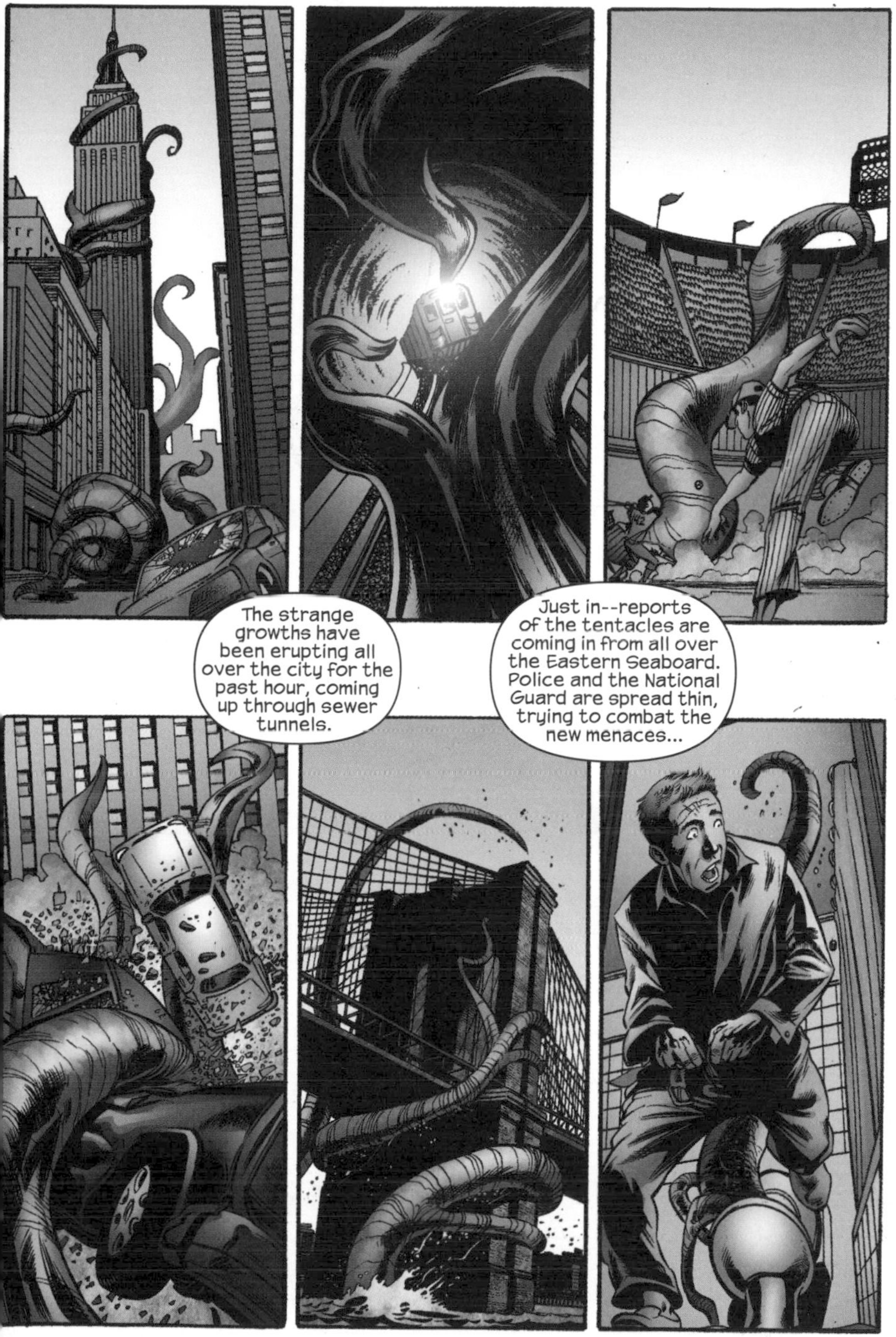
The strange growths have been erupting all over the city for the past hour, coming up through sewer tunnels.
Just in--reports of the tentacles are coming in from all over the Eastern Seaboard. Police and the National Guard are spread thin, trying to combat the new menaces...

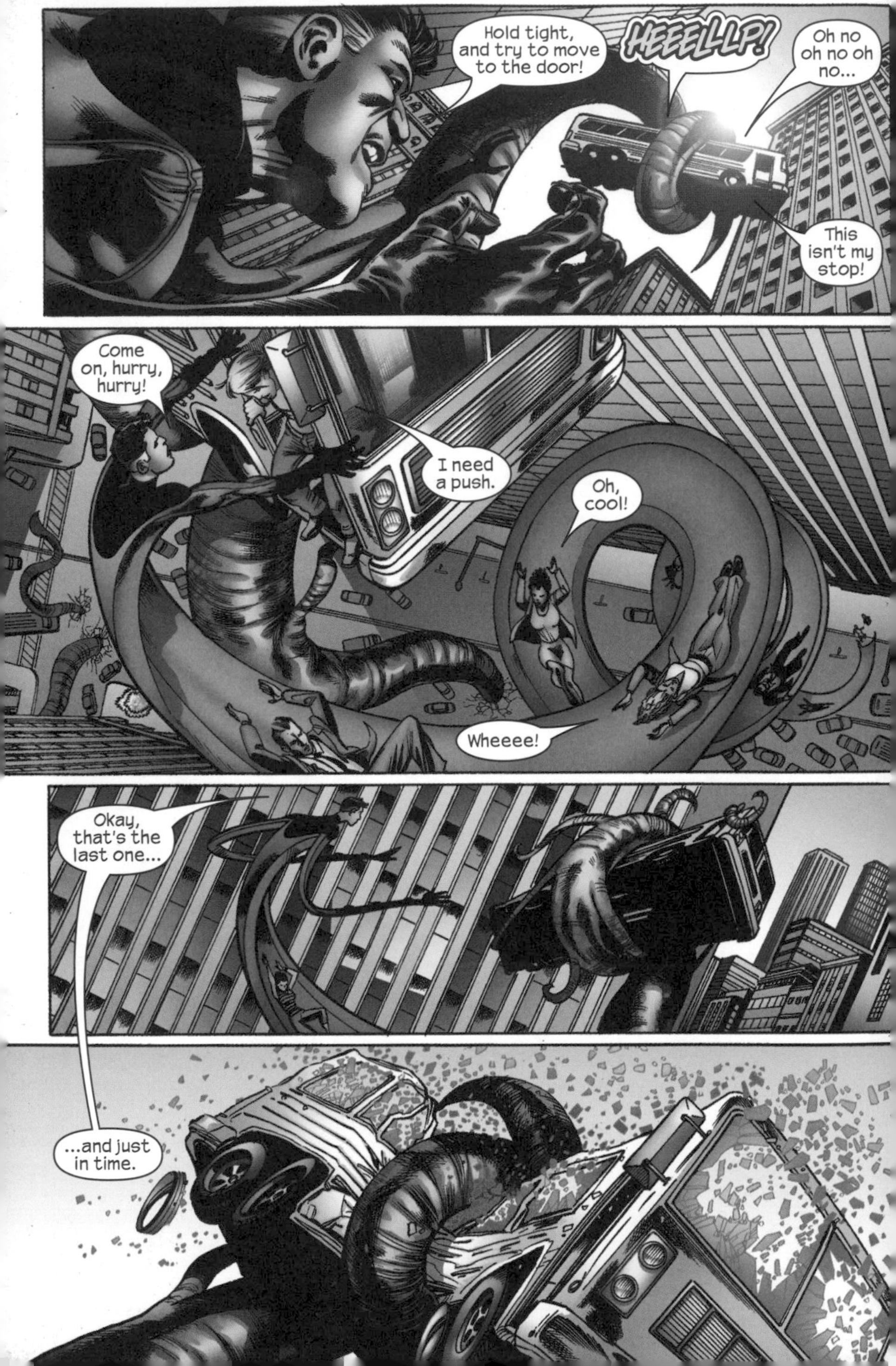
Hold tight, and try to move to the door!
HEEELLLP!
Oh no oh no oh no...
This isn't my stop!
Come on, hurry, hurry!
I need a push.
Oh, cool!
Wheeee!
Okay, that's the last one...
...and just in time.

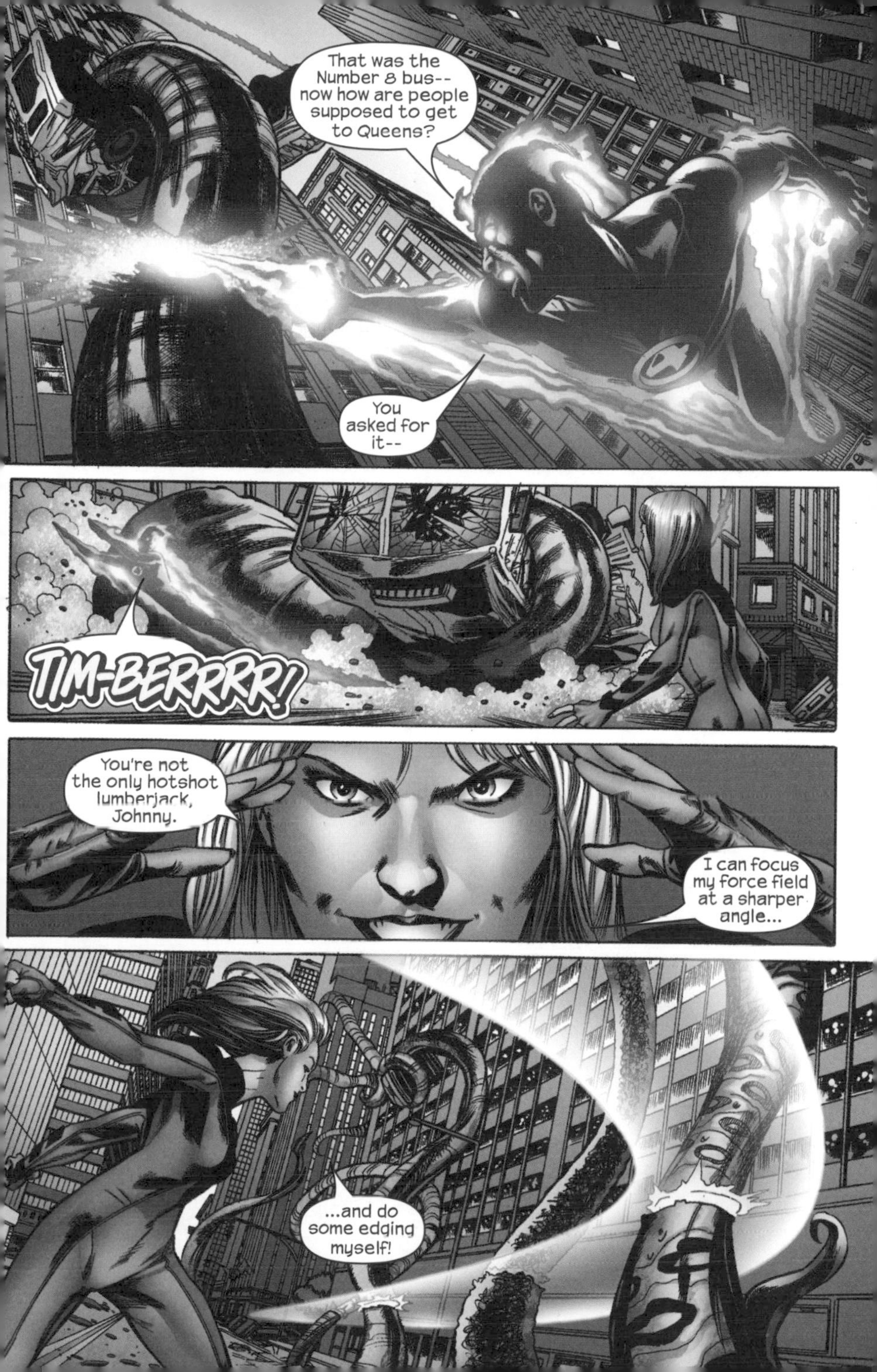
That was the Number 8 bus--now how are people supposed to get to Queens?
You asked for it--
TIM-BERRRR!
You're not the only hotshot lumberjack, Johnny.
I can focus my force field at a sharper angle...
...and do some edging myself!

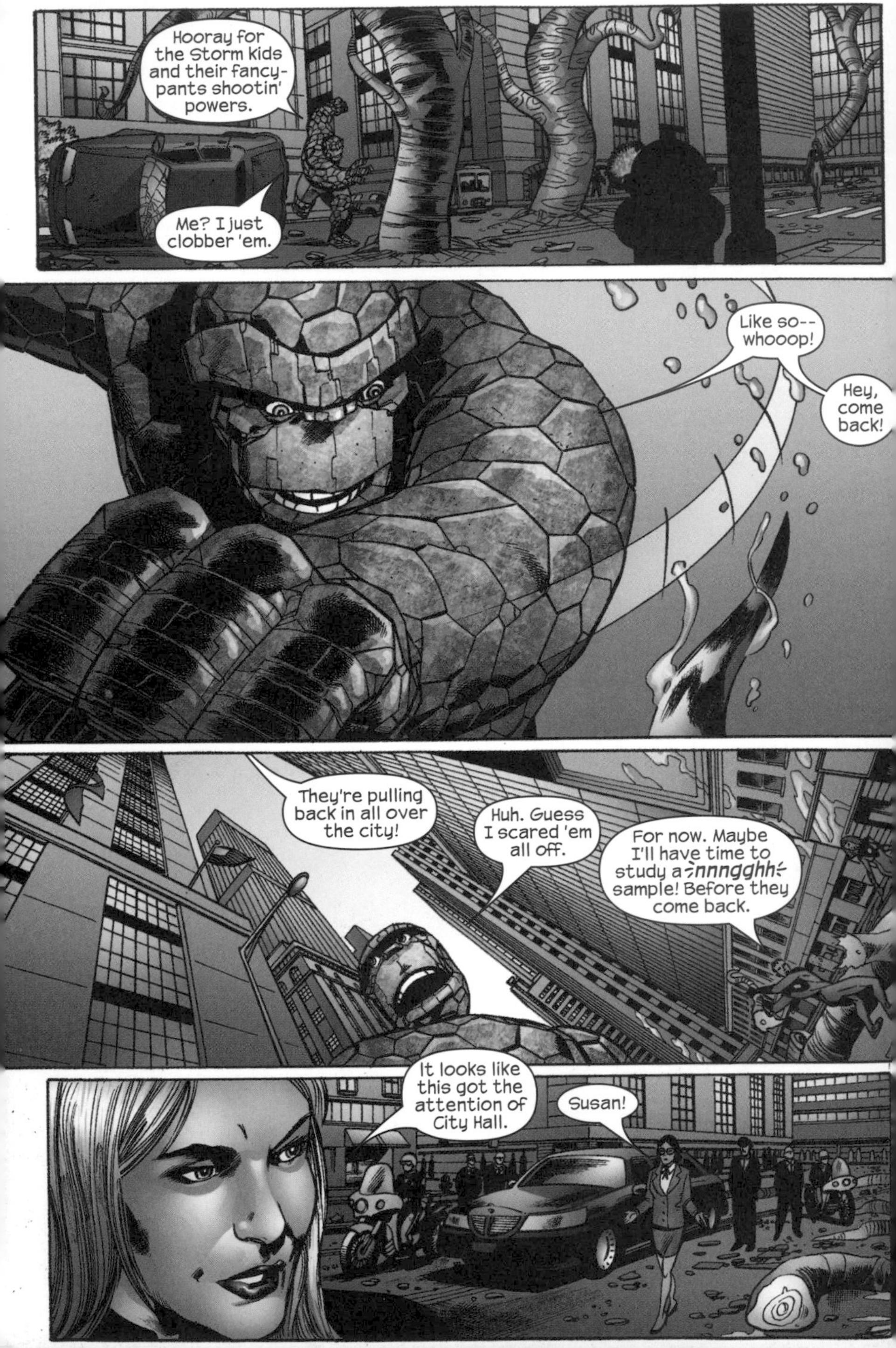
Hooray for the Storm kids and their fancy-pants shootin' powers.
Me? I just clobber 'em.
Like so--whooop!
Hey, come back!
They're pulling back in all over the city!
Huh. Guess I scared 'em all off.
For now. Maybe I'll have time to study a -nnngghh- sample! Before they come back.
It looks like this got the attention of City Hall.
Susan!

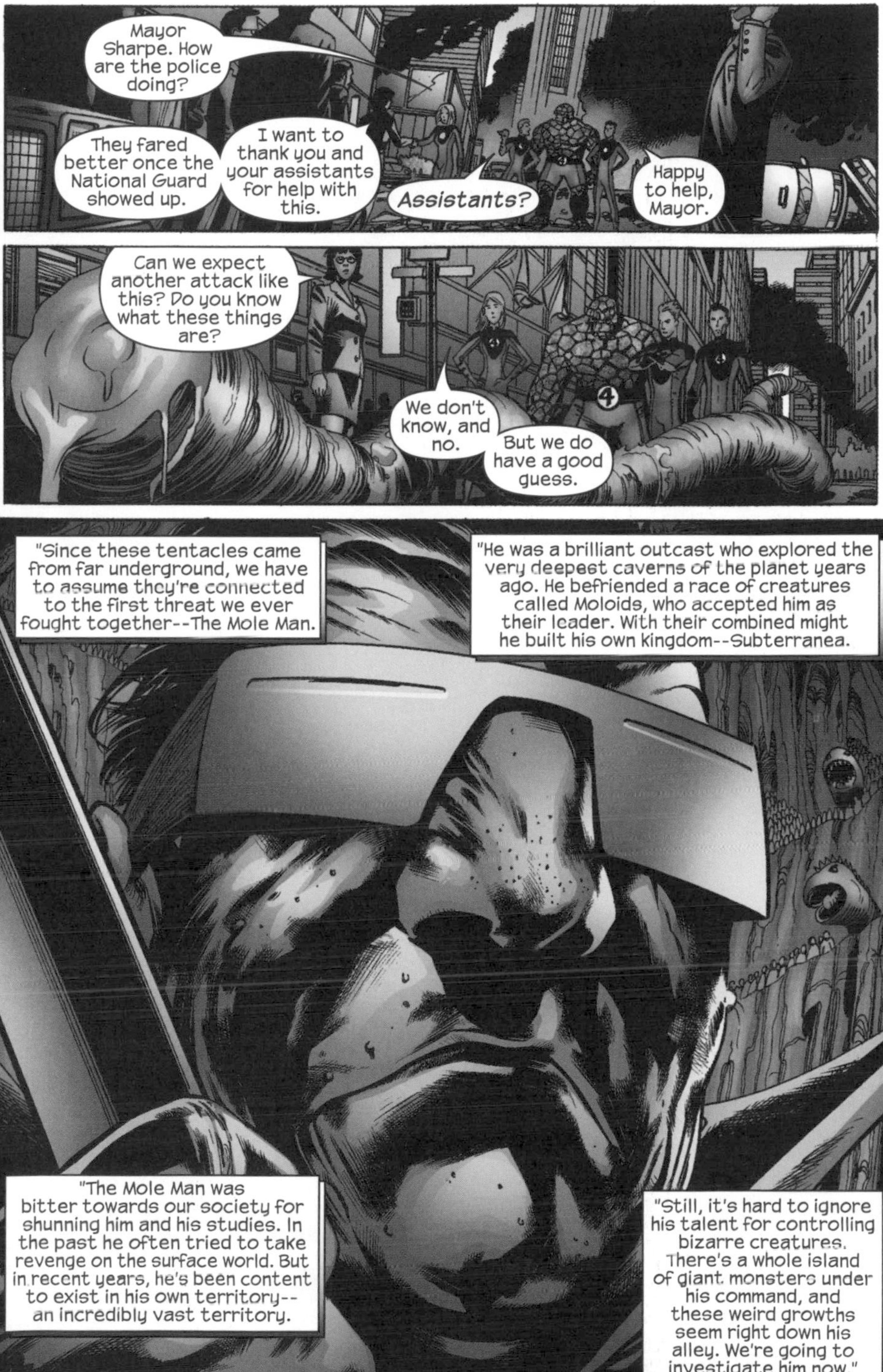
Mayor Sharpe. How are the police doing?
They fared better once the National Guard showed up.
I want to thank you and your assistants for help with this.
Assistants?
Happy to help, Mayor.
Can we expect another attack like this? Do you know what these things are?
We don't know, and no.
But we do have a good guess.
"Since these tentacles came from far underground, we have to assume they're connected to the first threat we ever fought together--The Mole Man.
"He was a brilliant outcast who explored the very deepest caverns of the planet years ago. He befriended a race of creatures called Moloids, who accepted him as their leader. With their combined might he built his own kingdom--Subterranea.
"The Mole Man was bitter towards our society for shunning him and his studies. In the past he often tried to take revenge on the surface world. But in recent years, he's been content to exist in his own territory--an incredibly vast territory.
"Still, it's hard to ignore his talent for controlling bizarre creatures. There's a whole island of giant monsters under his command, and these weird growths seem right down his alley. We're going to investigate him now."

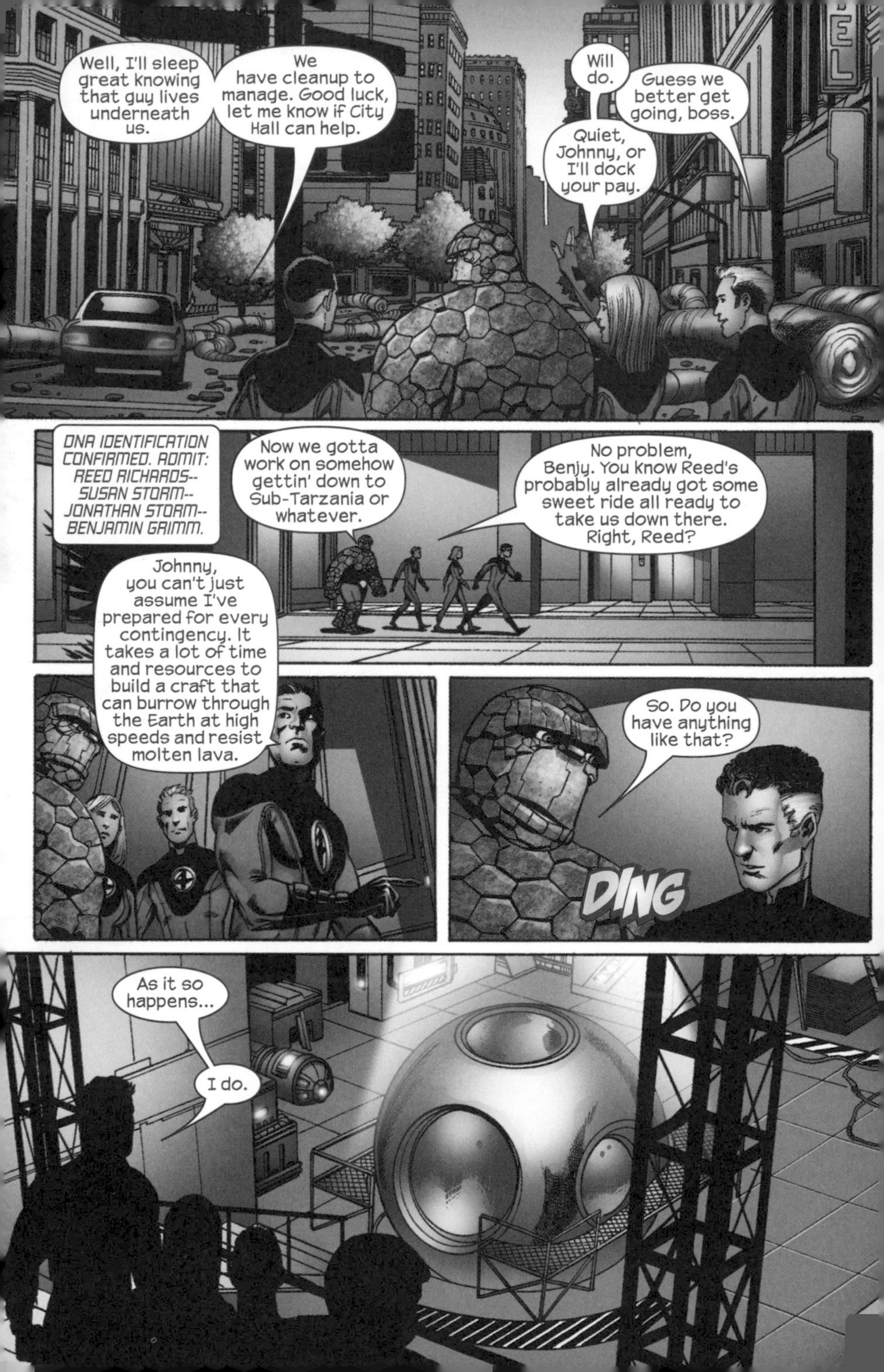
Well, I'll sleep great knowing that guy lives underneath us.
We have cleanup to manage. Good luck, let me know if City Hall can help.
Will do.
Guess we better get going, boss.
Quiet, Johnny, or I'll dock your pay.
DNA IDENTIFICATION CONFIRMED. ADMIT: REED RICHARDS-- SUSAN STORM-- JONATHAN STORM-- BENJAMIN GRIMM.
Now we gotta work on somehow gettin' down to Sub-Tarzania or whatever.
No problem, Benjy. You know Reed's probably already got some sweet ride all ready to take us down there. Right, Reed?
Johnny, you can't just assume I've prepared for every contingency. It takes a lot of time and resources to build a craft that can burrow through the Earth at high speeds and resist molten lava.
So. Do you have anything like that?
DING
As it so happens...
I do.

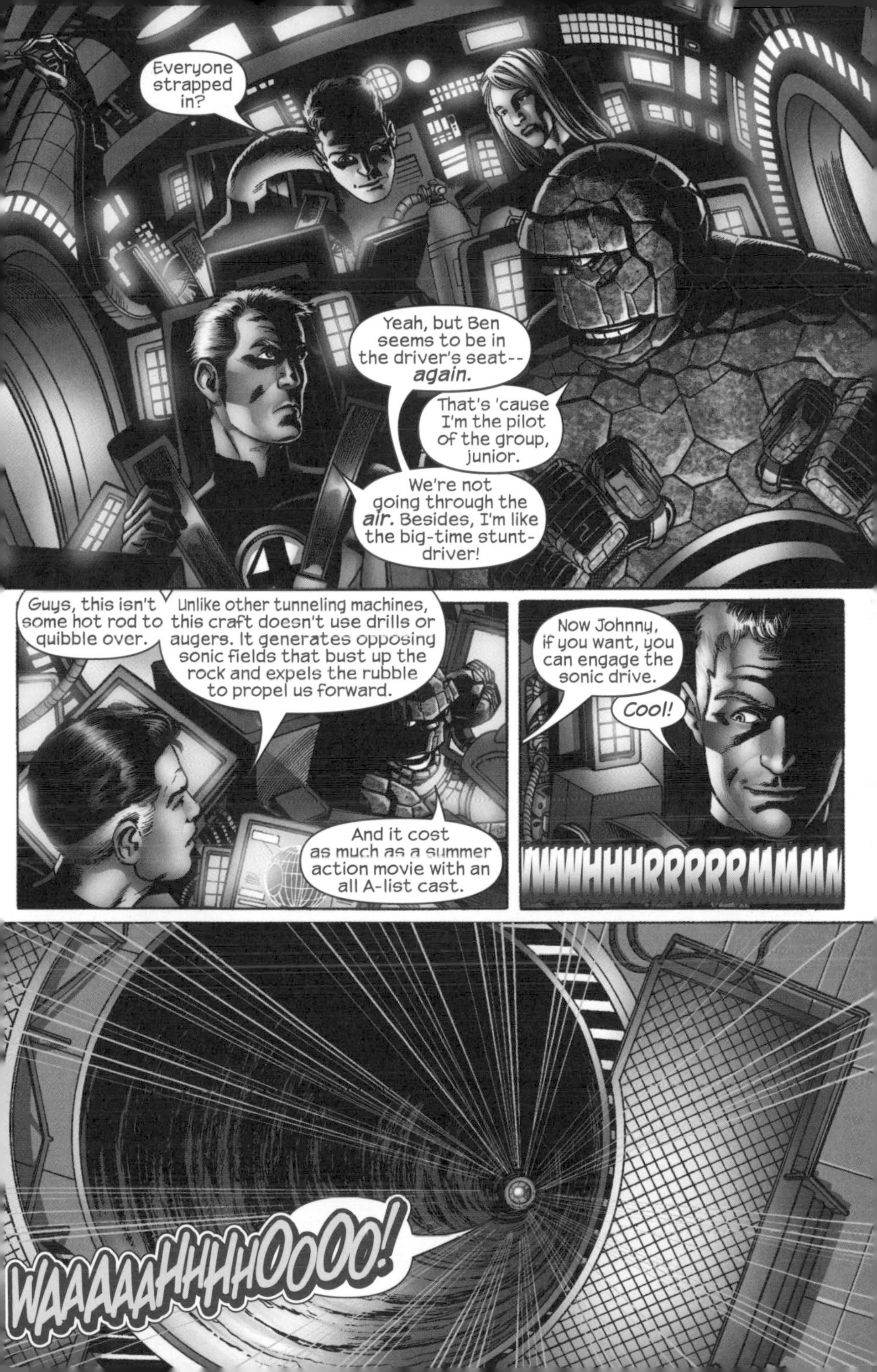

Everyone strapped in?
Yeah, but Ben seems to be in the driver's seat-- *again.*
That's 'cause I'm the pilot of the group, junior.
We're not going through the *air.* Besides, I'm like the big-time stunt-driver!
Guys, this isn't some hot rod to quibble over.
Unlike other tunneling machines, this craft doesn't use drills or augers. It generates opposing sonic fields that bust up the rock and expels the rubble to propel us forward.
And it cost as much as a summer action movie with an all A-list cast.
Now Johnny, if you want, you can engage the sonic drive.
Cool!
WWHHHRRRRRMMMN
WAAAAAAHHHHOOOOO!

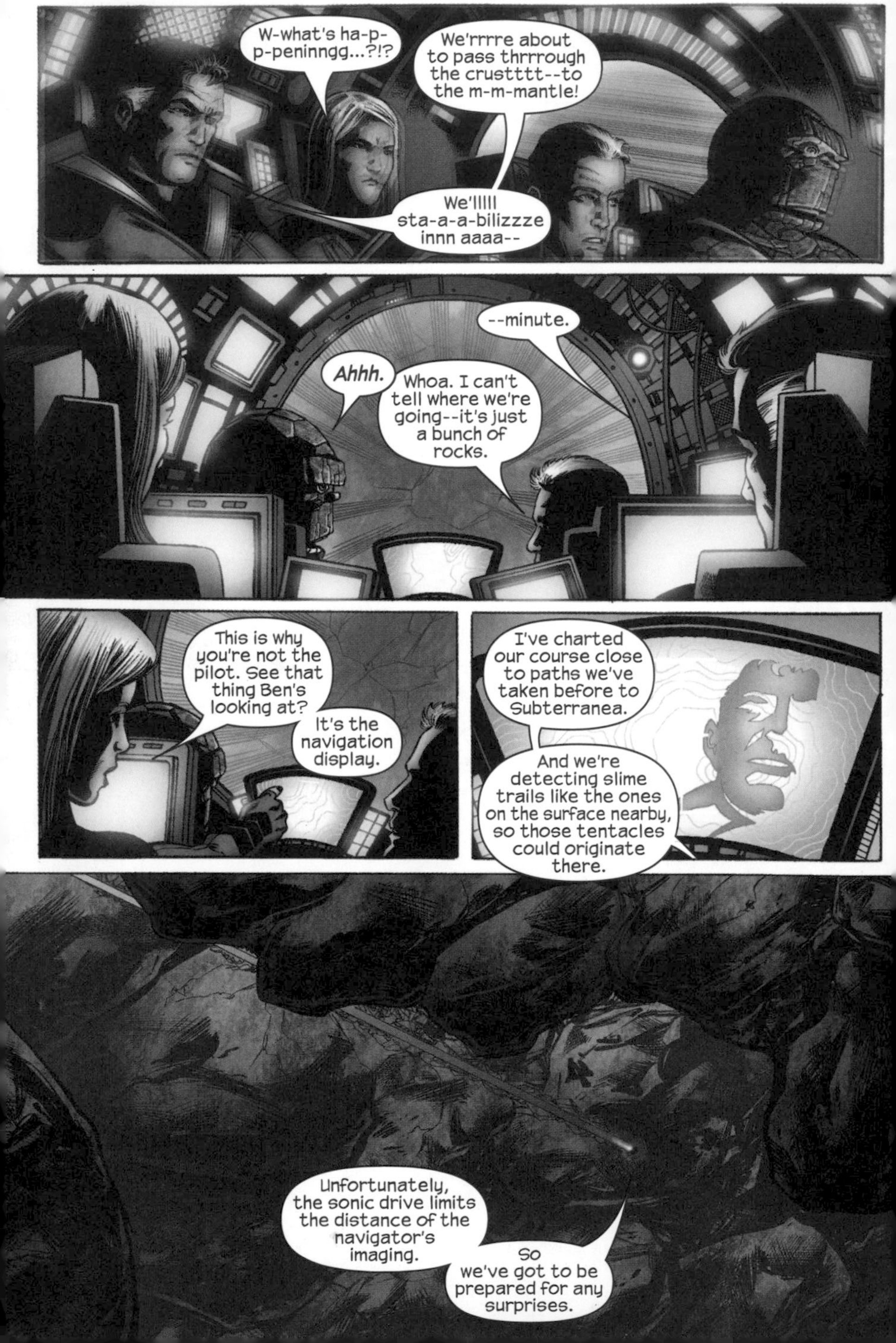
W-what's ha-p-p-peninngg...?!?
We'rrrre about to pass thrrrough the crustttt--to the m-m-mantle!
We'lllll sta-a-a-bilizzze innn aaaa--
--minute.
Ahhh.
Whoa. I can't tell where we're going--it's just a bunch of rocks.
This is why you're not the pilot. See that thing Ben's looking at?
It's the navigation display.
I've charted our course close to paths we've taken before to Subterranea.
And we're detecting slime trails like the ones on the surface nearby, so those tentacles could originate there.
Unfortunately, the sonic drive limits the distance of the navigator's imaging.
So we've got to be prepared for any surprises.

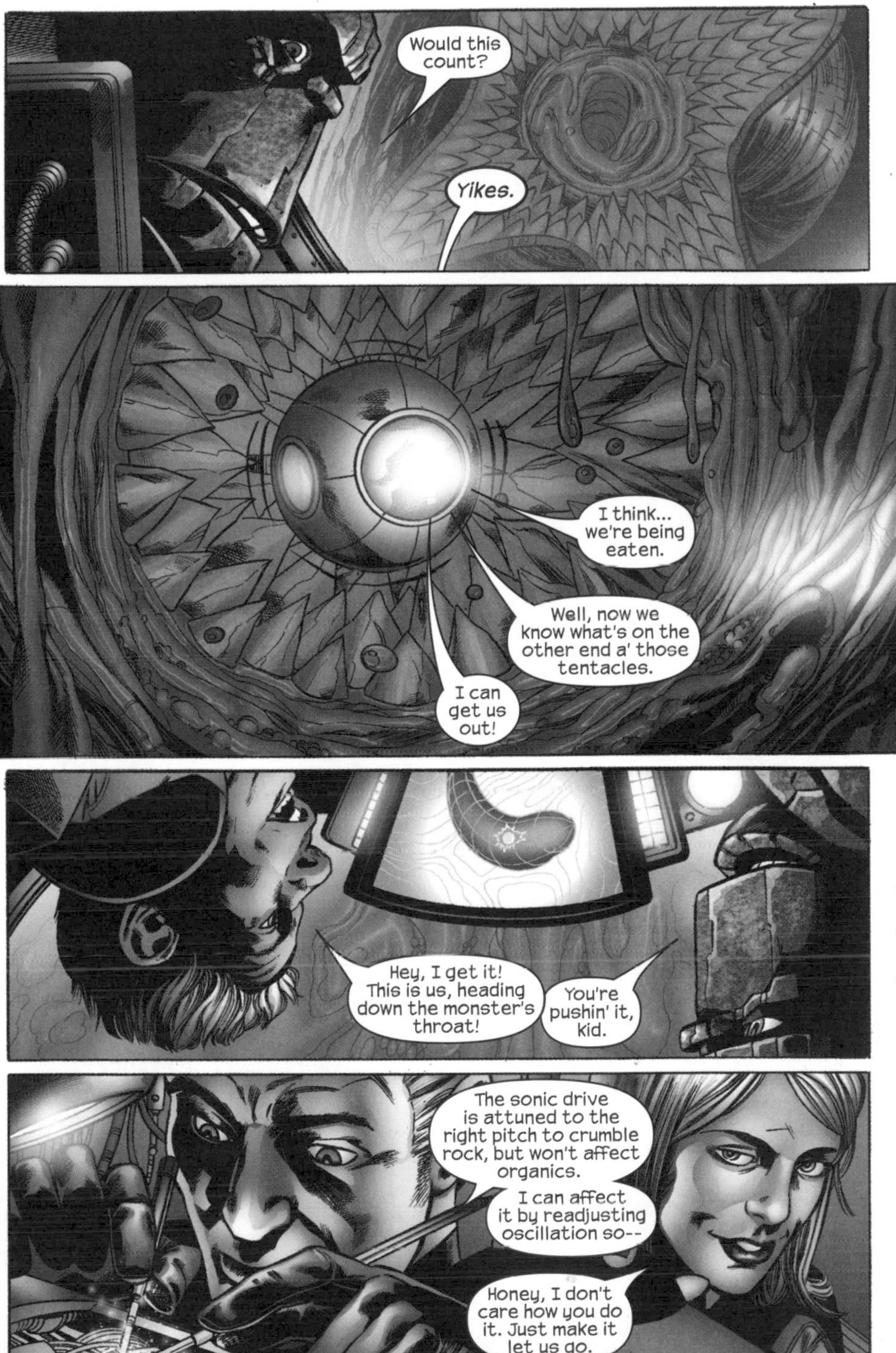
Would this count?
Yikes.
I think... we're being eaten.
Well, now we know what's on the other end a' those tentacles.
I can get us out!
Hey, I get it! This is us, heading down the monster's throat!
You're pushin' it, kid.
The sonic drive is attuned to the right pitch to crumble rock, but won't affect organics.
I can affect it by readjusting oscillation so--
Honey, I don't care how you do it. Just make it let us go.

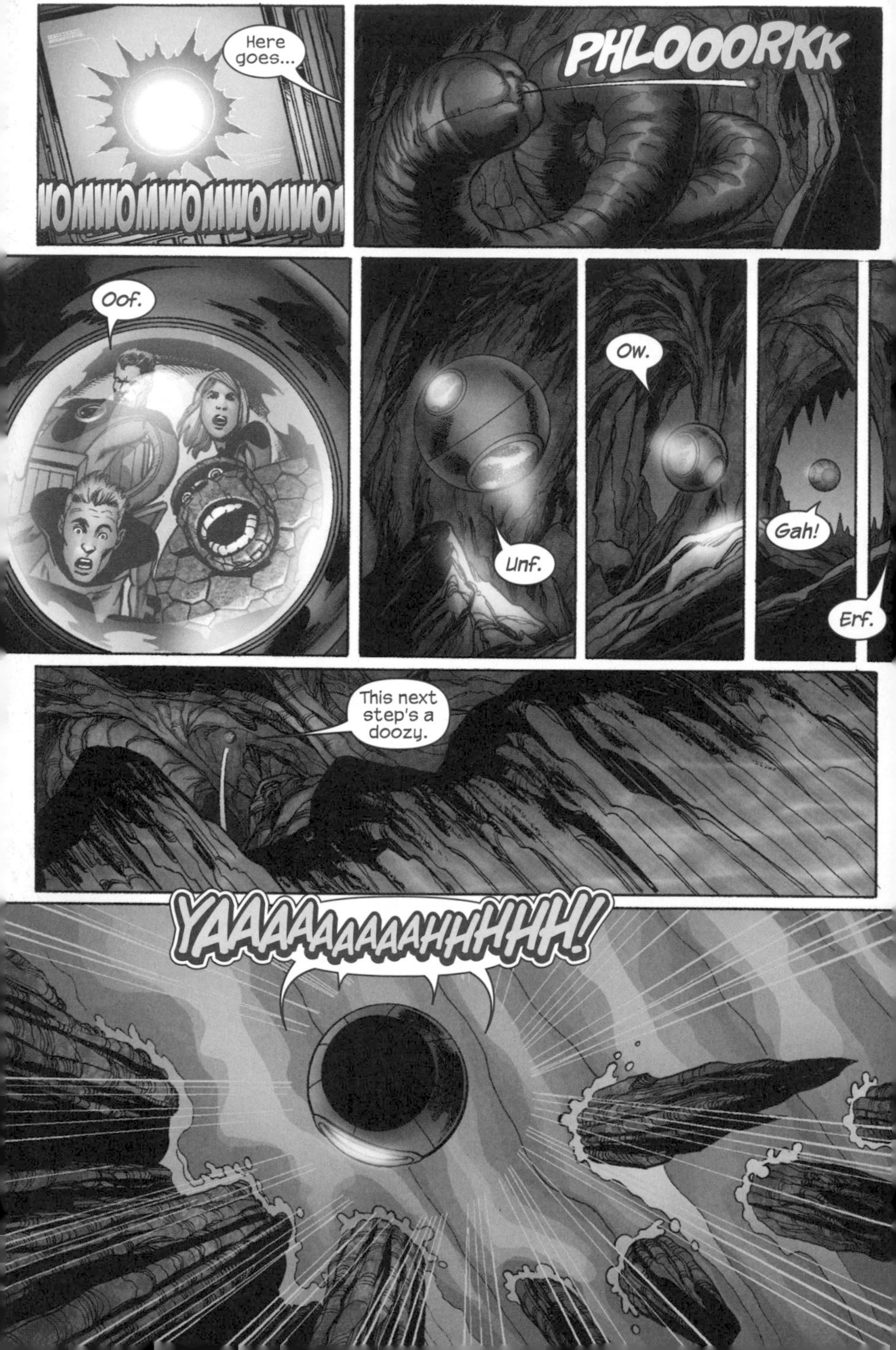
Here goes...
WOMWOMWOMWOMWOM
PHLOOORKK
Oof.
Unf.
Ow.
Gah!
Erf.
This next step's a doozy.
YAAAAAAAAAHHHHH!

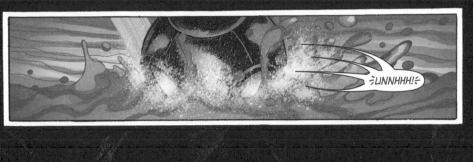

≶UNNHHH!≷

Wow.

Now...is this somewhere we want to be?

Yeah, we're not far from Subta-- Sub---the Mole Man's place.

This lava flow should come really close to an under- ground river. There.

The steam's a dead giveaway.

Maneuver us up into the stream, Ben. That feeds directly into the city.

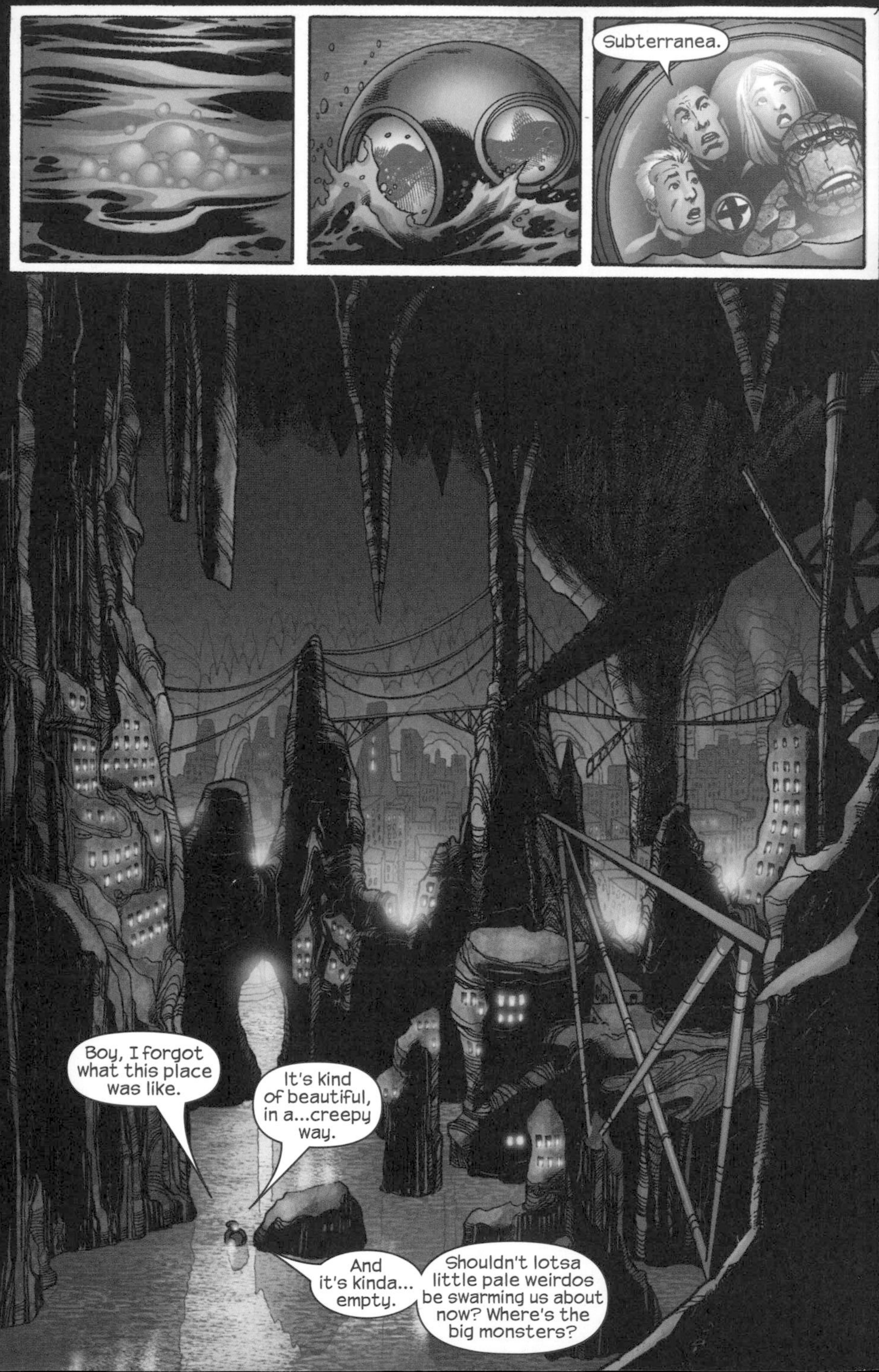
Subterranea.
Boy, I forgot what this place was like.
It's kind of beautiful, in a...creepy way.
And it's kinda... empty.
Shouldn't lotsa little pale weirdos be swarming us about now? Where's the big monsters?

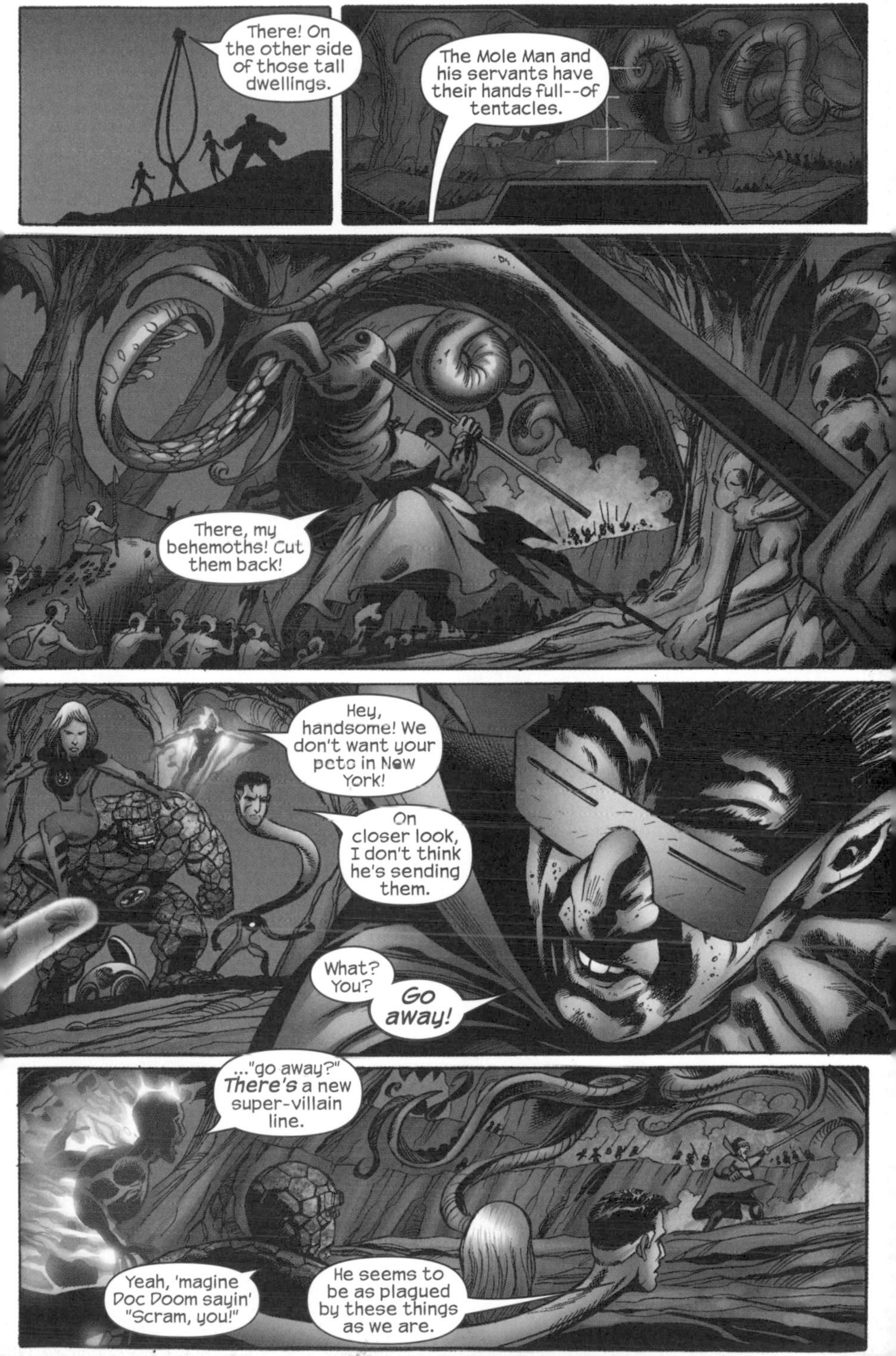
There! On the other side of those tall dwellings.
The Mole Man and his servants have their hands full--of tentacles.
There, my behemoths! Cut them back!
Hey, handsome! We don't want your pets in New York!
On closer look, I don't think he's sending them.
What? You? Go away!
..."go away?" There's a new super-villain line.
Yeah, 'magine Doc Doom sayin' "Scram, you!"
He seems to be as plagued by these things as we are.

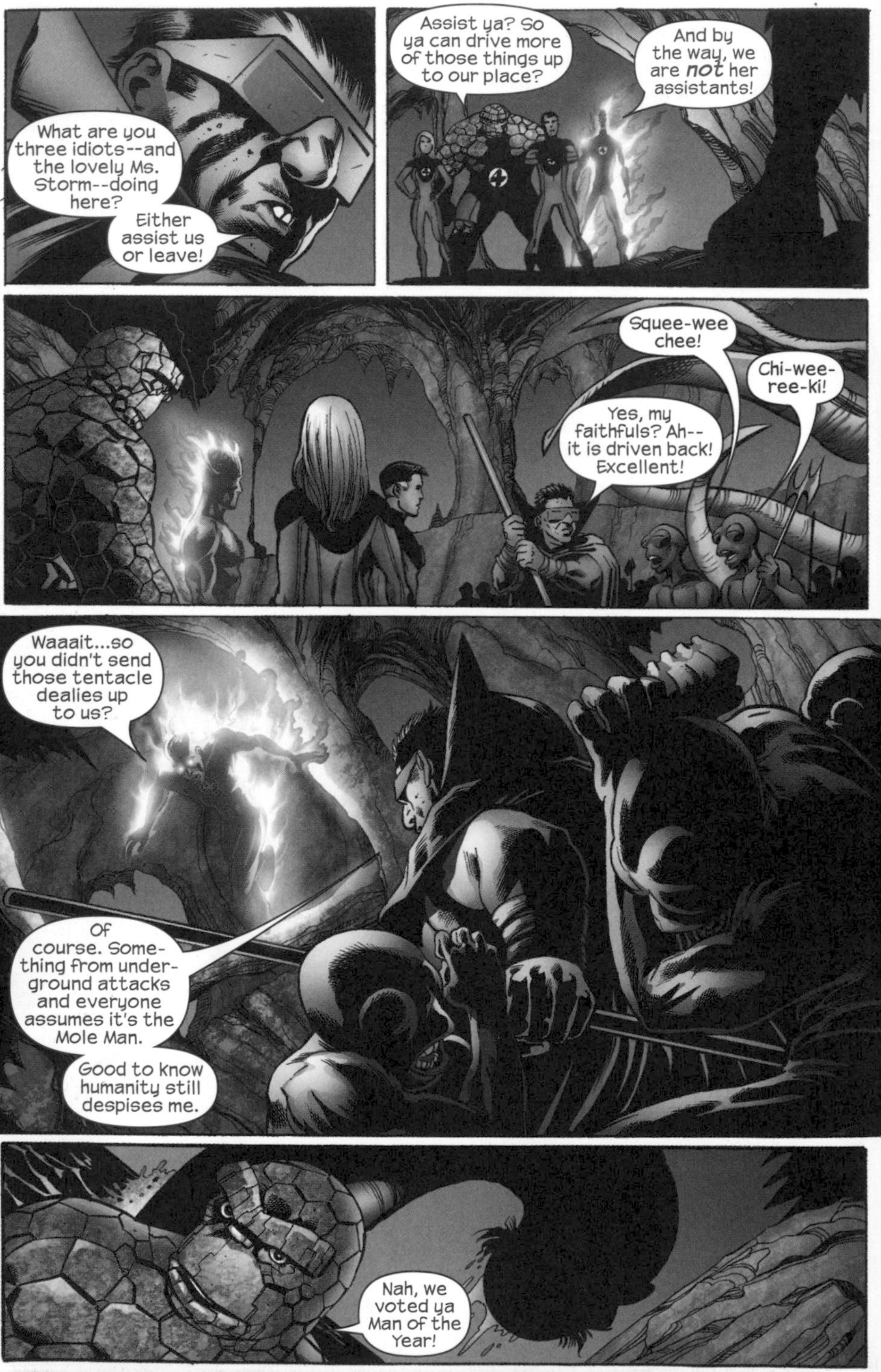
What are you three idiots--and the lovely Ms. Storm--doing here?
Either assist us or leave!
Assist ya? So ya can drive more of those things up to our place?
And by the way, we are **not** her assistants!
Squee-wee chee!
Chi-wee-ree-ki!
Yes, my faithfuls? Ah--it is driven back! Excellent!
Waaait...so you didn't send those tentacle dealies up to us?
Of course. Something from underground attacks and everyone assumes it's the Mole Man.
Good to know humanity still despises me.
Nah, we voted ya Man of the Year!

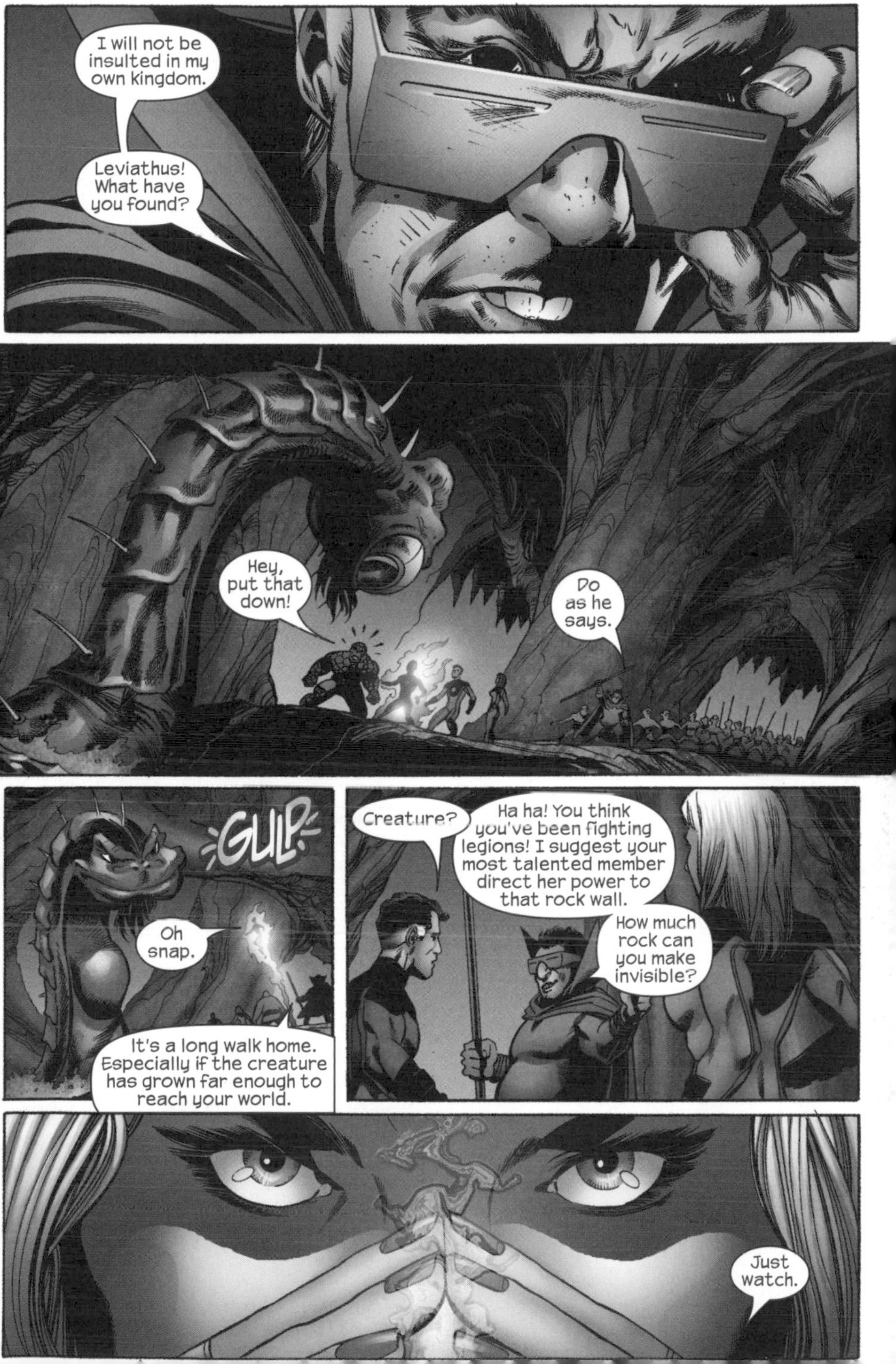
I will not be insulted in my own kingdom.
Leviathus! What have you found?
Hey, put that down!
Do as he says.
GULP
Oh snap.
It's a long walk home. Especially if the creature has grown far enough to reach your world.
Creature?
Ha ha! You think you've been fighting legions! I suggest your most talented member direct her power to that rock wall.
How much rock can you make invisible?
Just watch.

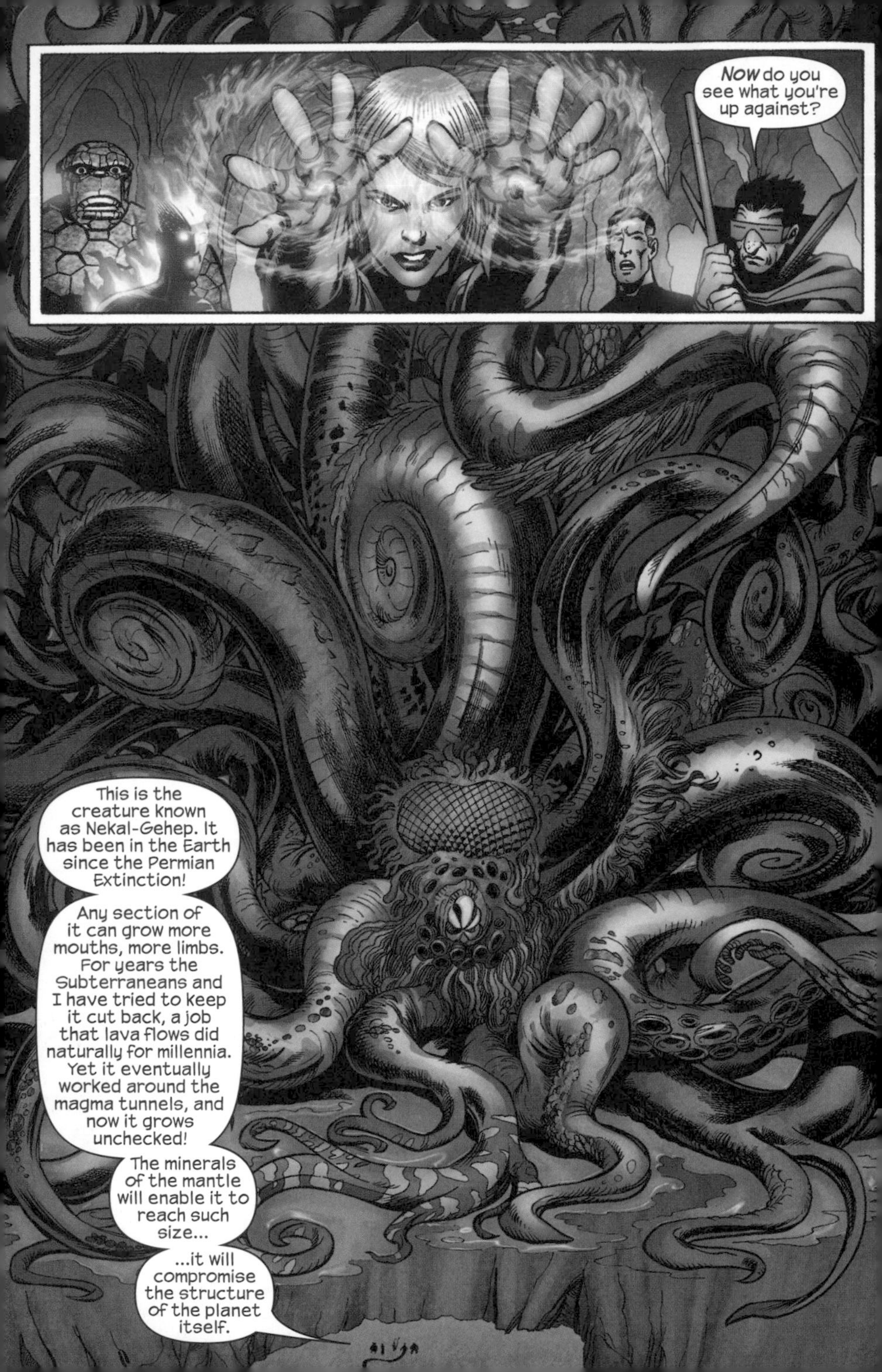

NOW do you see what you're up against?
This is the creature known as Nekal-Gehep. It has been in the Earth since the Permian Extinction!
Any section of it can grow more mouths, more limbs. For years the Subterraneans and I have tried to keep it cut back, a job that lava flows did naturally for millennia. Yet it eventually worked around the magma tunnels, and now it grows unchecked!
The minerals of the mantle will enable it to reach such size...
...it will compromise the structure of the planet itself.

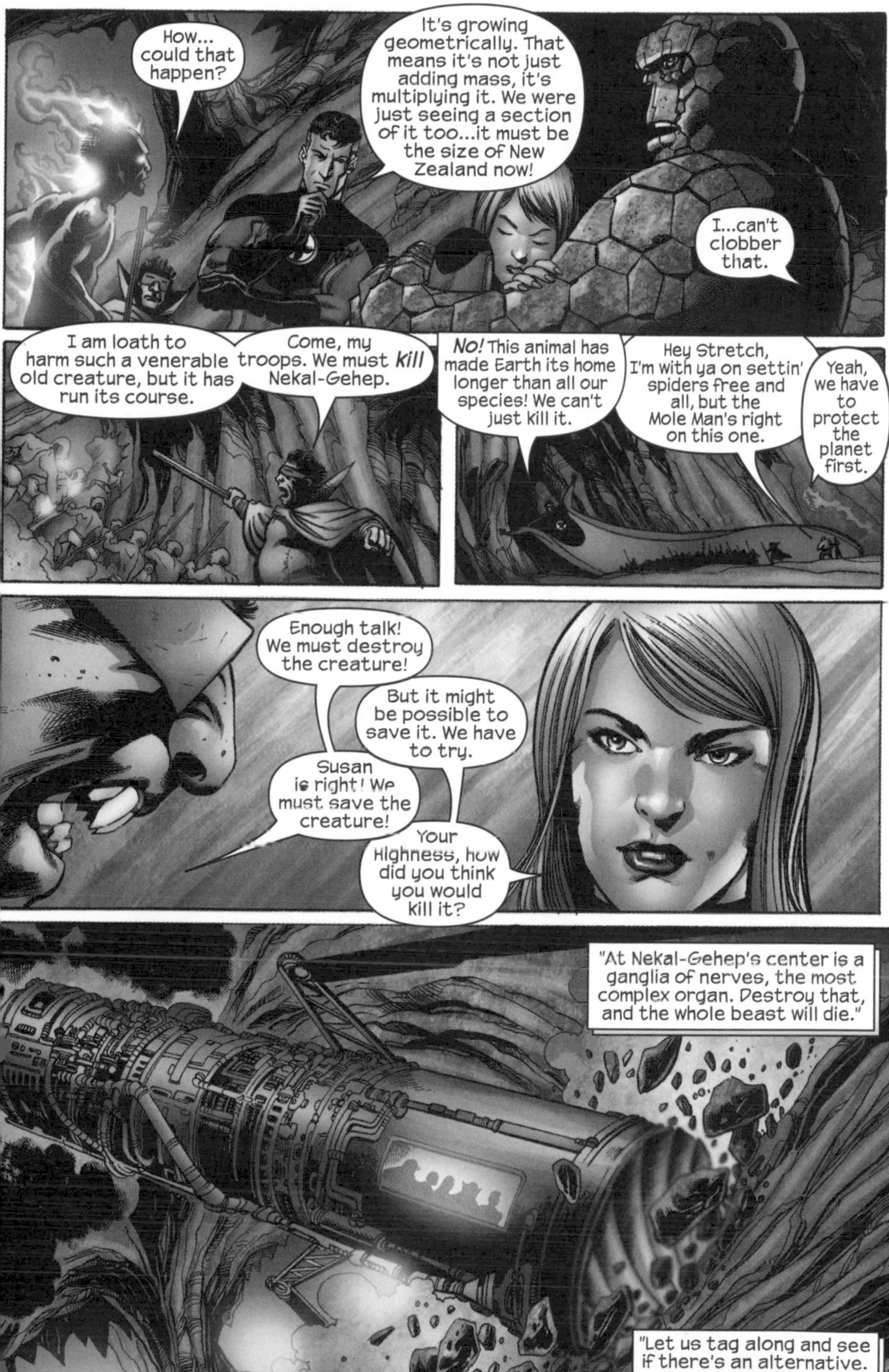

How... could that happen?
It's growing geometrically. That means it's not just adding mass, it's multiplying it. We were just seeing a section of it too...it must be the size of New Zealand now!
I...can't clobber that.
I am loath to harm such a venerable old creature, but it has run its course.
Come, my troops. We must *kill* Nekal-Gehep.
No! This animal has made Earth its home longer than all our species! We can't just kill it.
Hey Stretch, I'm with ya on settin' spiders free and all, but the Mole Man's right on this one.
Yeah, we have to protect the planet first.
Enough talk! We must destroy the creature!
But it might be possible to save it. We have to try.
Susan is right! We must save the creature!
Your Highness, how did you think you would kill it?
"At Nekal-Gehep's center is a ganglia of nerves, the most complex organ. Destroy that, and the whole beast will die."
"Let us tag along and see if there's an alternative. We won't fight you."

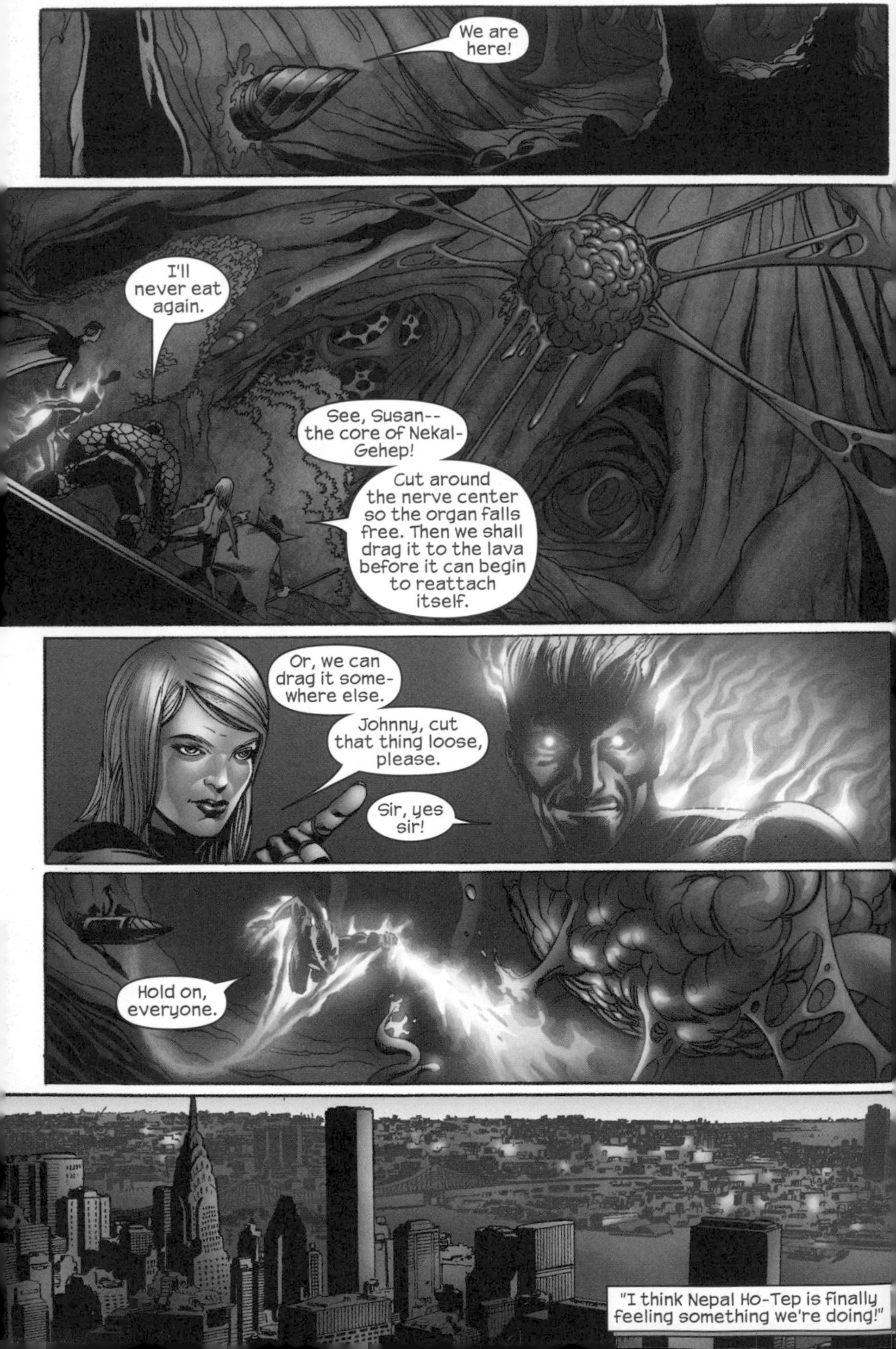
We are here!
I'll never eat again.
See, Susan-- the core of Nekal-Gehep!
Cut around the nerve center so the organ falls free. Then we shall drag it to the lava before it can begin to reattach itself.
Or, we can drag it some-where else.
Johnny, cut that thing loose, please.
Sir, yes sir!
Hold on, everyone.
"I think Nepal Ho-Tep is finally feeling something we're doing!"

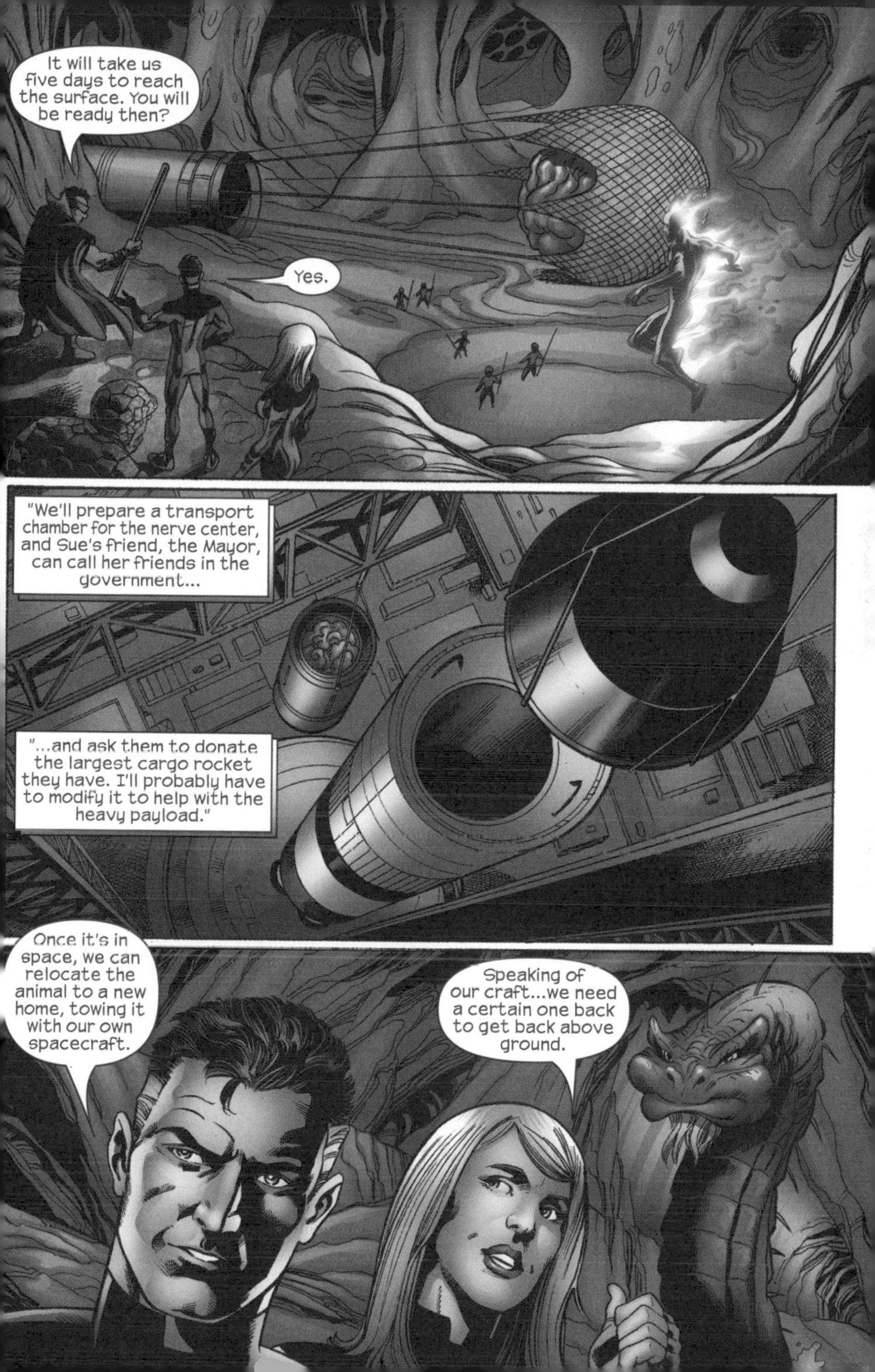
It will take us five days to reach the surface. You will be ready then?
Yes.
"We'll prepare a transport chamber for the nerve center, and Sue's friend, the Mayor, can call her friends in the government...
"...and ask them to donate the largest cargo rocket they have. I'll probably have to modify it to help with the heavy payload."
Once it's in space, we can relocate the animal to a new home, towing it with our own spacecraft.
Speaking of our craft...we need a certain one back to get back above ground.

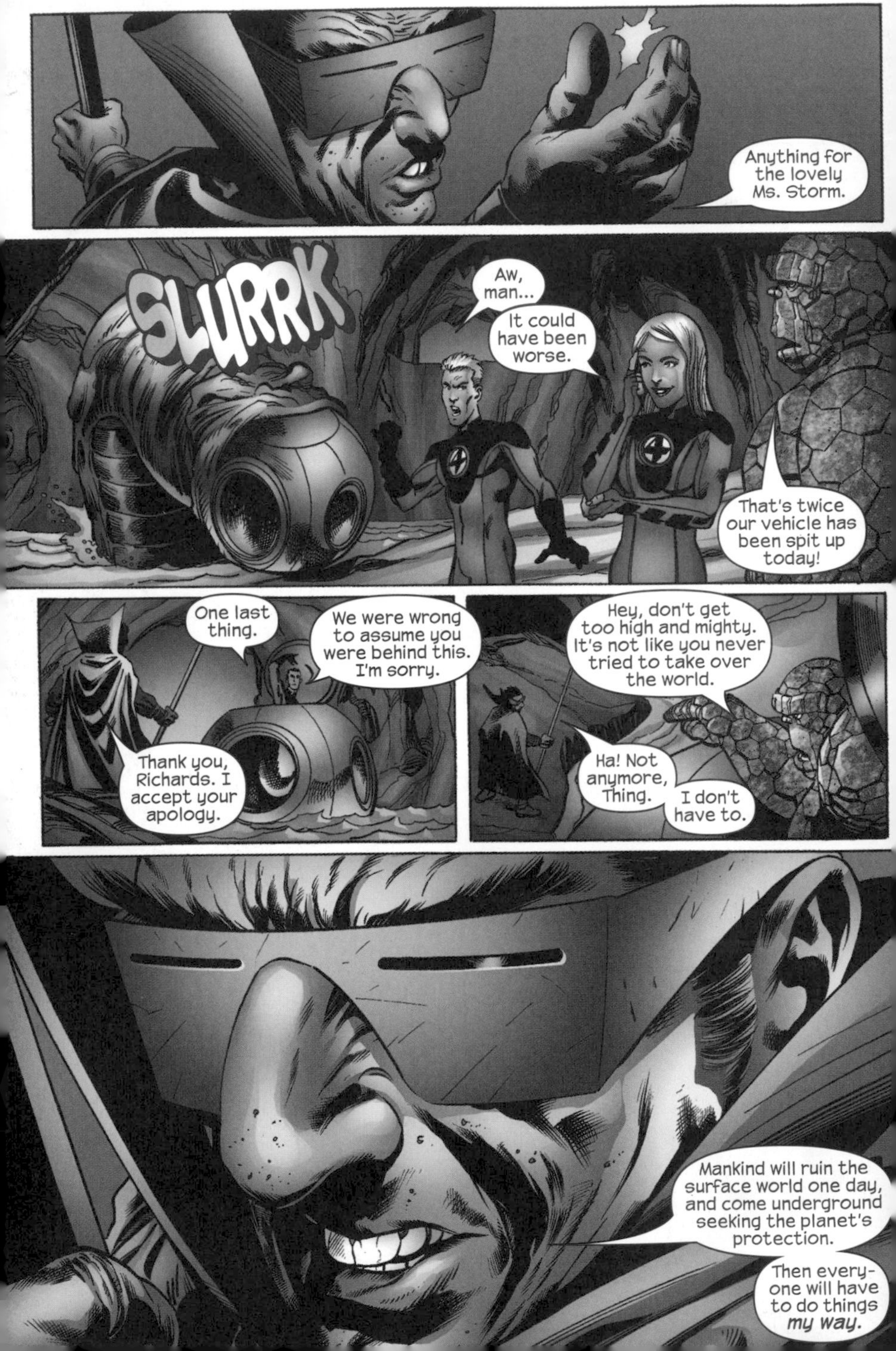
Anything for the lovely Ms. Storm.
SLURRK
Aw, man...
It could have been worse.
That's twice our vehicle has been spit up today!
One last thing.
We were wrong to assume you were behind this. I'm sorry.
Thank you, Richards. I accept your apology.
Hey, don't get too high and mighty. It's not like you never tried to take over the world.
Ha! Not anymore, Thing.
I don't have to.
Mankind will ruin the surface world one day, and come underground seeking the planet's protection.
Then every-one will have to do things *my way*.

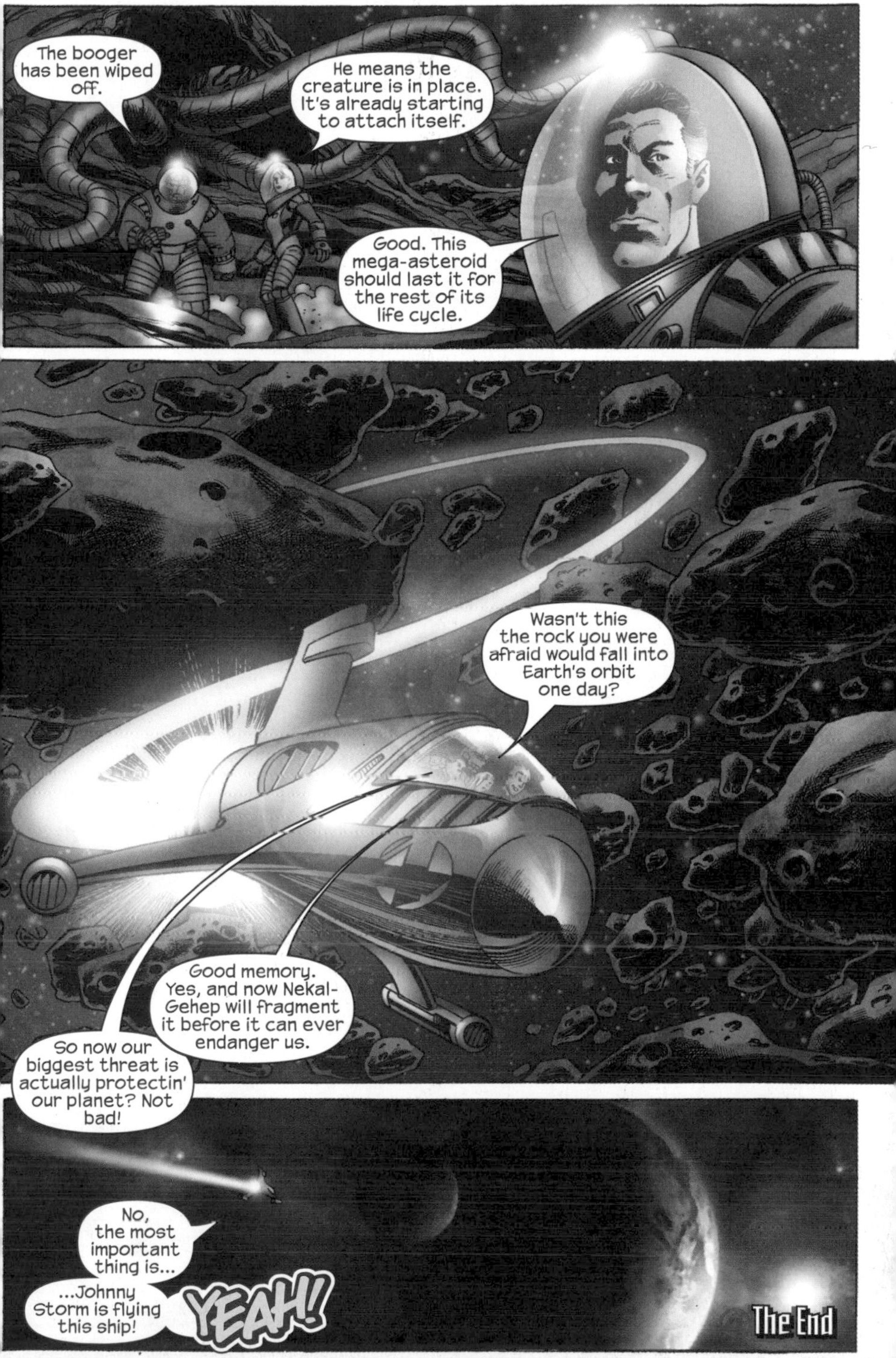
The booger has been wiped off.
He means the creature is in place. It's already starting to attach itself.
Good. This mega-asteroid should last it for the rest of its life cycle.
Wasn't this the rock you were afraid would fall into Earth's orbit one day?
Good memory. Yes, and now Nekal-Gehep will fragment it before it can ever endanger us.
So now our biggest threat is actually protectin' our planet? Not bad!
No, the most important thing is...
...Johnny Storm is flying this ship!
YEAH!!
The End

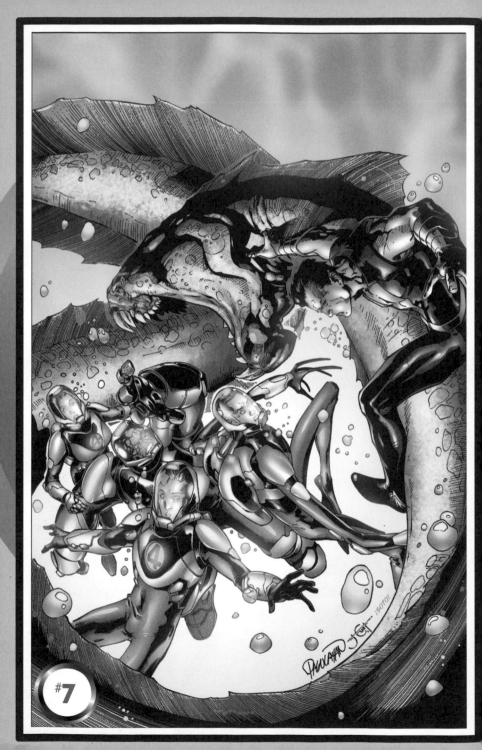

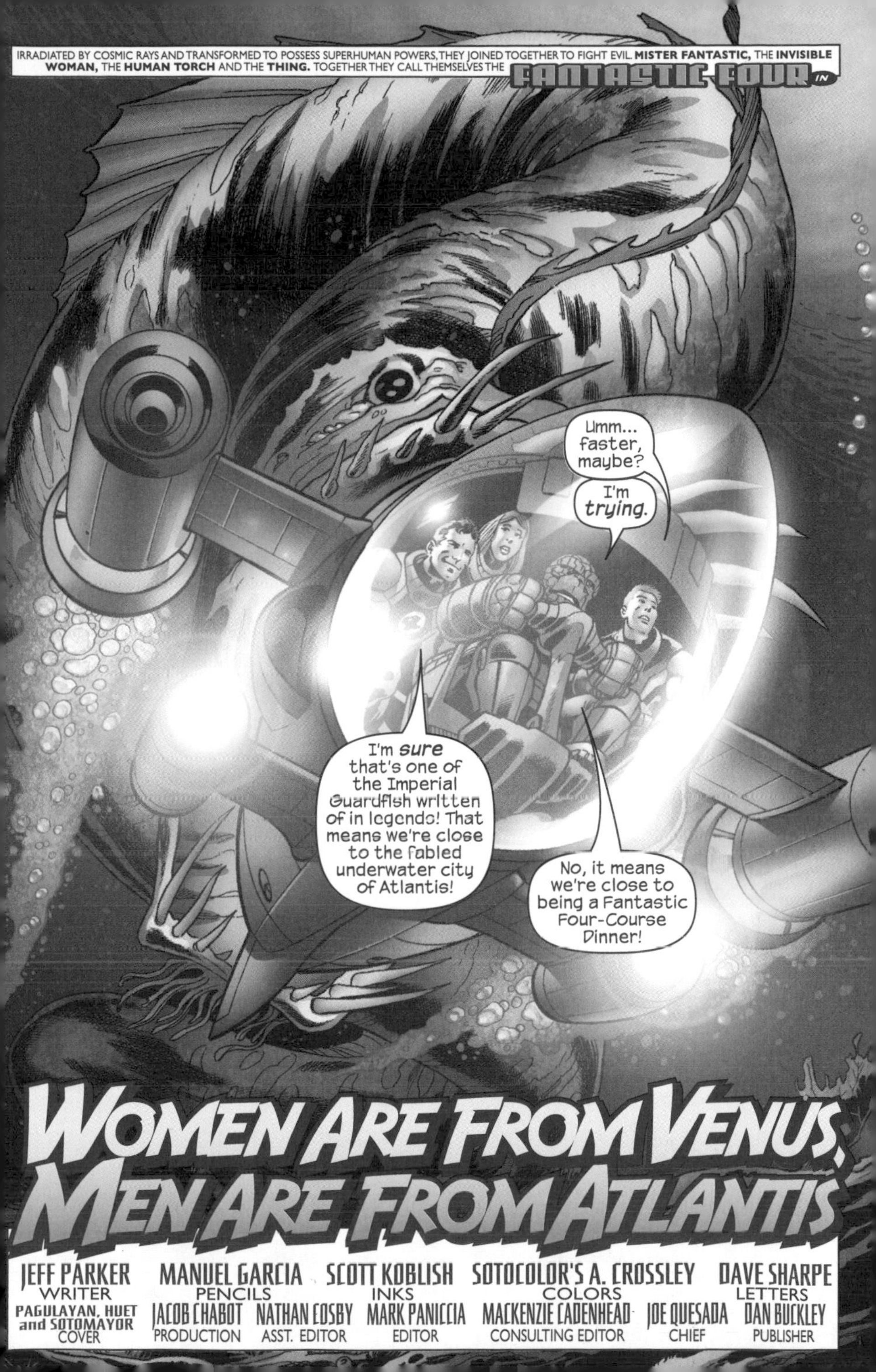
IRRADIATED BY COSMIC RAYS AND TRANSFORMED TO POSSESS SUPERHUMAN POWERS, THEY JOINED TOGETHER TO FIGHT EVIL. MISTER FANTASTIC, THE INVISIBLE WOMAN, THE HUMAN TORCH AND THE THING. TOGETHER THEY CALL THEMSELVES THE FANTASTIC FOUR IN
Umm... faster, maybe?
I'm trying.
I'm sure that's one of the Imperial Guardfish written of in legends! That means we're close to the fabled underwater city of Atlantis!
No, it means we're close to being a Fantastic Four-Course Dinner!
WOMEN ARE FROM VENUS, MEN ARE FROM ATLANTIS
JEFF PARKER WRITER
MANUEL GARCIA PENCILS
SCOTT KOBLISH INKS
SOTOCOLOR'S A. CROSSLEY COLORS
DAVE SHARPE LETTERS
PAGULAYAN, HUET and SOTOMAYOR COVER
JACOB CHABOT PRODUCTION
NATHAN COSBY ASST. EDITOR
MARK PANICCIA EDITOR
MACKENZIE CADENHEAD CONSULTING EDITOR
JOE QUESADA CHIEF
DAN BUCKLEY PUBLISHER

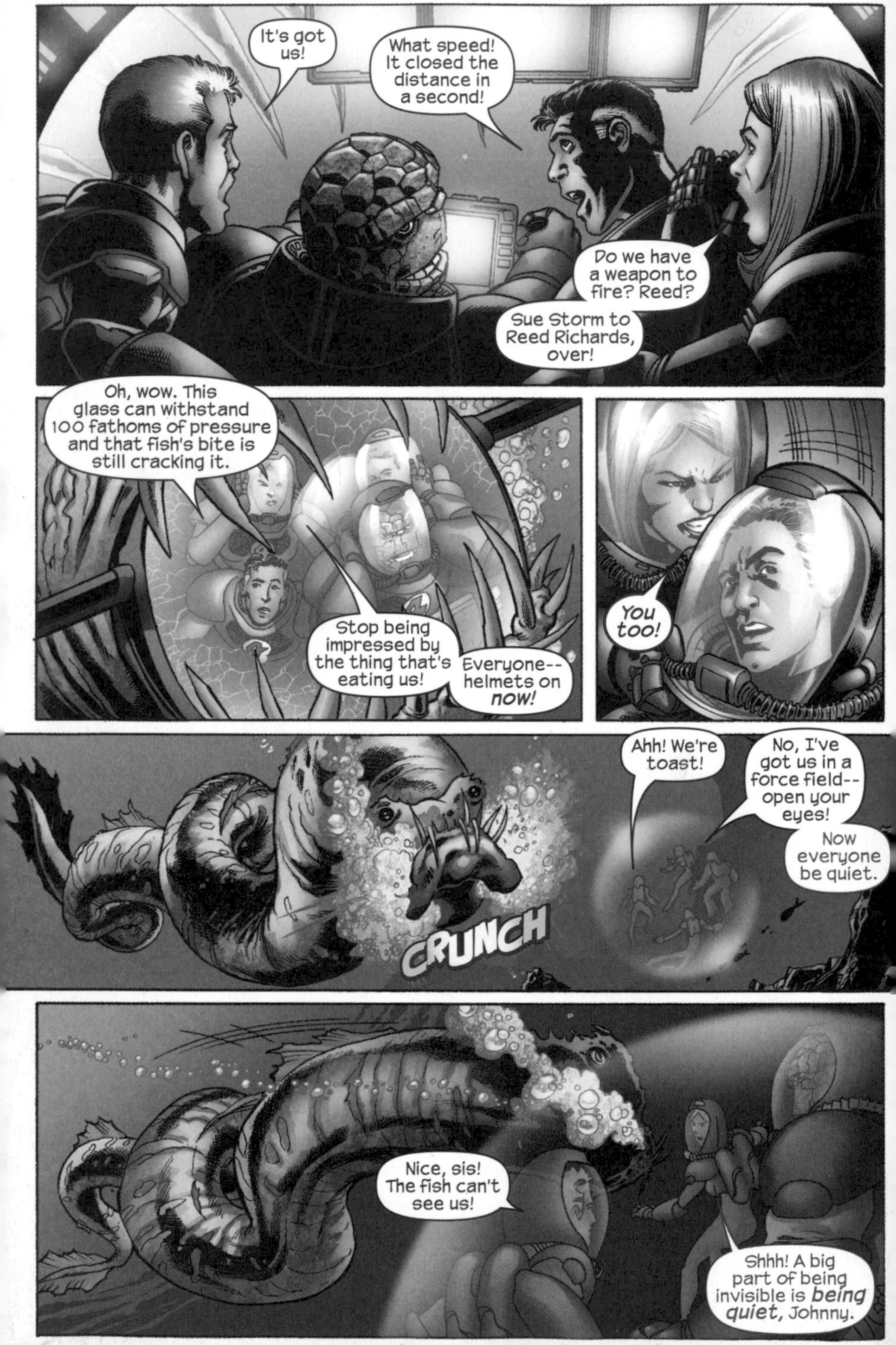

It's got us!
What speed! It closed the distance in a second!
Do we have a weapon to fire? Reed?
Sue Storm to Reed Richards, over!
Oh, wow. This glass can withstand 100 fathoms of pressure and that fish's bite is still cracking it.
Stop being impressed by the thing that's eating us!
Everyone-- helmets on *now!*
You too!
CRUNCH
Ahh! We're toast!
No, I've got us in a force field-- open your eyes!
Now everyone be quiet.
Nice, sis! The fish can't see us!
Shhh! A big part of being invisible is ***being quiet***, Johnny.

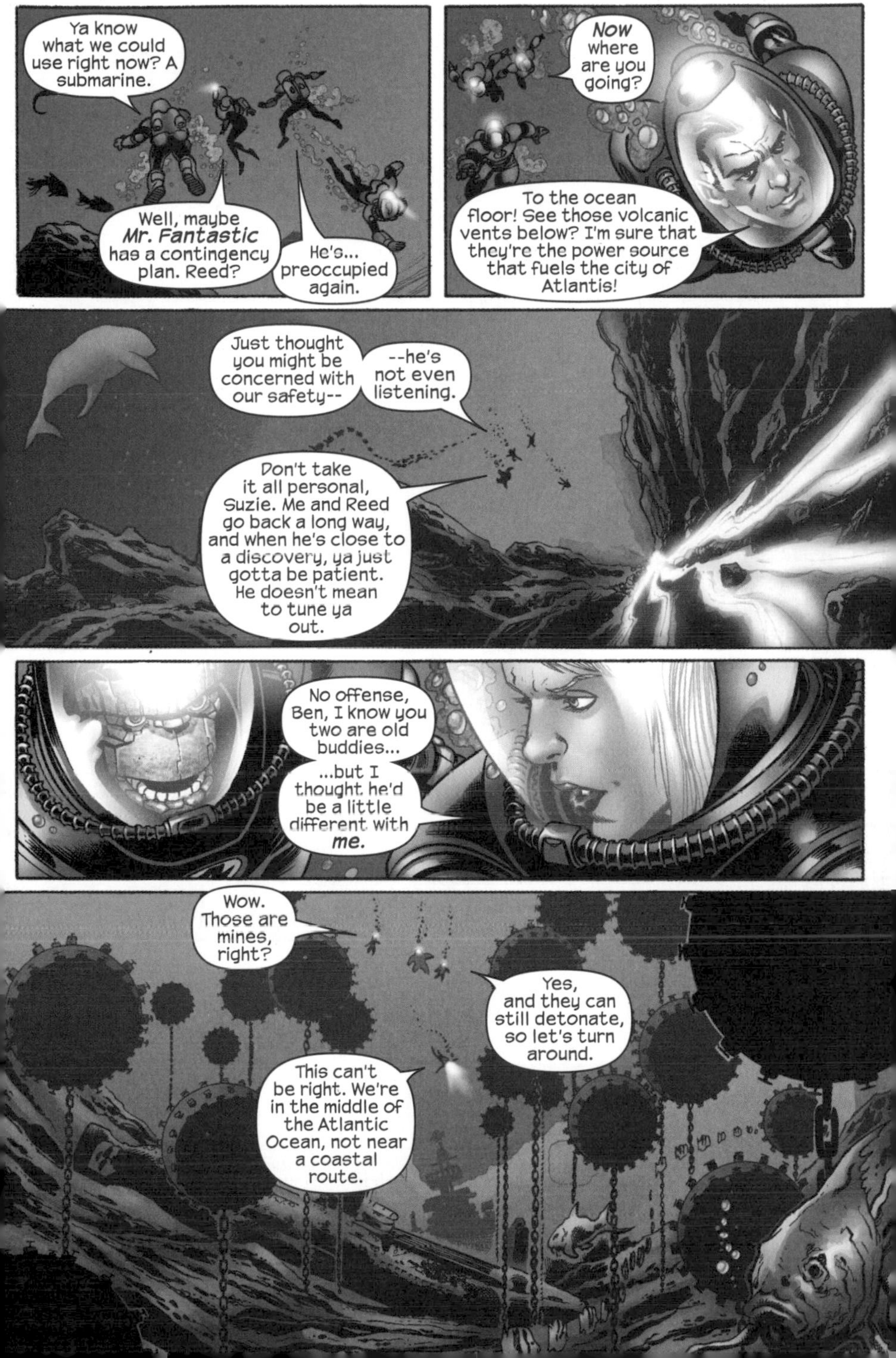
Ya know what we could use right now? A submarine.
Well, maybe *Mr. Fantastic* has a contingency plan. Reed?
He's... preoccupied again.
Now where are you going?
To the ocean floor! See those volcanic vents below? I'm sure that they're the power source that fuels the city of Atlantis!
Just thought you might be concerned with our safety--
--he's not even listening.
Don't take it all personal, Suzie. Me and Reed go back a long way, and when he's close to a discovery, ya just gotta be patient. He doesn't mean to tune ya out.
No offense, Ben, I know you two are old buddies...
...but I thought he'd be a little different with *me.*
Wow. Those are mines, right?
Yes, and they can still detonate, so let's turn around.
This can't be right. We're in the middle of the Atlantic Ocean, not near a coastal route.

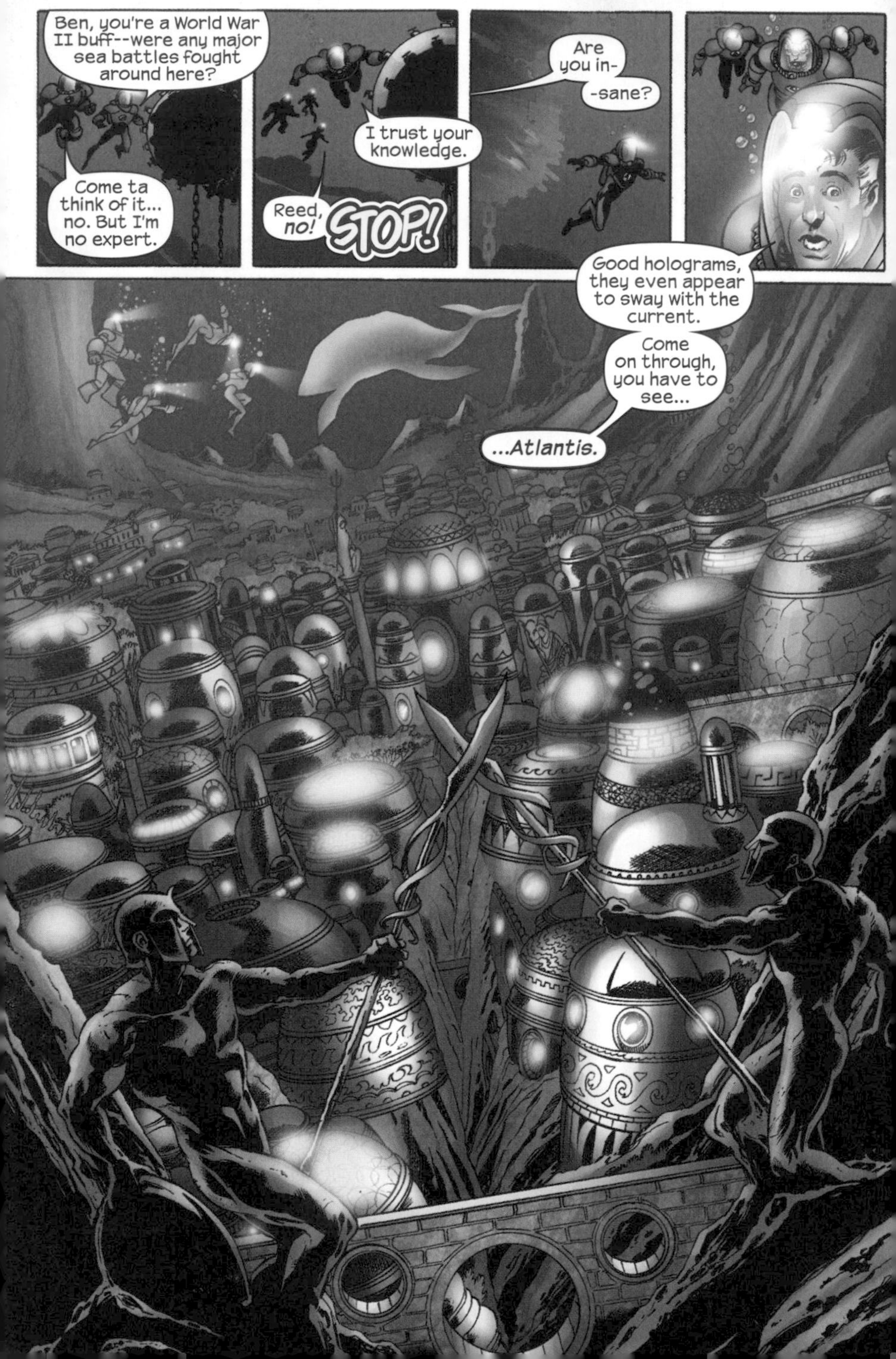
Ben, you're a World War II buff--were any major sea battles fought around here?
Come ta think of it... no. But I'm no expert.
I trust your knowledge.
Reed, no!
STOP!
Are you in-
-sane?
Good holograms, they even appear to sway with the current.
Come on through, you have to see...
...Atlantis.

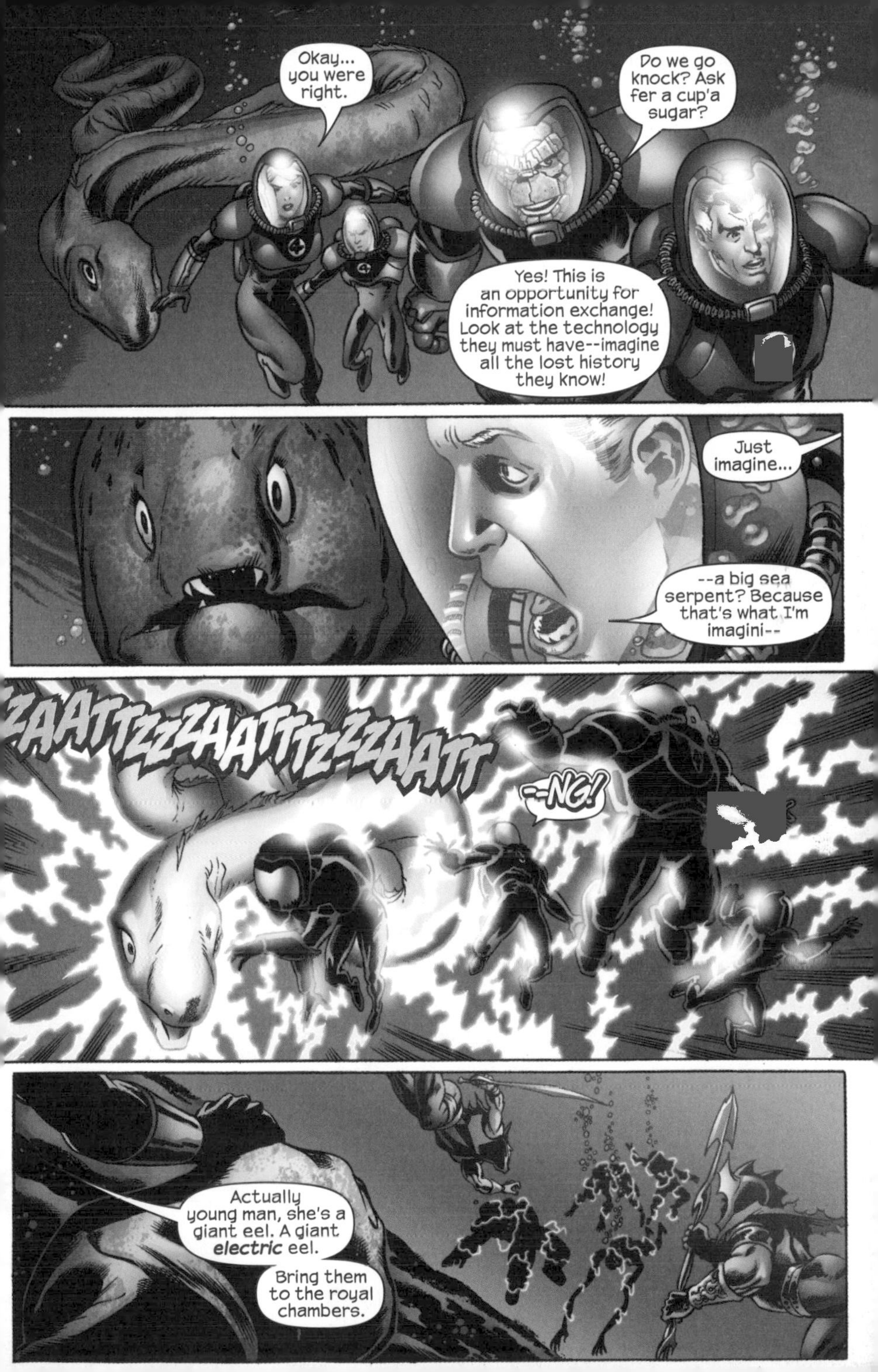

Okay... you were right.
Do we go knock? Ask fer a cup'a sugar?
Yes! This is an opportunity for information exchange! Look at the technology they must have--imagine all the lost history they know!
Just imagine...
--a big sea serpent? Because that's what I'm imagini--
ZAATTZZZAATTTZZZAATT
--NG!
Actually young man, she's a giant eel. A giant *electric* eel.
Bring them to the royal chambers.

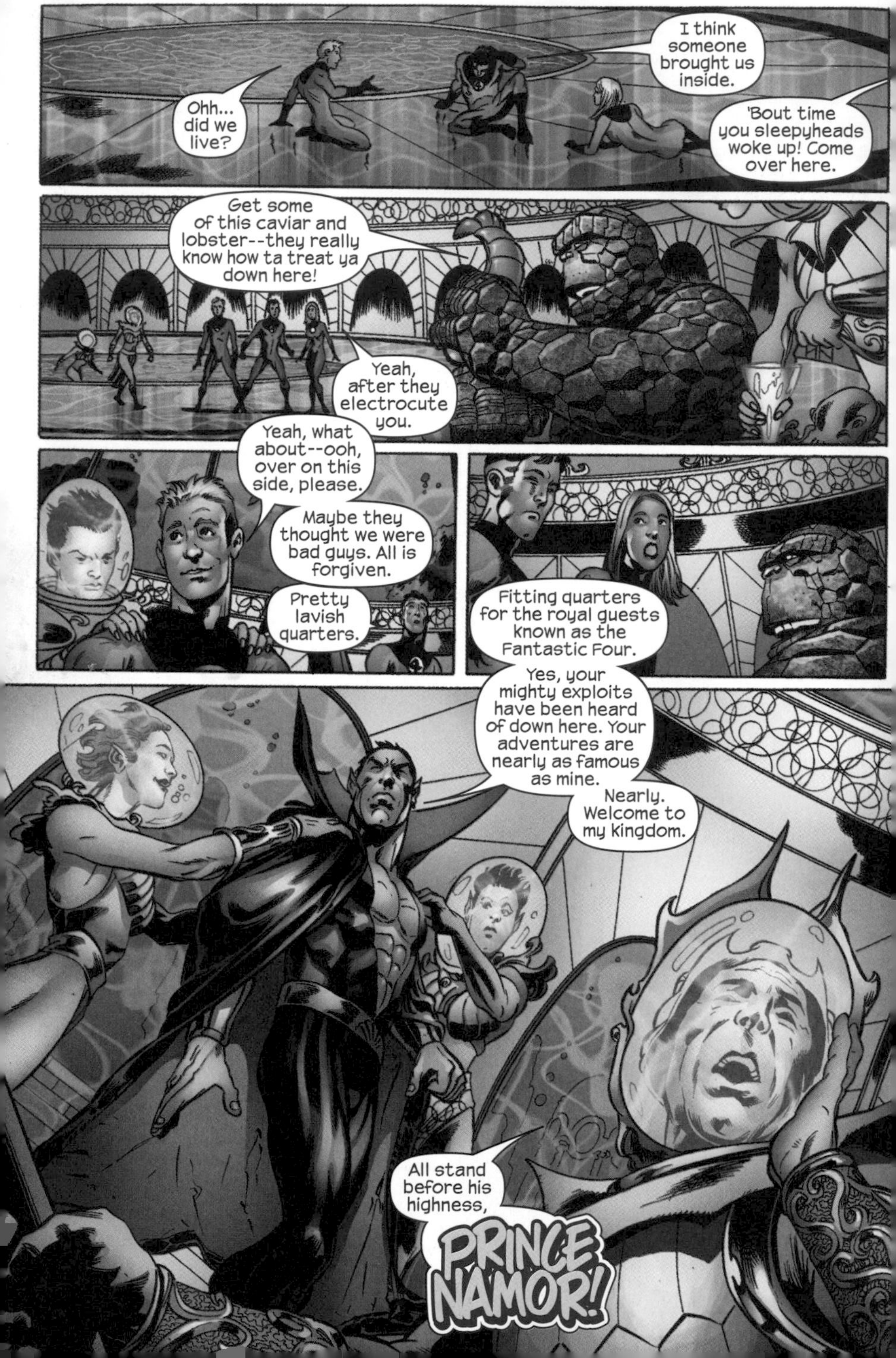
Ohh... did we live?
I think someone brought us inside.
'Bout time you sleepyheads woke up! Come over here.
Get some of this caviar and lobster--they really know how ta treat ya down here!
Yeah, after they electrocute you.
Yeah, what about--ooh, over on this side, please.
Maybe they thought we were bad guys. All is forgiven.
Pretty lavish quarters.
Fitting quarters for the royal guests known as the Fantastic Four.
Yes, your mighty exploits have been heard of down here. Your adventures are nearly as famous as mine.
Nearly. Welcome to my kingdom.
All stand before his highness,
PRINCE NAMOR!

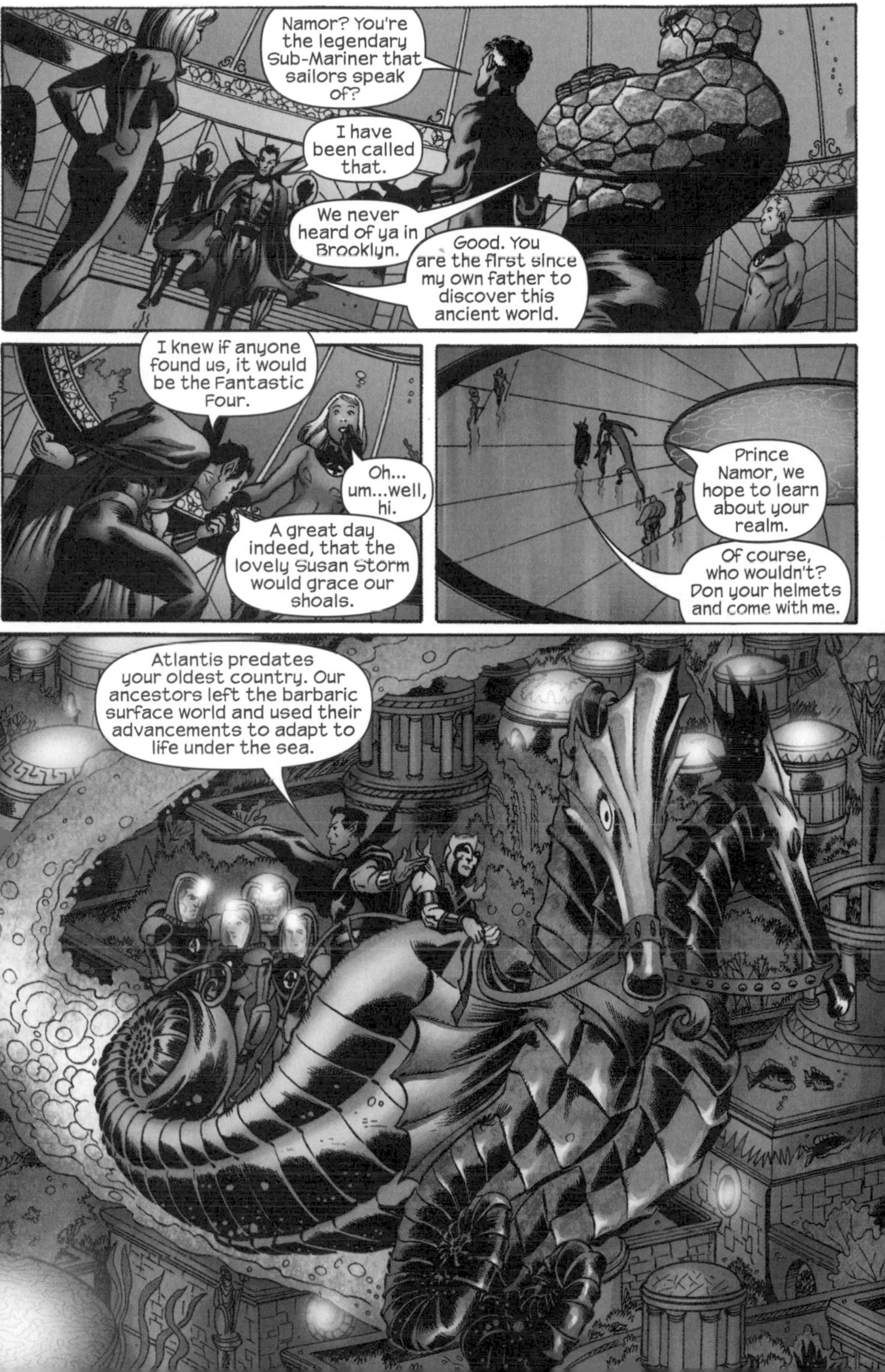
Namor? You're the legendary Sub-Mariner that sailors speak of?
I have been called that.
We never heard of ya in Brooklyn.
Good. You are the first since my own father to discover this ancient world.
I knew if anyone found us, it would be the Fantastic Four.
Oh... um...well, hi.
A great day indeed, that the lovely Susan Storm would grace our shoals.
Prince Namor, we hope to learn about your realm.
Of course, who wouldn't? Don your helmets and come with me.
Atlantis predates your oldest country. Our ancestors left the barbaric surface world and used their advancements to adapt to life under the sea.

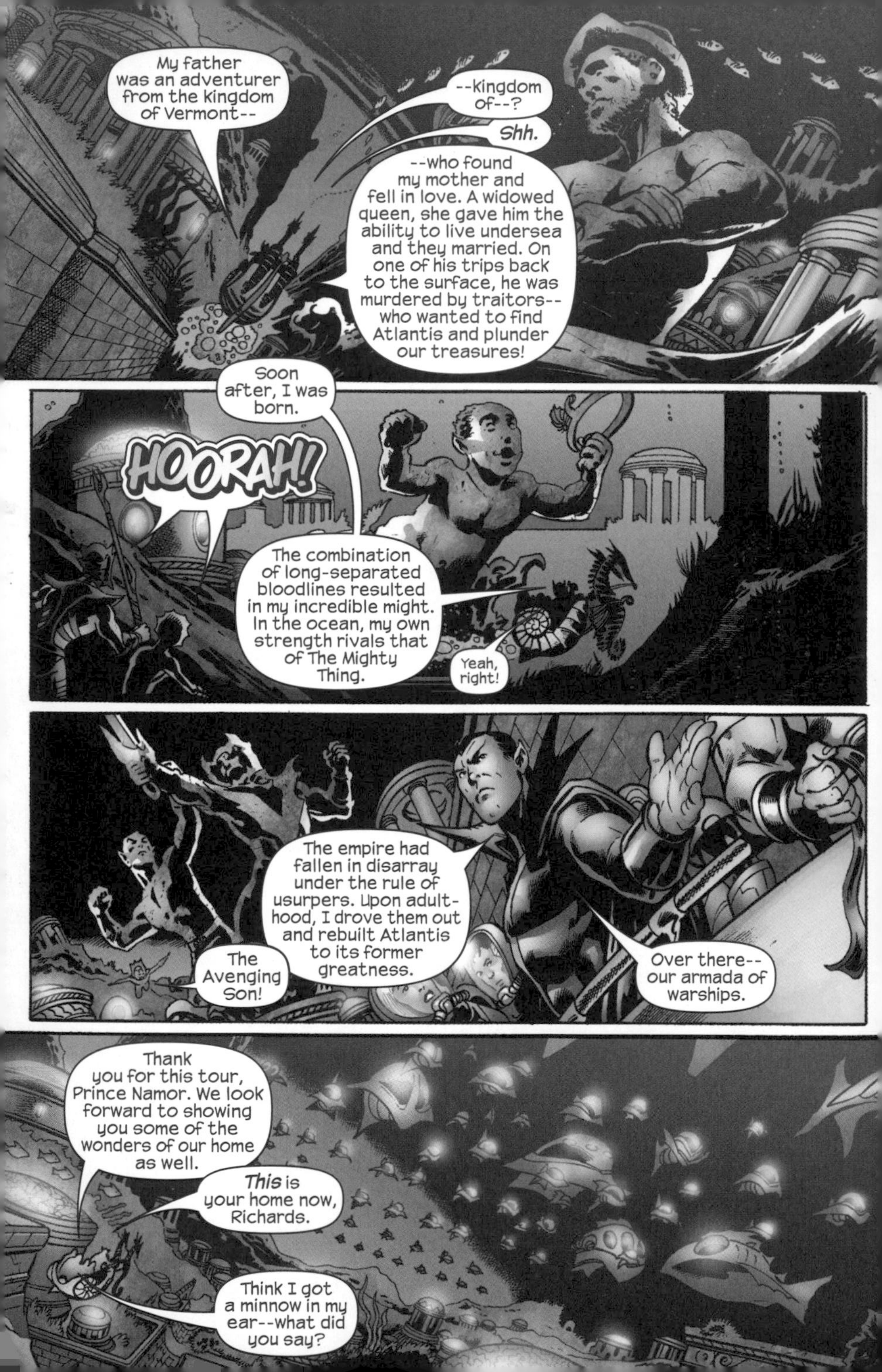
My father was an adventurer from the kingdom of Vermont--
--kingdom of--?
Shh.
--who found my mother and fell in love. A widowed queen, she gave him the ability to live undersea and they married. On one of his trips back to the surface, he was murdered by traitors-- who wanted to find Atlantis and plunder our treasures!
Soon after, I was born.
HOORAH!!
The combination of long-separated bloodlines resulted in my incredible might. In the ocean, my own strength rivals that of The Mighty Thing.
Yeah, right!
The empire had fallen in disarray under the rule of usurpers. Upon adult-hood, I drove them out and rebuilt Atlantis to its former greatness.
The Avenging Son!
Over there-- our armada of warships.
Thank you for this tour, Prince Namor. We look forward to showing you some of the wonders of our home as well.
This is your home now, Richards.
Think I got a minnow in my ear--what did you say?

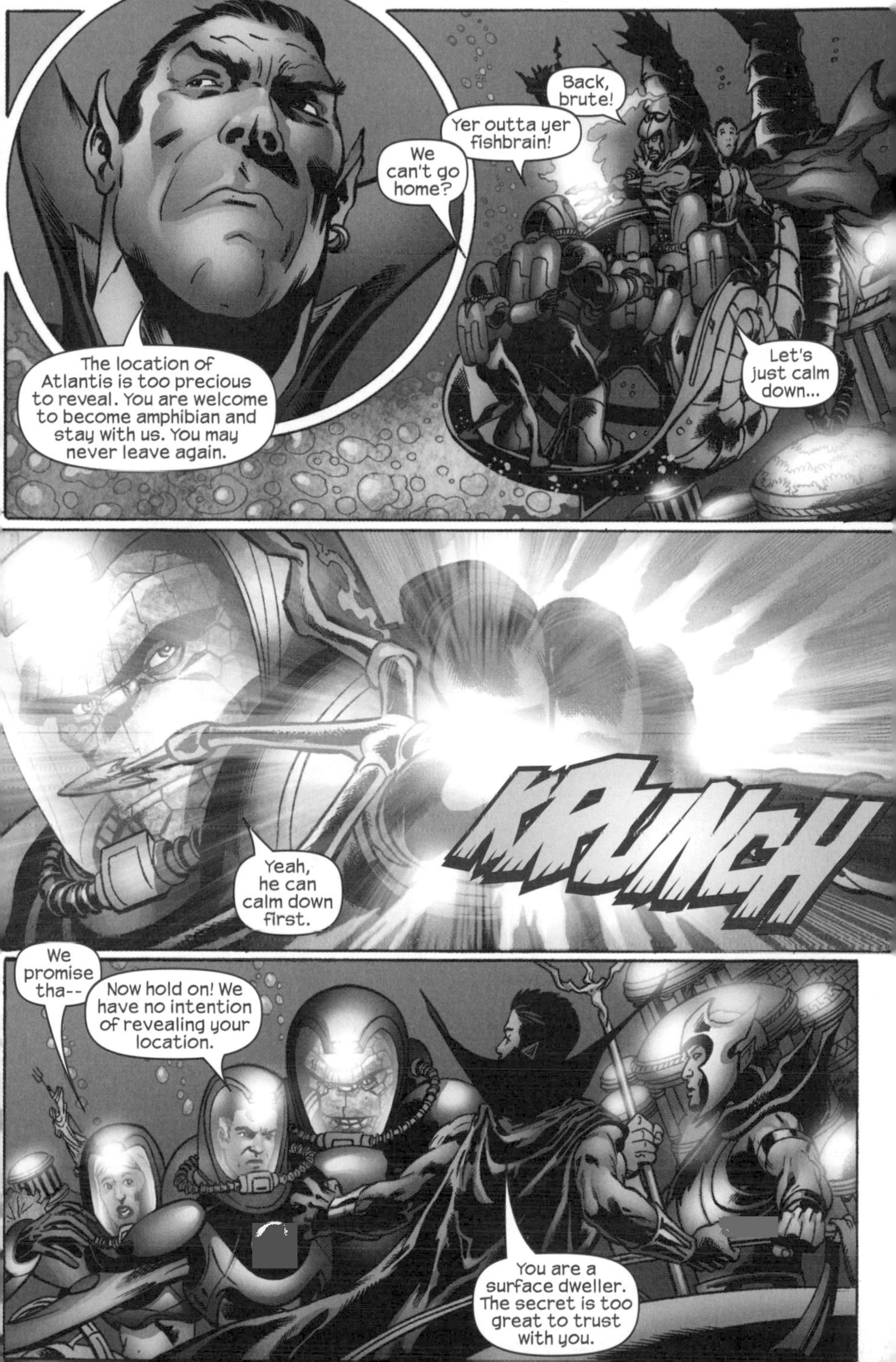
The location of Atlantis is too precious to reveal. You are welcome to become amphibian and stay with us. You may never leave again.
We can't go home?
Yer outta yer fishbrain!
Back, brute!
Let's just calm down...
KRUNCH
Yeah, he can calm down first.
We promise tha--
Now hold on! We have no intention of revealing your location.
You are a surface dweller. The secret is too great to trust with you.

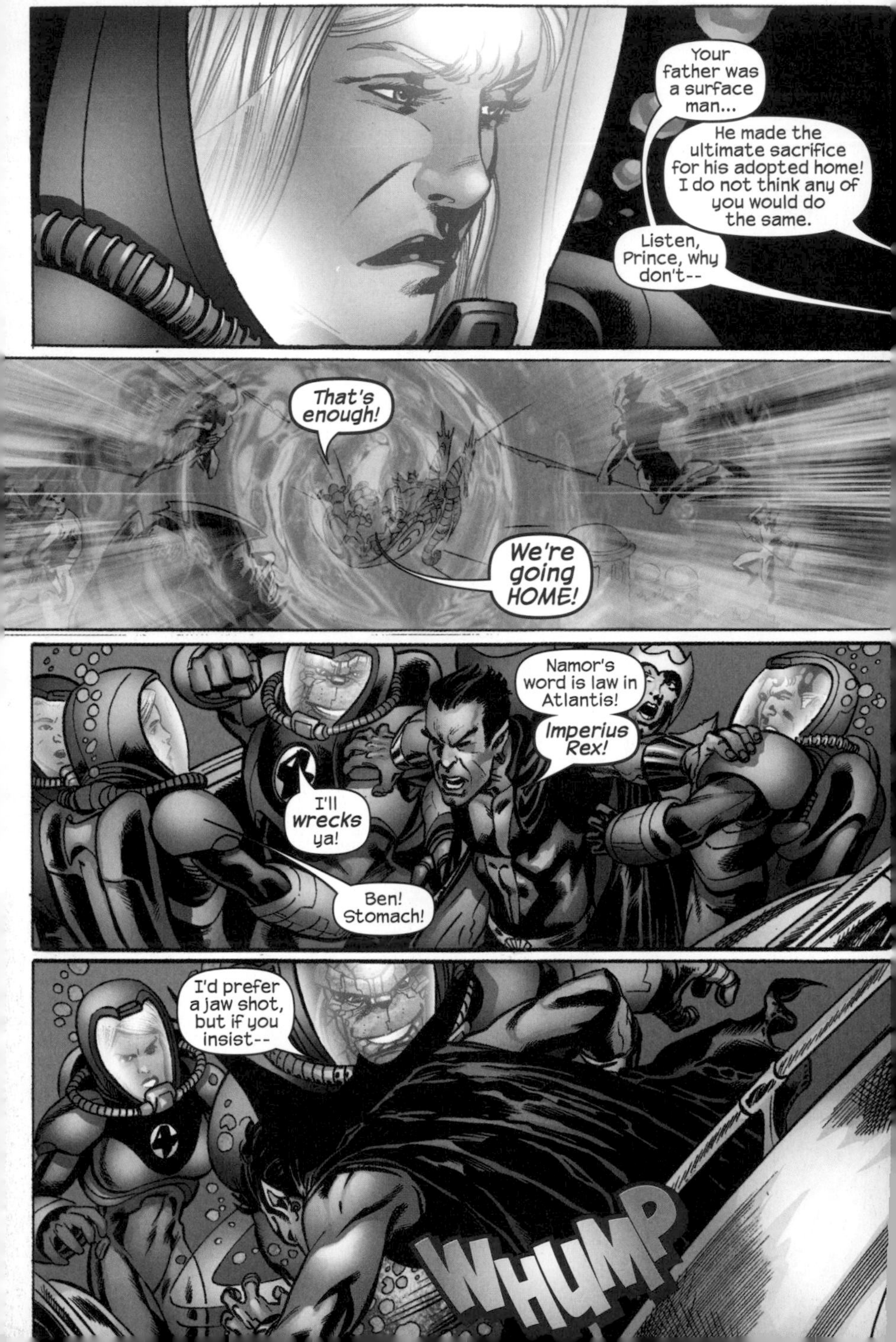
Your father was a surface man...
He made the ultimate sacrifice for his adopted home! I do not think any of you would do the same.
Listen, Prince, why don't--
That's enough!
We're going HOME!
Namor's word is law in Atlantis!
Imperius Rex!
I'll wrecks ya!
Ben! Stomach!
I'd prefer a jaw shot, but if you insist--
WHUMP

My wrath wi--

Thanks, I didn't want him to get a breath. Johnny, steer us over to that open ship.

Cool!

We are *in there.*

Good, let's get that door closed.

Reed, make this thing go!

Okay, but I think we could have--

Hurry, please, back-up is on the way.

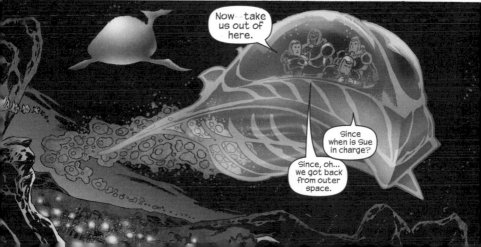

Now take us out of here.

Since when is Sue in charge?

Since, oh... we got back from outer space.

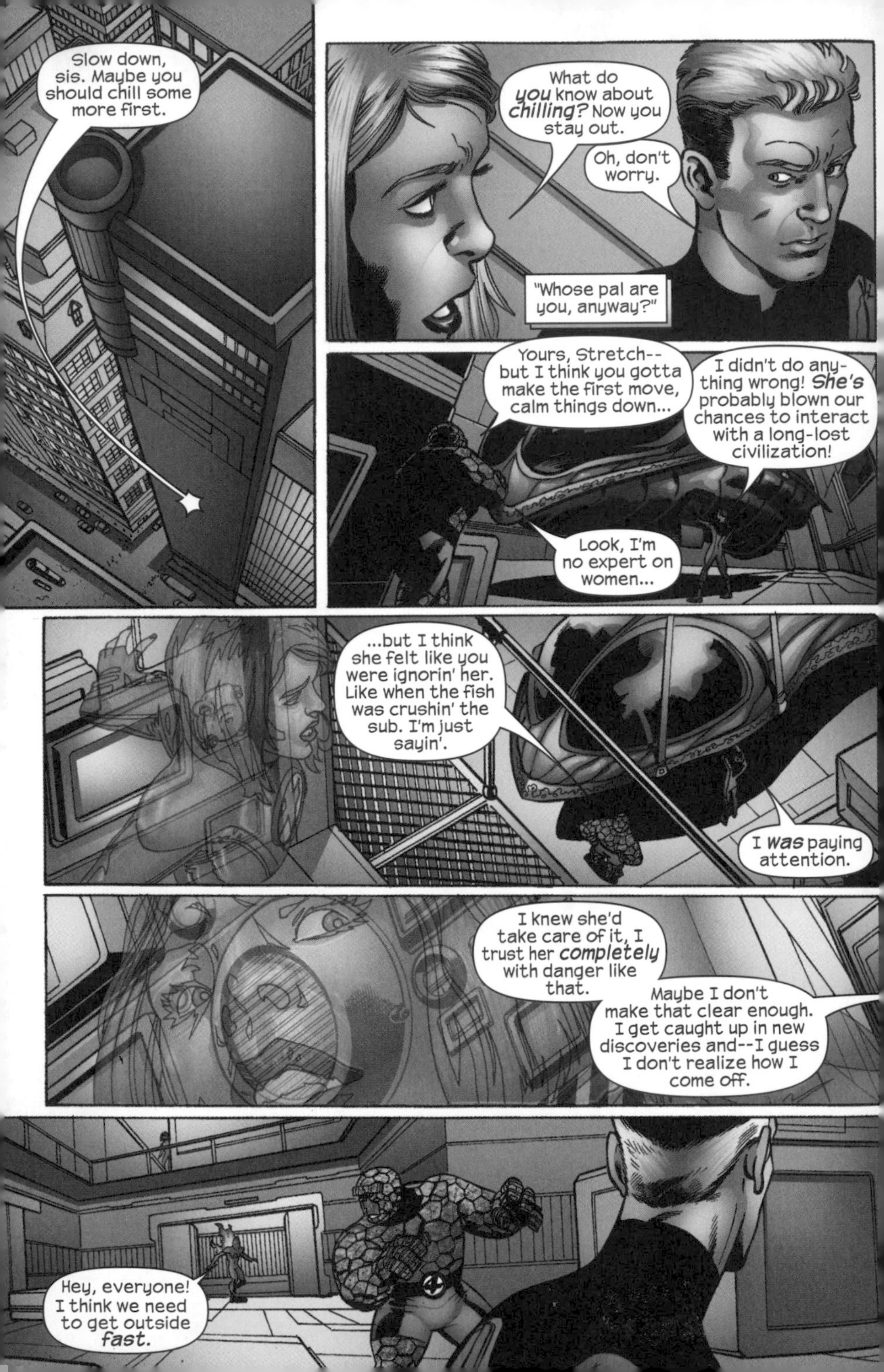
Slow down, sis. Maybe you should chill some more first.
What do *you* know about *chilling?* Now you stay out.
Oh, don't worry.
"Whose pal are you, anyway?"
Yours, Stretch--but I think you gotta make the first move, calm things down...
I didn't do any-thing wrong! *She's* probably blown our chances to interact with a long-lost civilization!
Look, I'm no expert on women...
...but I think she felt like you were ignorin' her. Like when the fish was crushin' the sub. I'm just sayin'.
I *was* paying attention.
I knew she'd take care of it, I trust her *completely* with danger like that.
Maybe I don't make that clear enough. I get caught up in new discoveries and--I guess I don't realize how I come off.
Hey, everyone! I think we need to get outside *fast.*

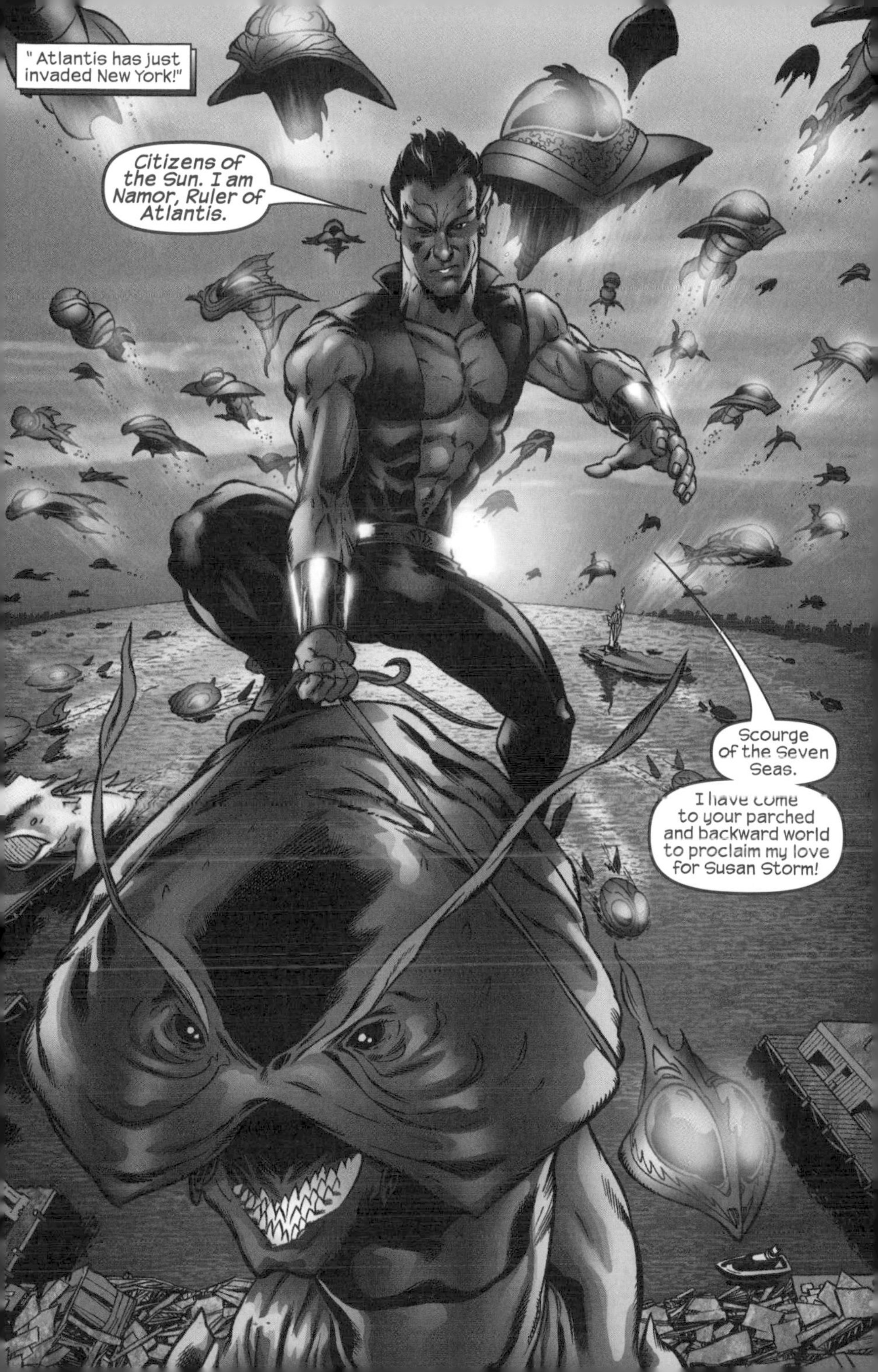
" Atlantis has just invaded New York!"
Citizens of the Sun. I am Namor, Ruler of Atlantis.
Scourge of the Seven Seas.
I have come to your parched and backward world to proclaim my love for Susan Storm!

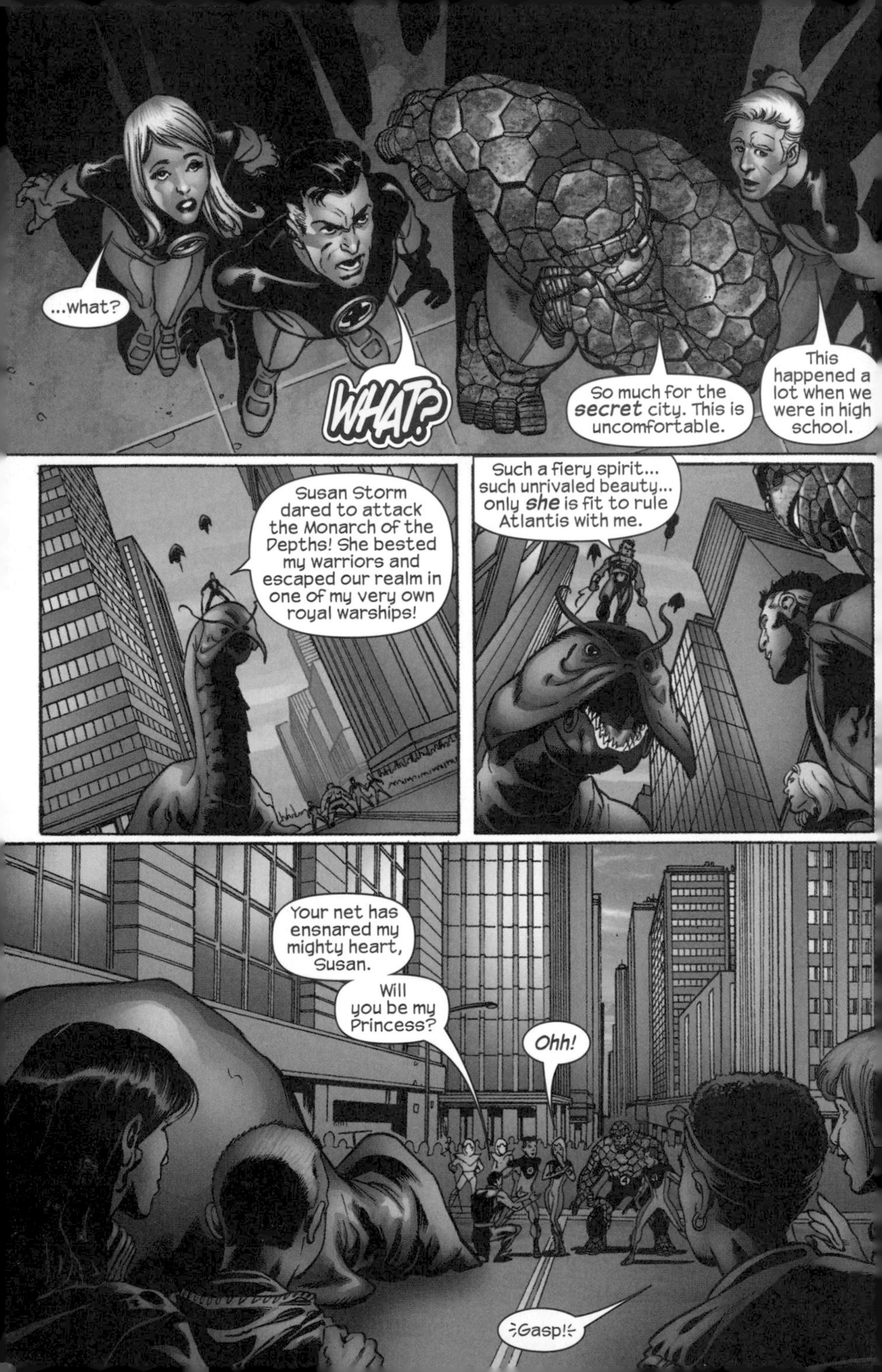
...what?
WHAT?
So much for the secret city. This is uncomfortable.
This happened a lot when we were in high school.
Susan Storm dared to attack the Monarch of the Depths! She bested my warriors and escaped our realm in one of my very own royal warships!
Such a fiery spirit... such unrivaled beauty... only she is fit to rule Atlantis with me.
Your net has ensnared my mighty heart, Susan.
Will you be my Princess?
Ohh!
Gasp!

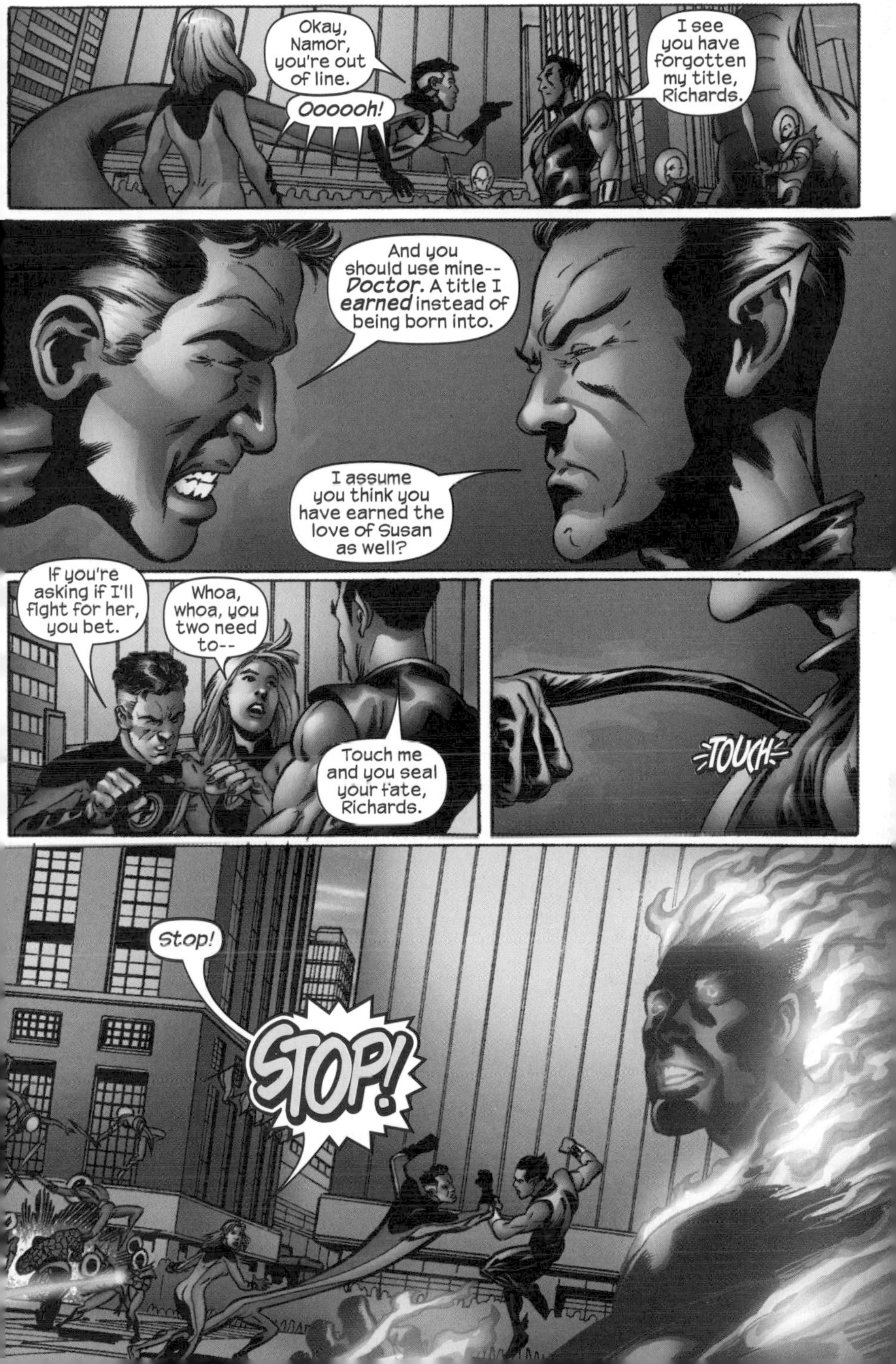
Okay, Namor, you're out of line.
Oooooh!
I see you have forgotten my title, Richards.
And you should use mine-- *Doctor*. A title I *earned* instead of being born into.
I assume you think you have earned the love of Susan as well?
If you're asking if I'll fight for her, you bet.
Whoa, whoa, you two need to--
Touch me and you seal your fate, Richards.
TOUCH
Stop!
STOP!

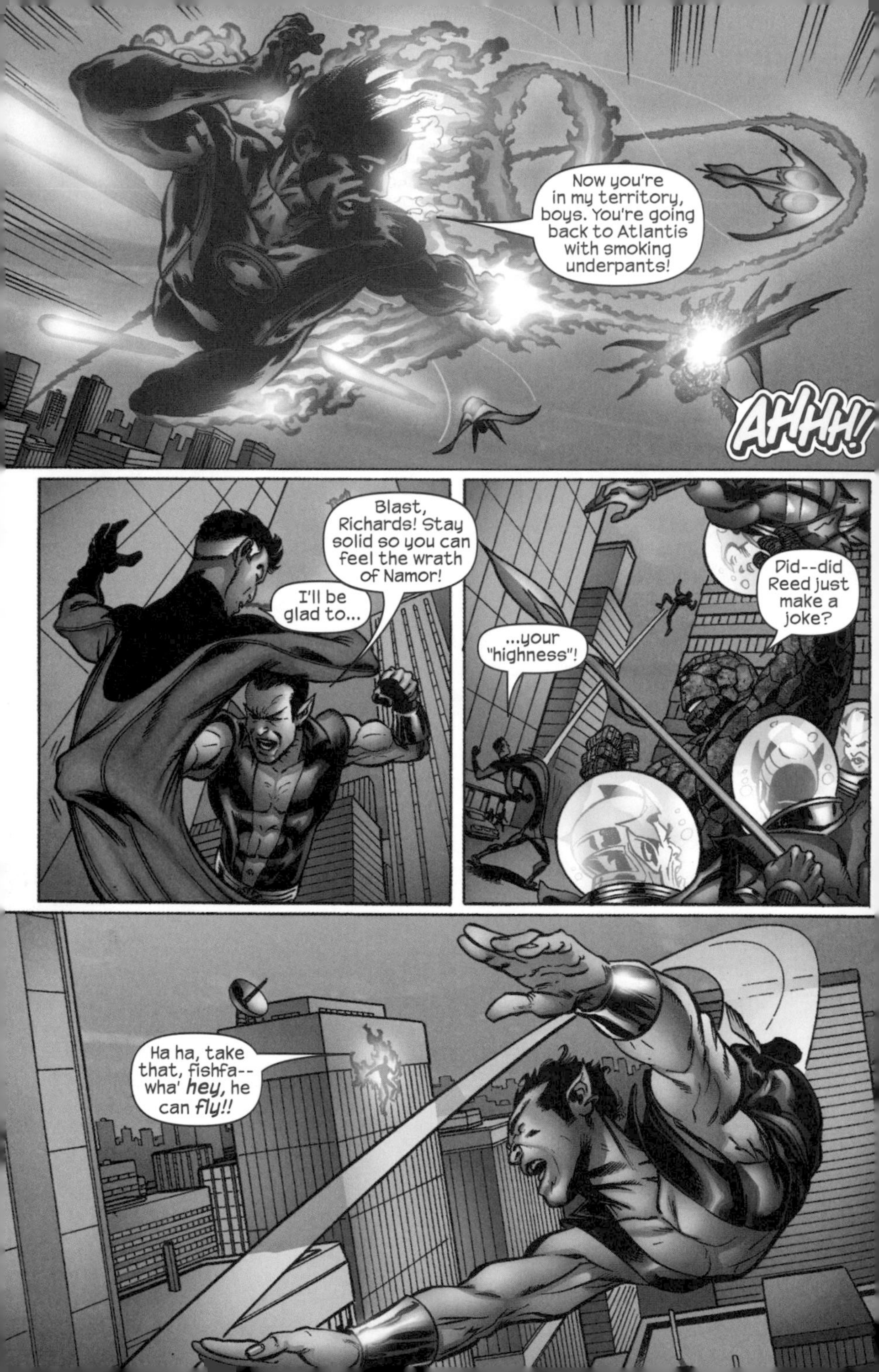
Now you're in my territory, boys. You're going back to Atlantis with smoking underpants!
AHHH!
Blast, Richards! Stay solid so you can feel the wrath of Namor!
I'll be glad to...
...your "highness"!
Did--did Reed just make a joke?
Ha ha, take that, fishfa-- wha' *hey*, he can *fly*!!

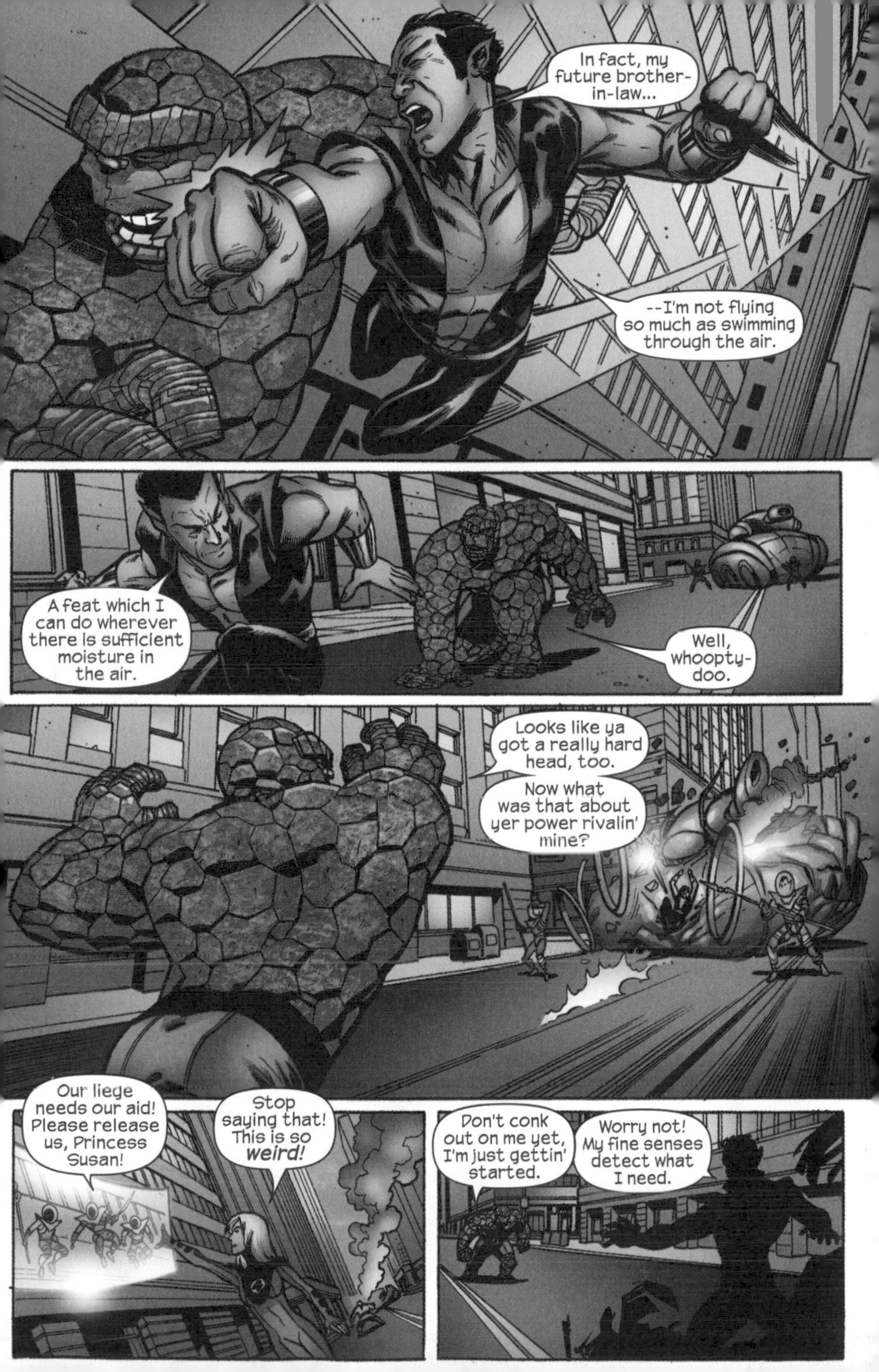
In fact, my future brother-in-law...
--I'm not flying so much as swimming through the air.
A feat which I can do wherever there is sufficient moisture in the air.
Well, whoopty-doo.
Looks like ya got a really hard head, too.
Now what was that about yer power rivalin' mine?
Our liege needs our aid! Please release us, Princess Susan!
Stop saying that! This is so *weird!*
Don't conk out on me yet, I'm just gettin' started.
Worry not! My fine senses detect what I need.

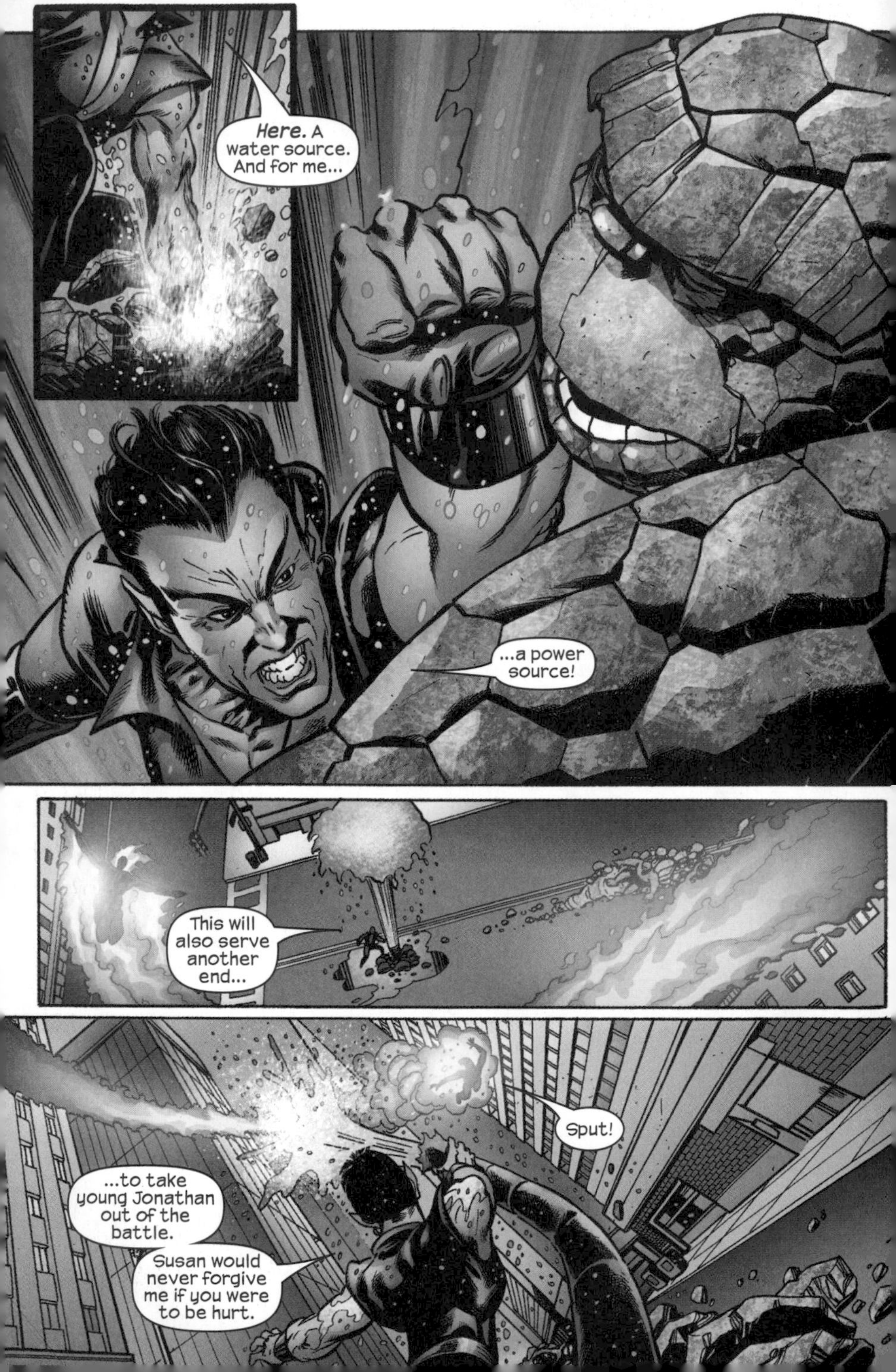
Here. A water source. And for me...
...a power source!
This will also serve another end...
Sput!
...to take young Jonathan out of the battle.
Susan would never forgive me if you were to be hurt.

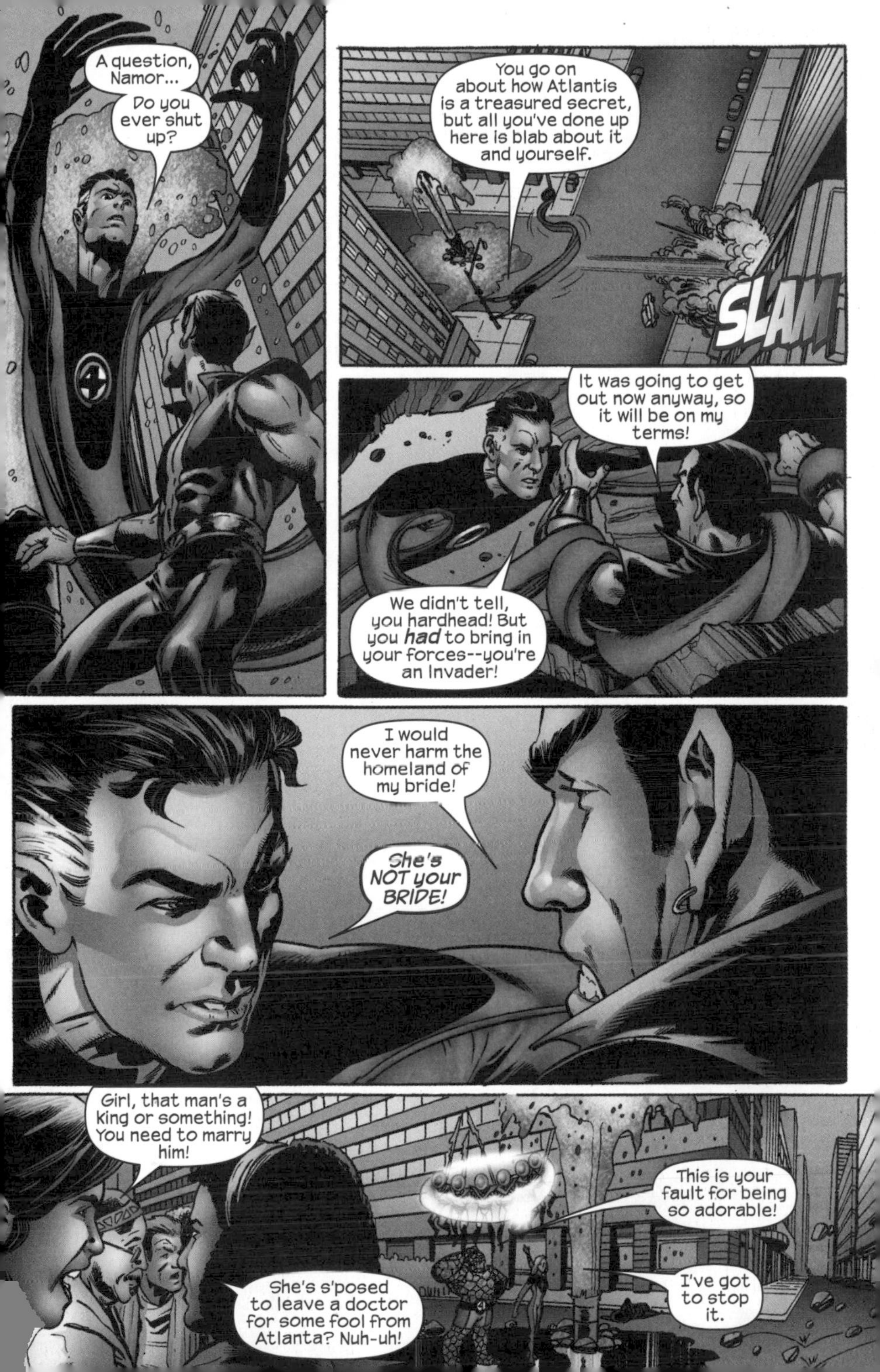

A question, Namor...
Do you ever shut up?
You go on about how Atlantis is a treasured secret, but all you've done up here is blab about it and yourself.
SLAM
It was going to get out now anyway, so it will be on my terms!
We didn't tell, you hardhead! But you *had* to bring in your forces--you're an Invader!
I would never harm the homeland of my bride!
She's NOT your BRIDE!
Girl, that man's a king or something! You need to marry him!
This is your fault for being so adorable!
She's s'posed to leave a doctor for some fool from Atlanta? Nuh-uh!
I've got to stop it.

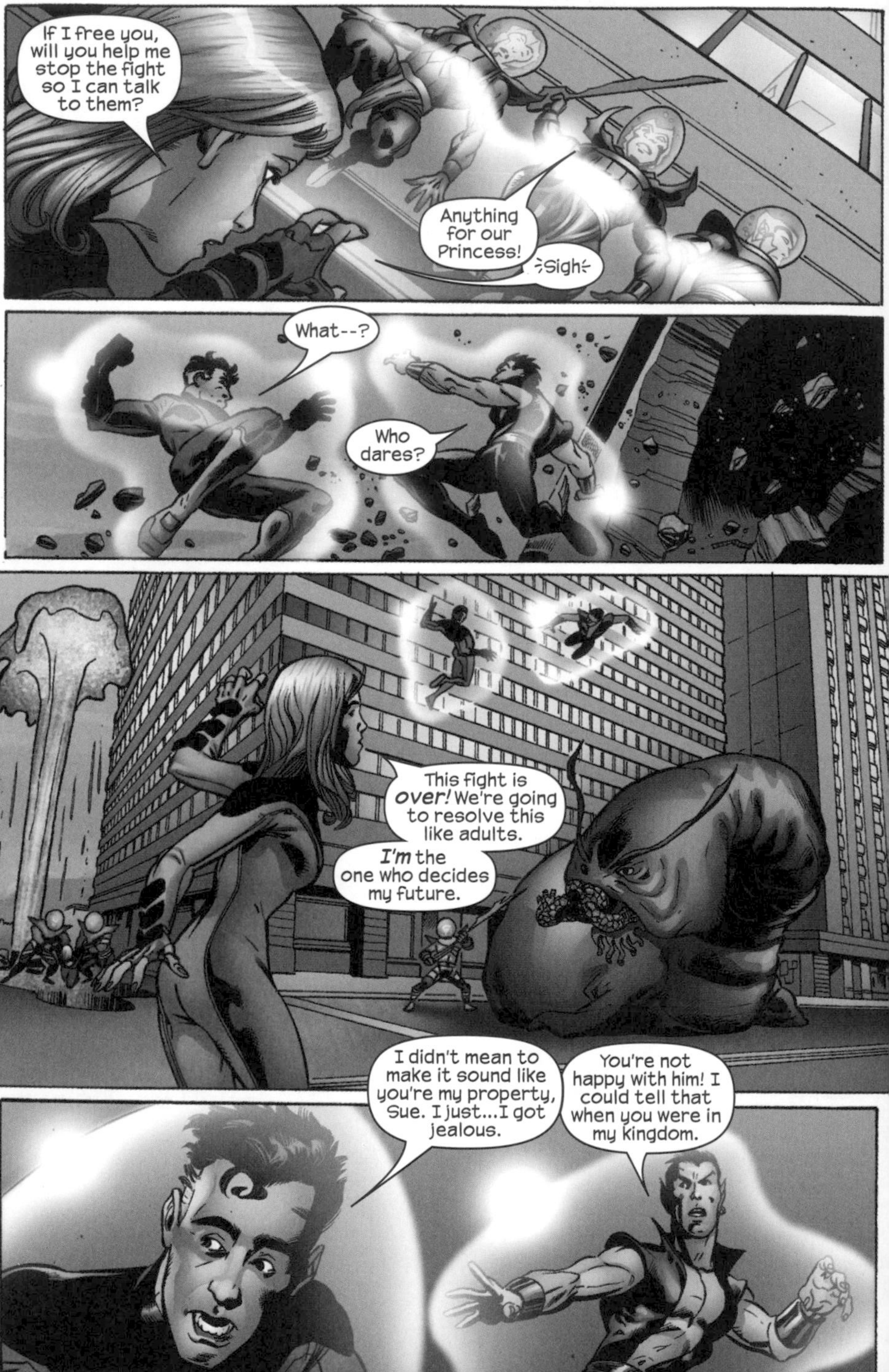
If I free you, will you help me stop the fight so I can talk to them?
Anything for our Princess!
Sigh
What--?
Who dares?
This fight is over! We're going to resolve this like adults.
I'm the one who decides my future.
I didn't mean to make it sound like you're my property, Sue. I just...I got jealous.
You're not happy with him! I could tell that when you were in my kingdom.

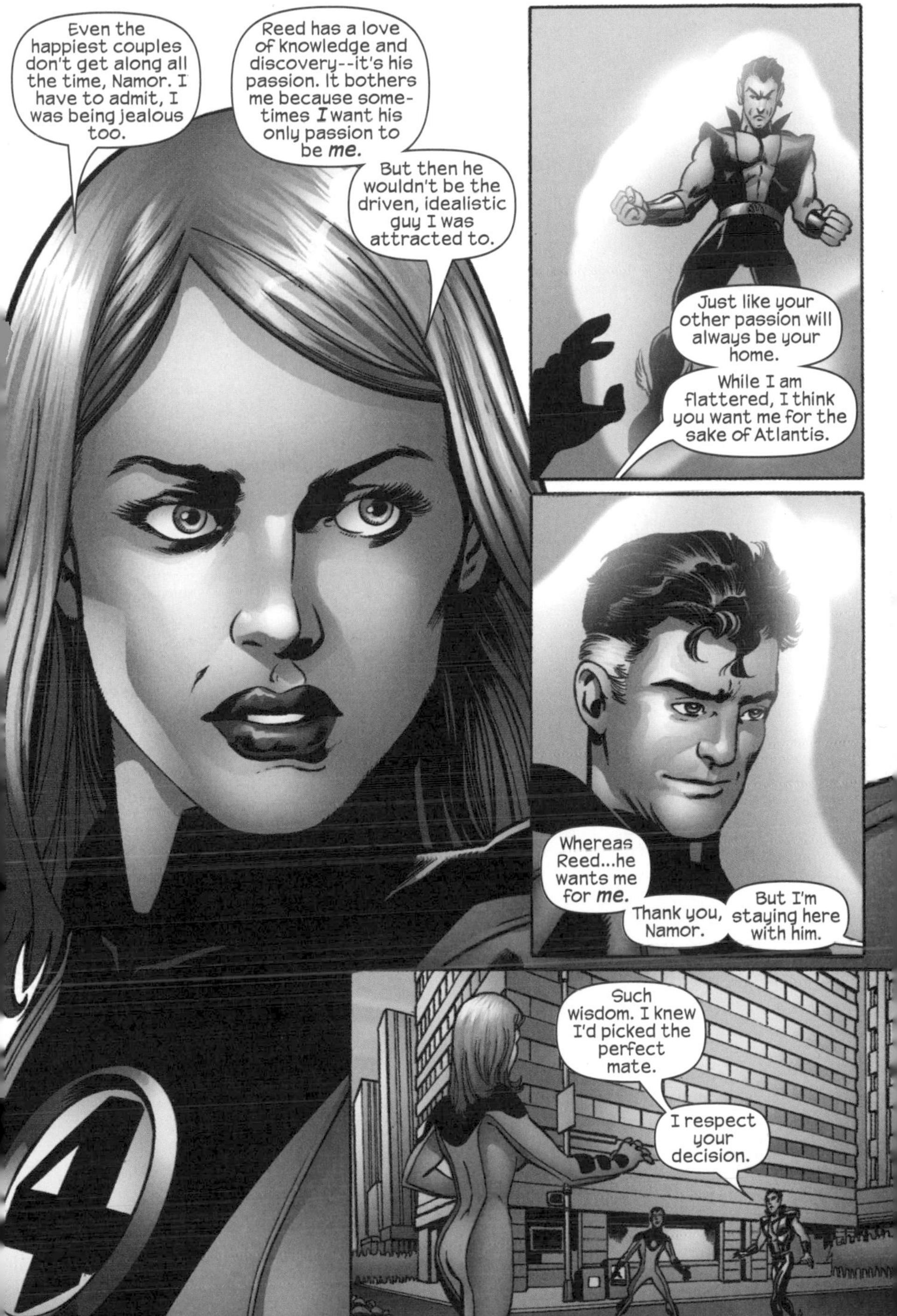

Even the happiest couples don't get along all the time, Namor. I have to admit, I was being jealous too.
Reed has a love of knowledge and discovery--it's his passion. It bothers me because sometimes *I* want his only passion to be ***me.***
But then he wouldn't be the driven, idealistic guy I was attracted to.
Just like your other passion will always be your home.
While I am flattered, I think you want me for the sake of Atlantis.
Whereas Reed...he wants me for ***me.***
Thank you, Namor.
But I'm staying here with him.
Such wisdom. I knew I'd picked the perfect mate.
I respect your decision.

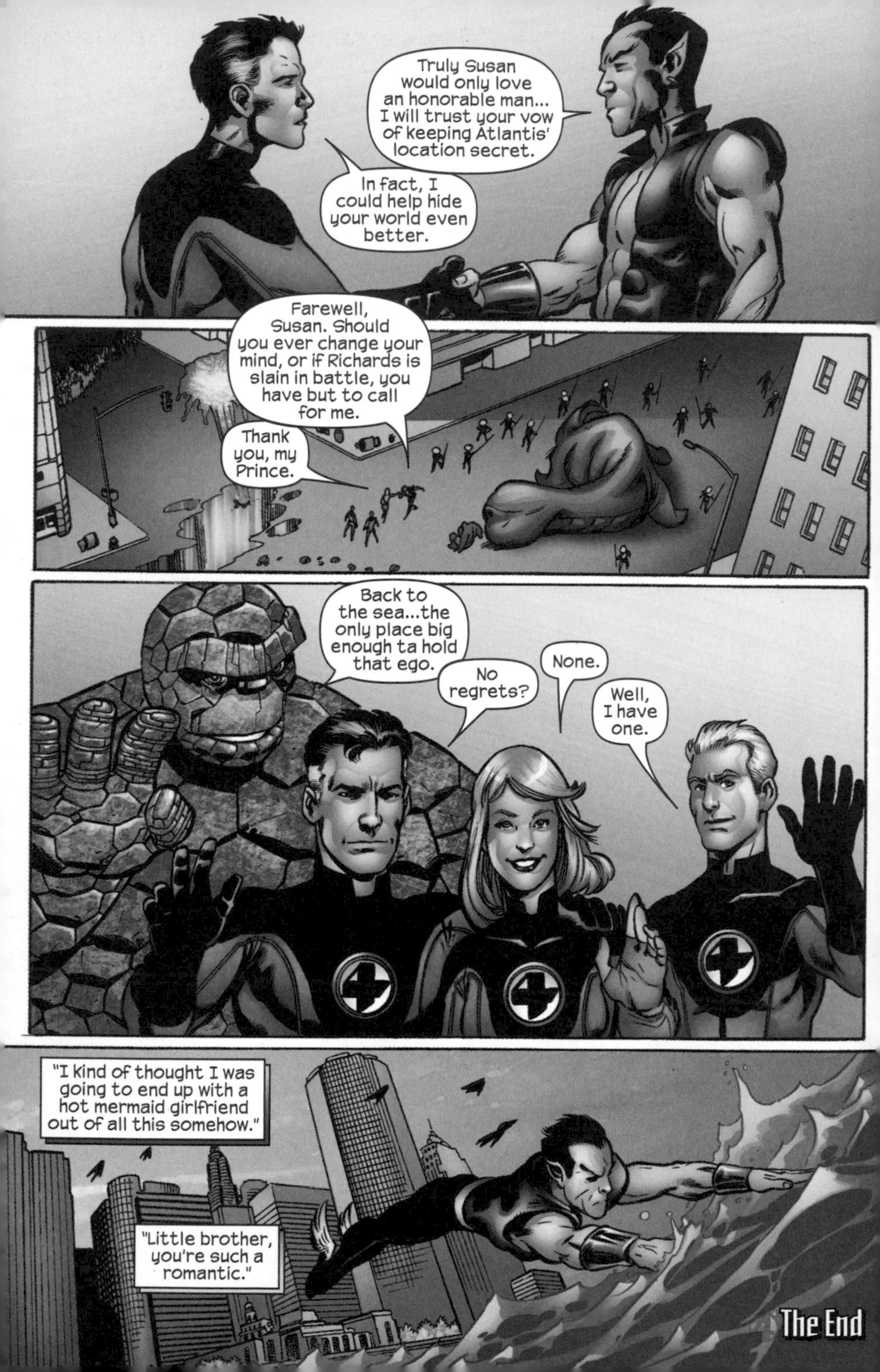
Truly Susan would only love an honorable man... I will trust your vow of keeping Atlantis' location secret.
In fact, I could help hide your world even better.
Farewell, Susan. Should you ever change your mind, or if Richards is slain in battle, you have but to call for me.
Thank you, my Prince.
Back to the sea...the only place big enough ta hold that ego.
No regrets?
None.
Well, I have one.
"I kind of thought I was going to end up with a hot mermaid girlfriend out of all this somehow."
"Little brother, you're such a romantic."
The End

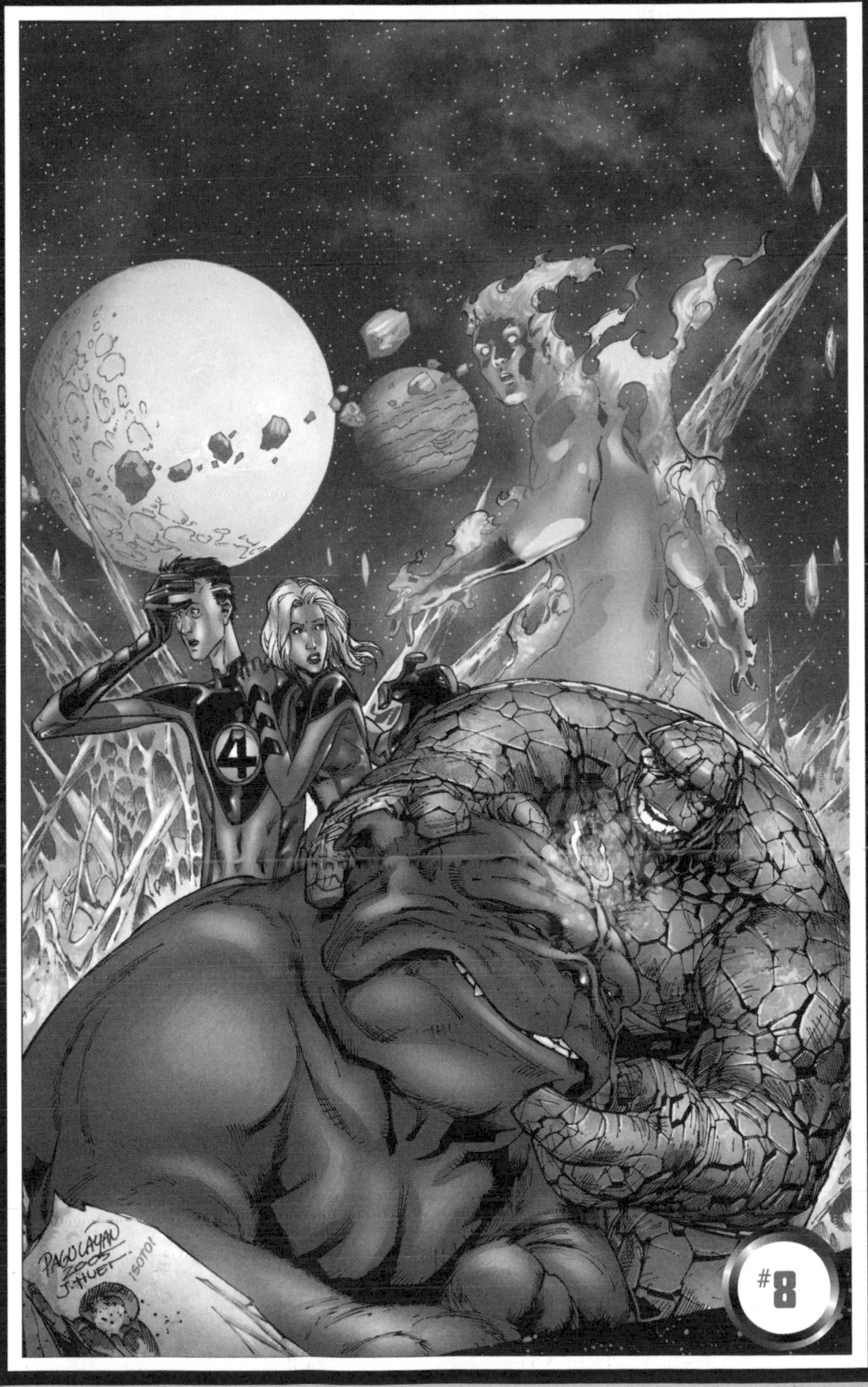
PAGULAYAN 2005 J. HUET ¡SOTO!
#8

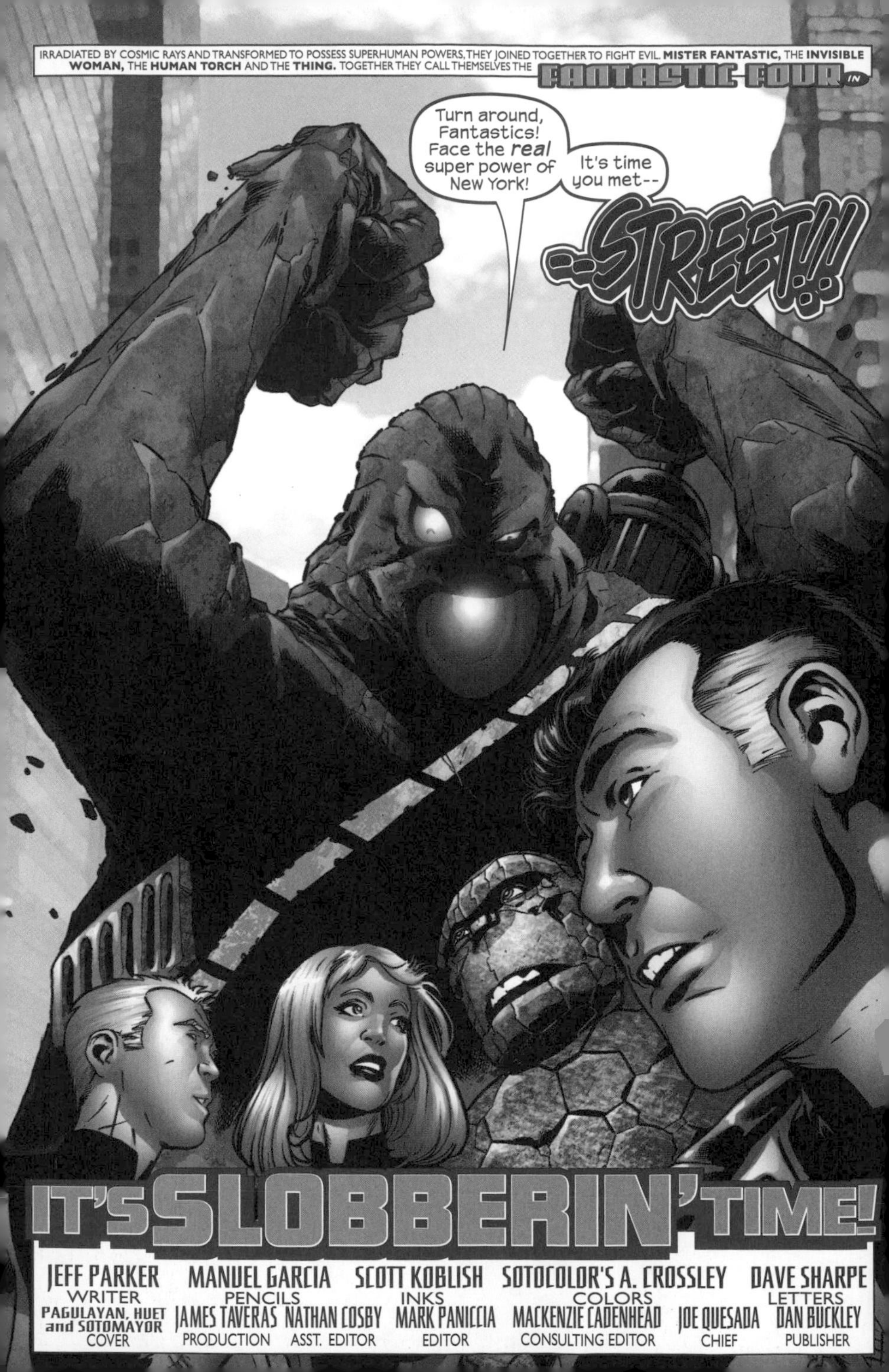
IRRADIATED BY COSMIC RAYS AND TRANSFORMED TO POSSESS SUPERHUMAN POWERS, THEY JOINED TOGETHER TO FIGHT EVIL. MISTER FANTASTIC, THE INVISIBLE WOMAN, THE HUMAN TORCH AND THE THING. TOGETHER THEY CALL THEMSELVES THE FANTASTIC FOUR IN
Turn around, Fantastics! Face the *real* super power of New York!
It's time you met--
--STREET!!!
IT'S SLOBBERIN' TIME!
JEFF PARKER WRITER
MANUEL GARCIA PENCILS
SCOTT KOBLISH INKS
SOTOCOLOR'S A. CROSSLEY COLORS
DAVE SHARPE LETTERS
PAGULAYAN, HUET and SOTOMAYOR COVER
JAMES TAVERAS PRODUCTION
NATHAN COSBY ASST. EDITOR
MARK PANICCIA EDITOR
MACKENZIE CADENHEAD CONSULTING EDITOR
JOE QUESADA CHIEF
DAN BUCKLEY PUBLISHER

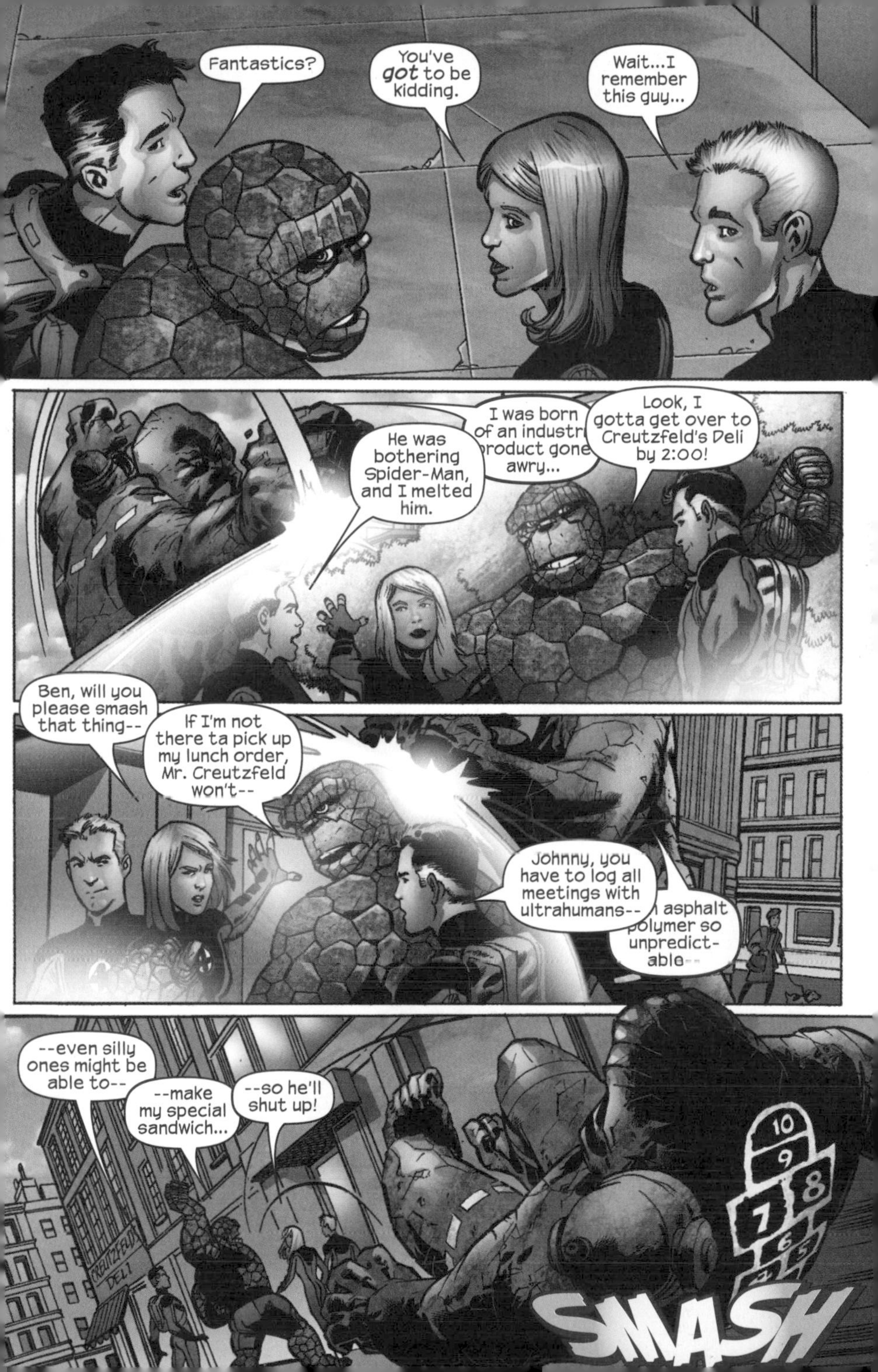
Fantastics?
You've *got* to be kidding.
Wait...I remember this guy...
He was bothering Spider-Man, and I melted him.
I was born of an industri product gone awry...
Look, I gotta get over to Creutzfeld's Deli by 2:00!
Ben, will you please smash that thing--
If I'm not there ta pick up my lunch order, Mr. Creutzfeld won't--
Johnny, you have to log all meetings with ultrahumans--
asphalt polymer so unpredict-able--
--even silly ones might be able to--
--make my special sandwich...
--so he'll shut up!
10
9
8
7
6
5
CREUTZFELD'S DELI
SMASH

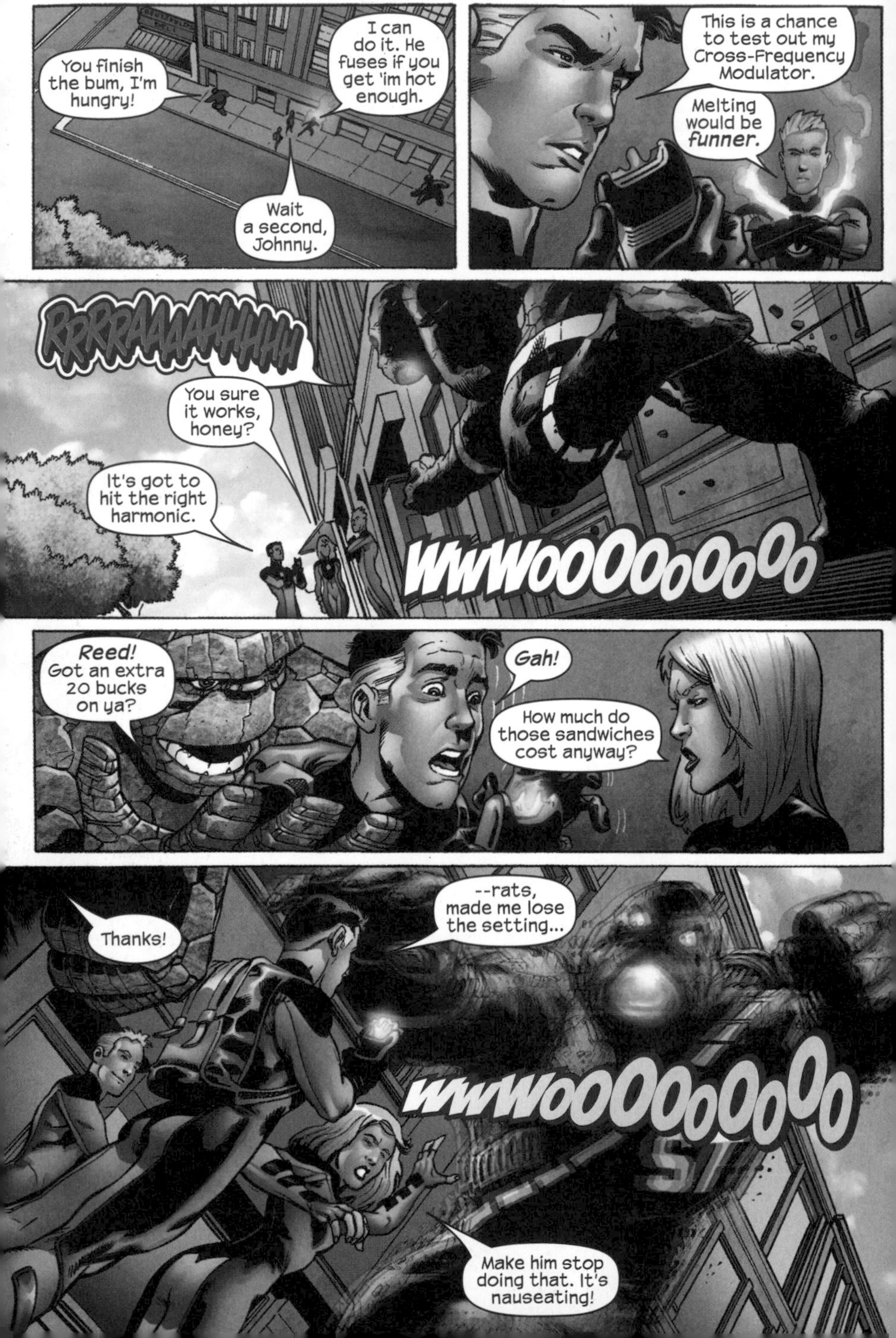
You finish the bum, I'm hungry!
I can do it. He fuses if you get 'im hot enough.
Wait a second, Johnny.
This is a chance to test out my Cross-Frequency Modulator.
Melting would be *funner.*
RRRRAAAAHHHHHH
You sure it works, honey?
It's got to hit the right harmonic.
WWWOOOOOOOOOO
Reed! Got an extra 20 bucks on ya?
Gah!
How much do those sandwiches cost anyway?
Thanks!
--rats, made me lose the setting...
WWWOOOOOOOOOOO
Make him stop doing that. It's nauseating!

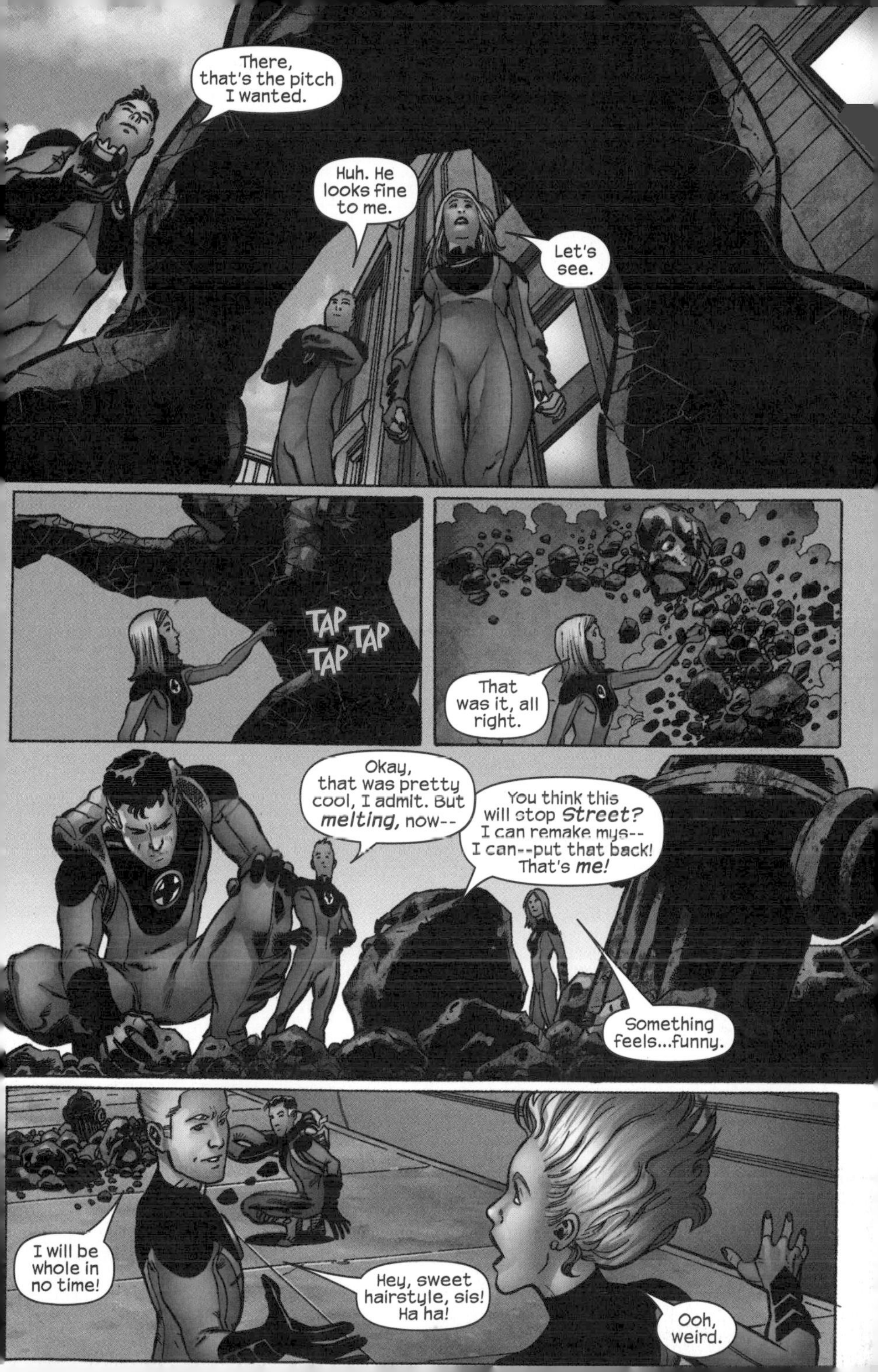
There, that's the pitch I wanted.
Huh. He looks fine to me.
Let's see.
TAP TAP TAP
That was it, all right.
Okay, that was pretty cool, I admit. But melting, now--
You think this will stop Street? I can remake mys-- I can--put that back! That's me!
Something feels...funny.
I will be whole in no time!
Hey, sweet hairstyle, sis! Ha ha!
Ooh, weird.

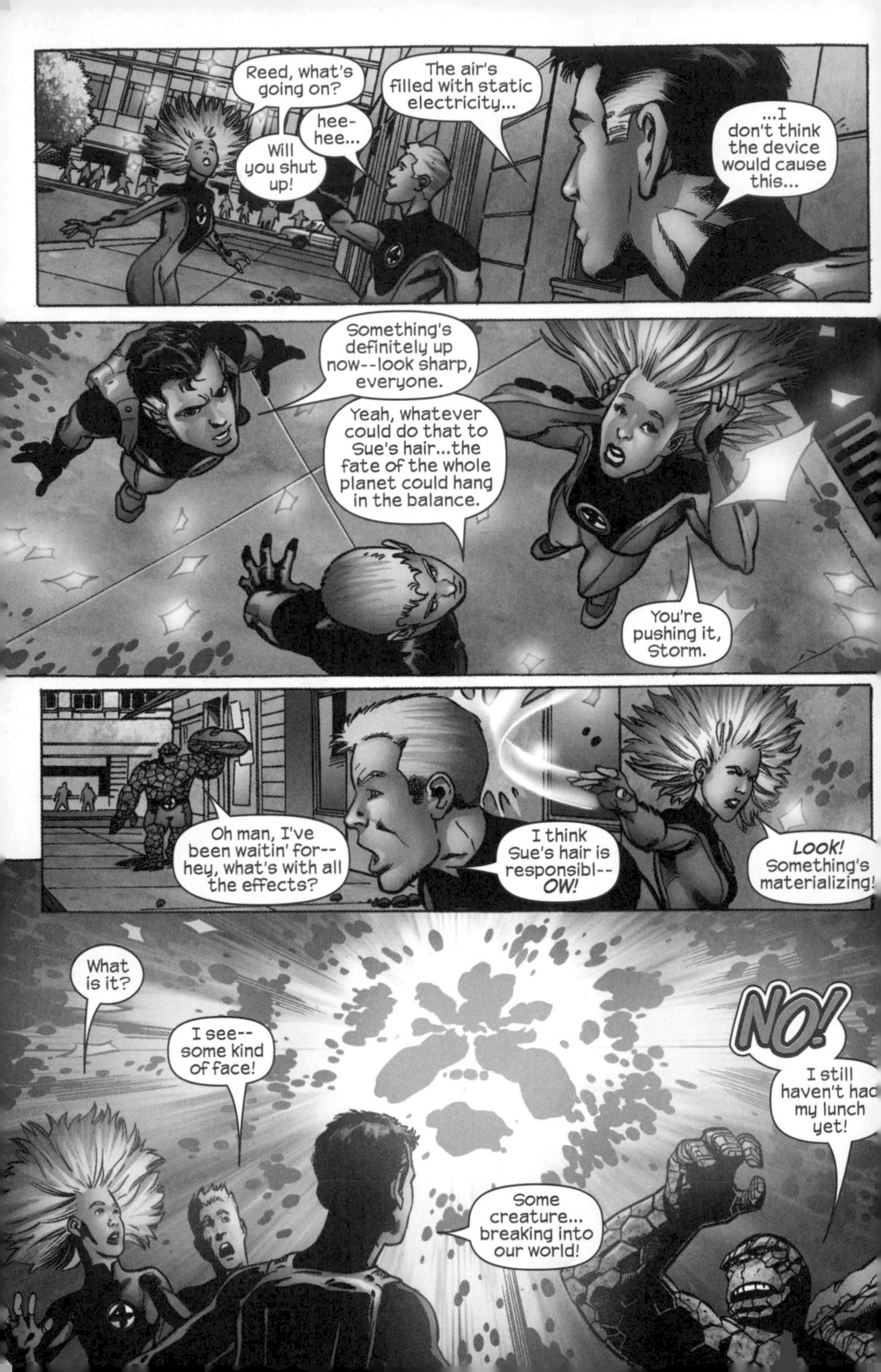
Reed, what's going on?
hee-hee...
Will you shut up!
The air's filled with static electricity...
...I don't think the device would cause this...
Something's definitely up now--look sharp, everyone.
Yeah, whatever could do that to Sue's hair...the fate of the whole planet could hang in the balance.
You're pushing it, Storm.
Oh man, I've been waitin' for--hey, what's with all the effects?
I think Sue's hair is responsibl--OW!
LOOK! Something's materializing!
What is it?
I see--some kind of face!
Some creature... breaking into our world!
NO!
I still haven't had my lunch yet!

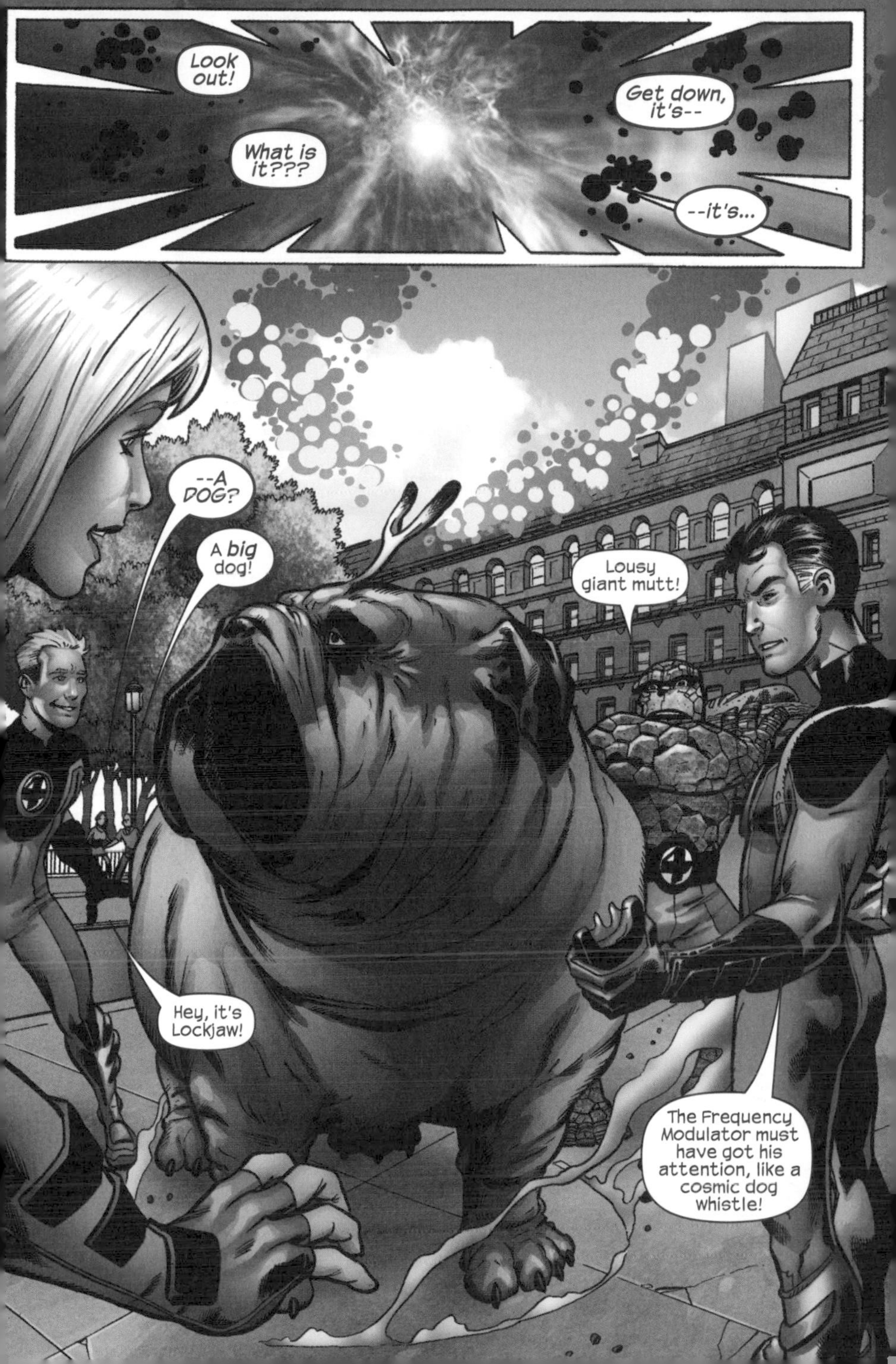

Look out!
What is it???
Get down, it's--
--it's...
--A DOG?
A big dog!
Lousy giant mutt!
Hey, it's Lockjaw!
The Frequency Modulator must have got his attention, like a cosmic dog whistle!

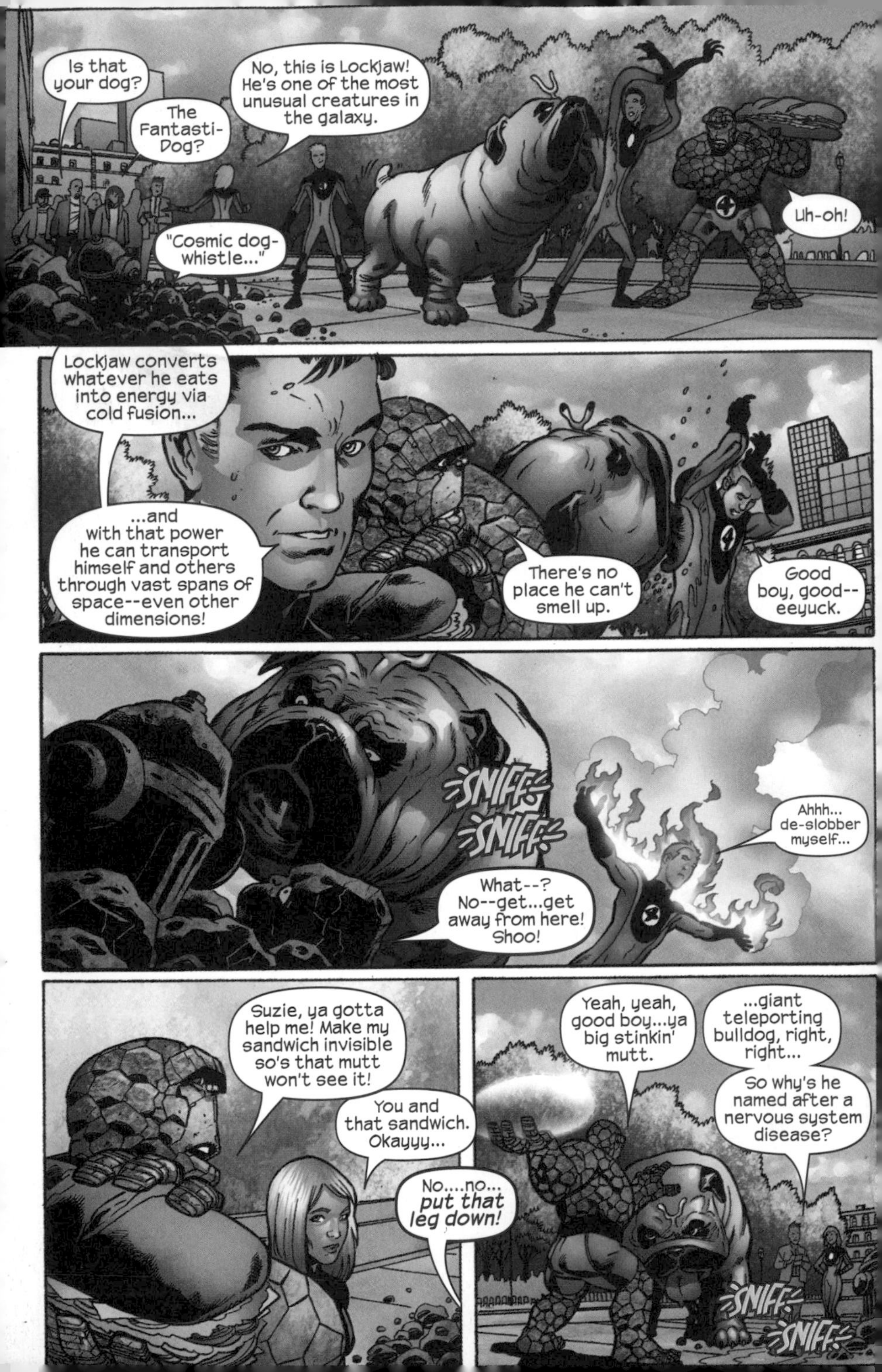
Is that your dog?
The Fantasti-Dog?
"Cosmic dog-whistle..."
No, this is Lockjaw! He's one of the most unusual creatures in the galaxy.
Uh-oh!
Lockjaw converts whatever he eats into energy via cold fusion...
...and with that power he can transport himself and others through vast spans of space--even other dimensions!
There's no place he can't smell up.
Good boy, good--eeyuck.
SNIFF SNIFF
What--? No--get...get away from here! Shoo!
Ahhh... de-slobber myself...
Suzie, ya gotta help me! Make my sandwich invisible so's that mutt won't see it!
You and that sandwich. Okayyy...
No....no... put that leg down!
Yeah, yeah, good boy...ya big stinkin' mutt.
...giant teleporting bulldog, right, right...
So why's he named after a nervous system disease?
SNIFF SNIFF

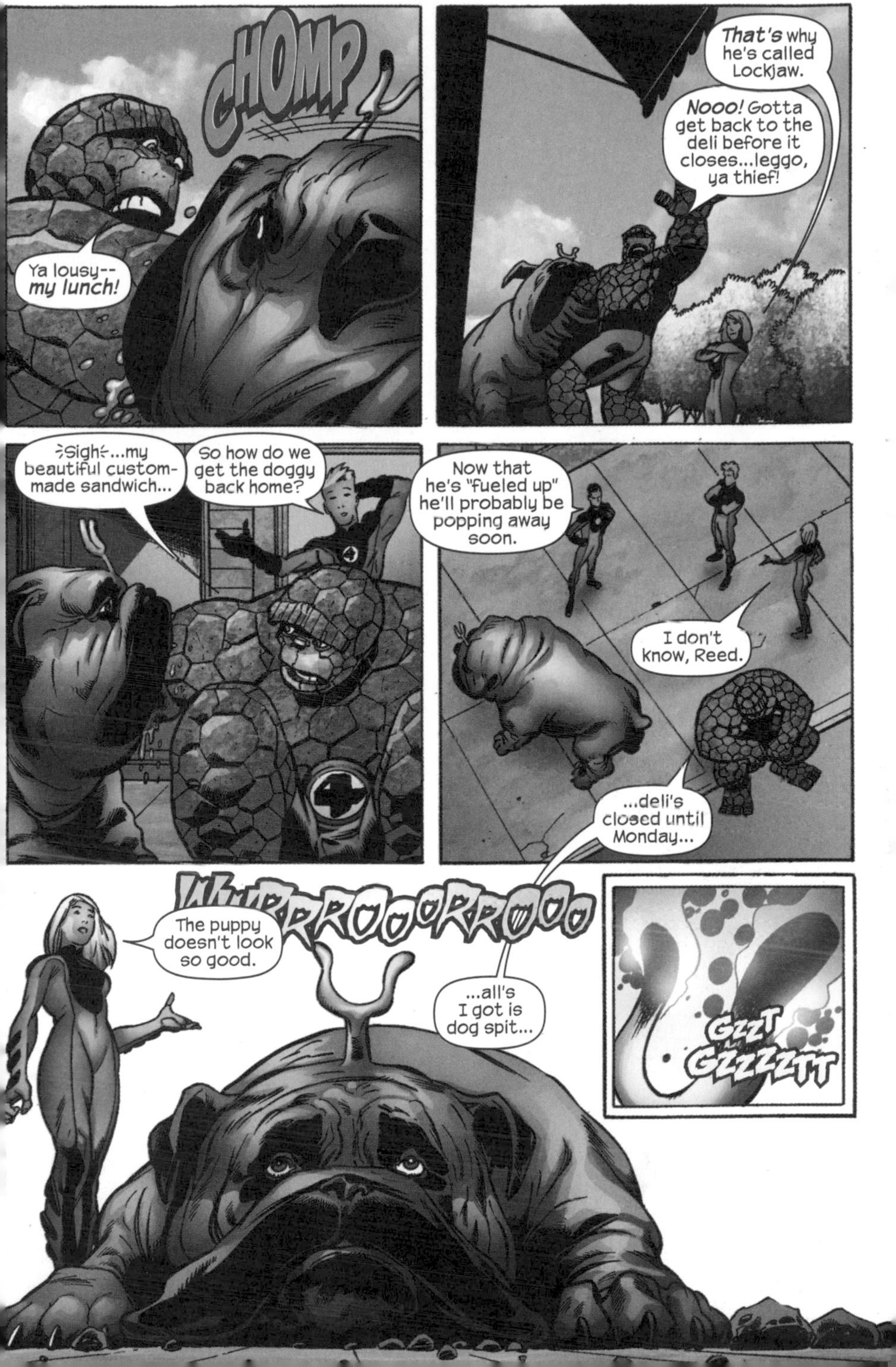

CHOMP
Ya lousy-- my lunch!
That's why he's called Lockjaw.
Nooo! Gotta get back to the deli before it closes...leggo, ya thief!
Sigh...my beautiful custom-made sandwich...
So how do we get the doggy back home?
Now that he's "fueled up" he'll probably be popping away soon.
I don't know, Reed.
...deli's closed until Monday...
The puppy doesn't look so good.
...all's I got is dog spit...
GZZT GZZZZTT

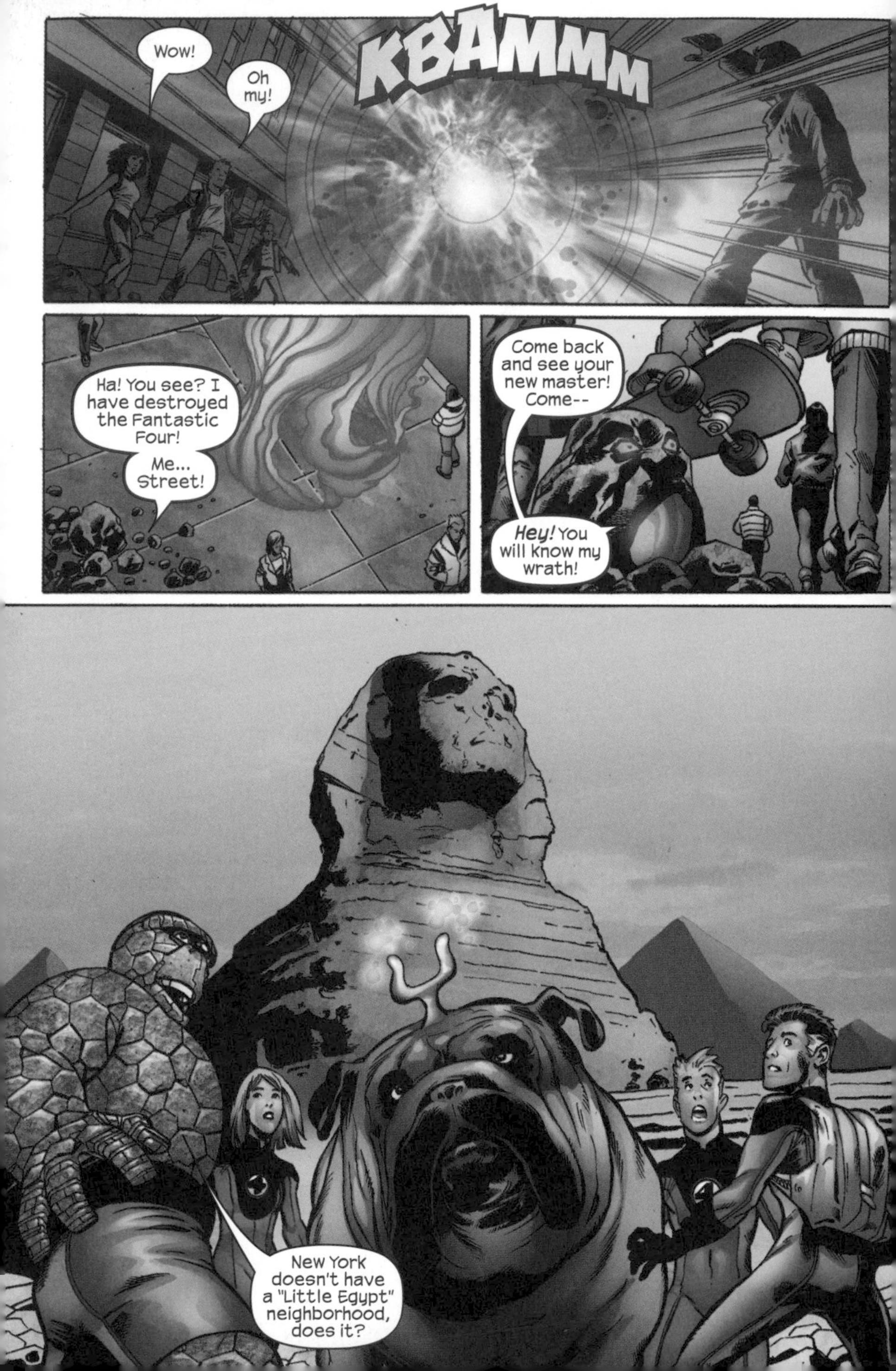
Wow!
Oh my!
KBAMMM
Ha! You see? I have destroyed the Fantastic Four!
Me... Street!
Come back and see your new master! Come--
Hey! You will know my wrath!
New York doesn't have a "Little Egypt" neighborhood, does it?

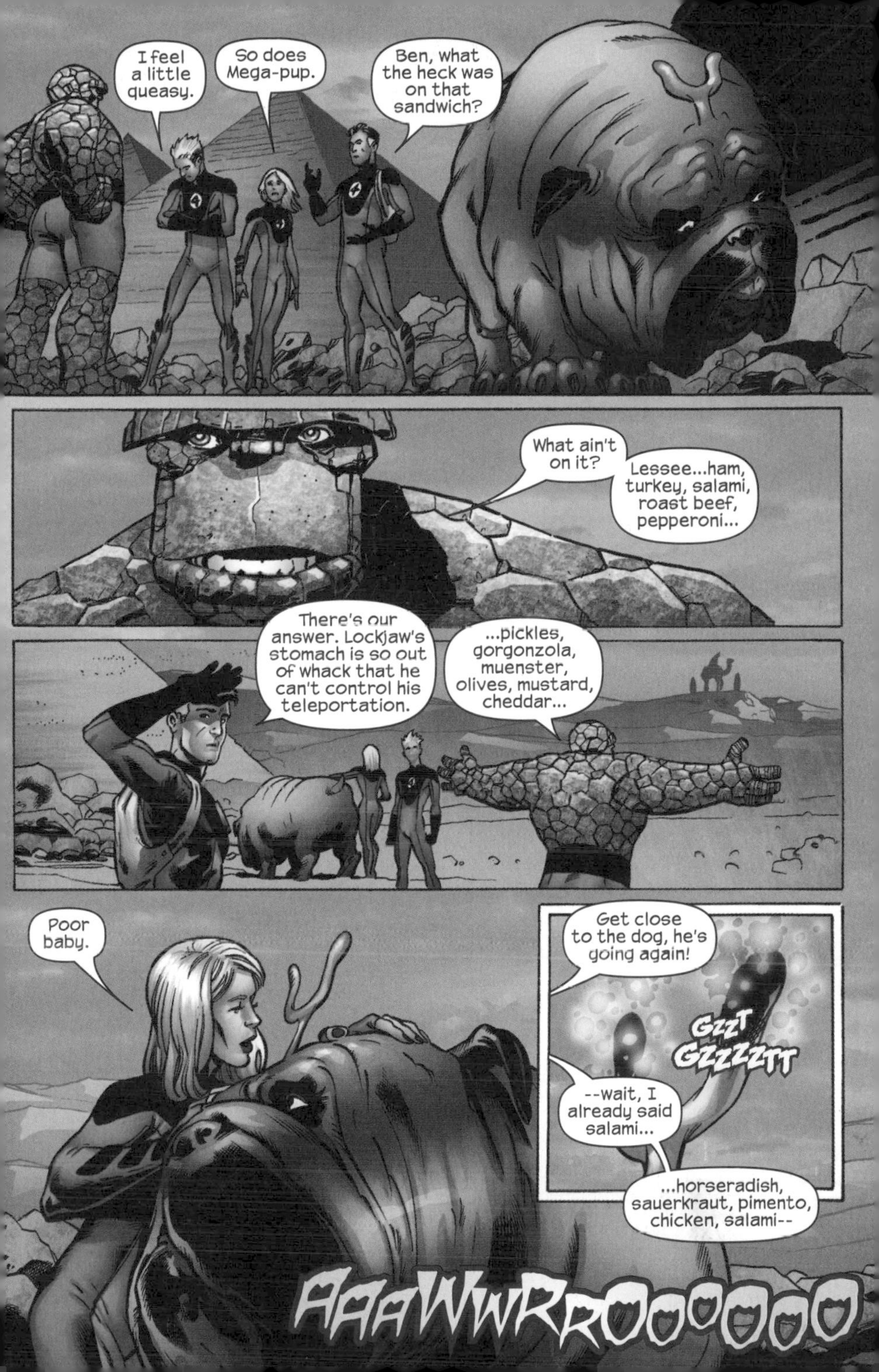
I feel a little queasy.
So does Mega-pup.
Ben, what the heck was on that sandwich?
What ain't on it?
Lessee...ham, turkey, salami, roast beef, pepperoni...
There's our answer. Lockjaw's stomach is so out of whack that he can't control his teleportation.
...pickles, gorgonzola, muenster, olives, mustard, cheddar...
Poor baby.
Get close to the dog, he's going again!
GZZT GZZZZTT
--wait, I already said salami...
...horseradish, sauerkraut, pimento, chicken, salami--
AAAWWRROOOOOOO

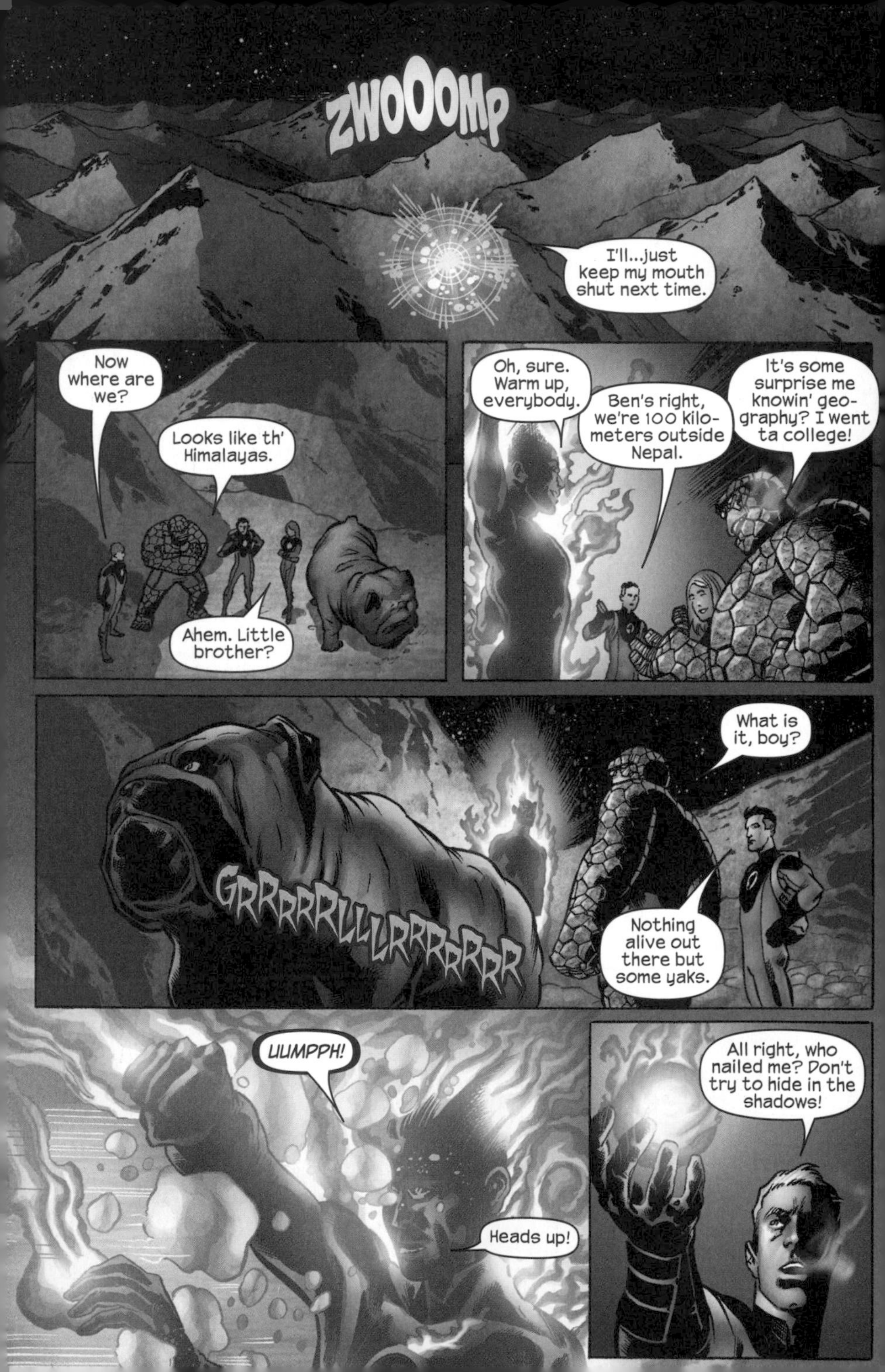
ZWOOOMP
I'll...just keep my mouth shut next time.
Now where are we?
Looks like th' Himalayas.
Ahem. Little brother?
Oh, sure. Warm up, everybody.
Ben's right, we're 100 kilometers outside Nepal.
It's some surprise me knowin' geography? I went ta college!
What is it, boy?
GRRRRRLLLRRRRRRR
Nothing alive out there but some yaks.
UUMPPH!
Heads up!
All right, who nailed me? Don't try to hide in the shadows!

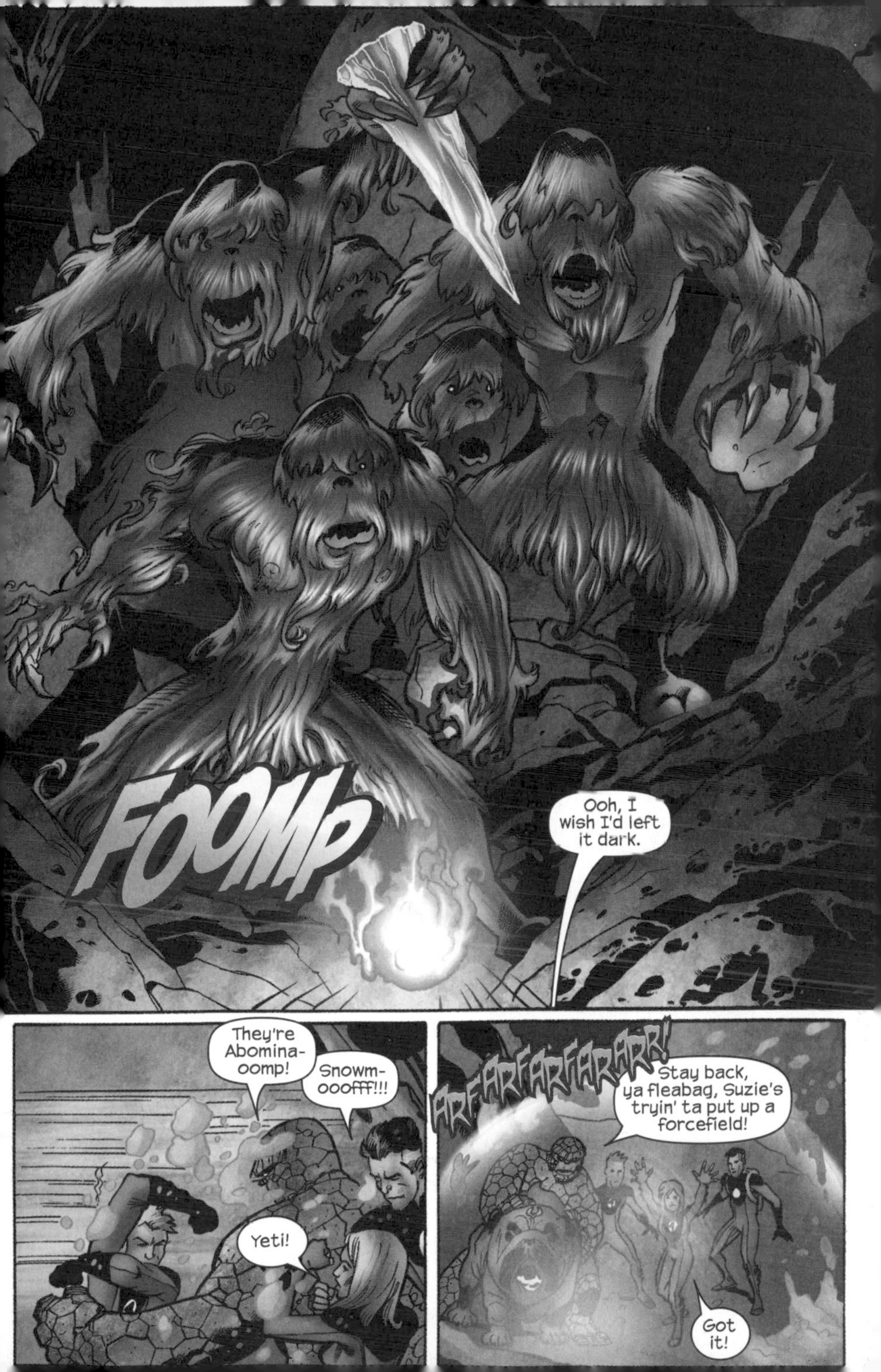
FOOMP
Ooh, I wish I'd left it dark.
They're Abomina-oomp!
Snowm-ooofff!!!
Yeti!
ARFARFARFARFARARR!
Stay back, ya fleabag, Suzie's tryin' ta put up a forcefield!
Got it!

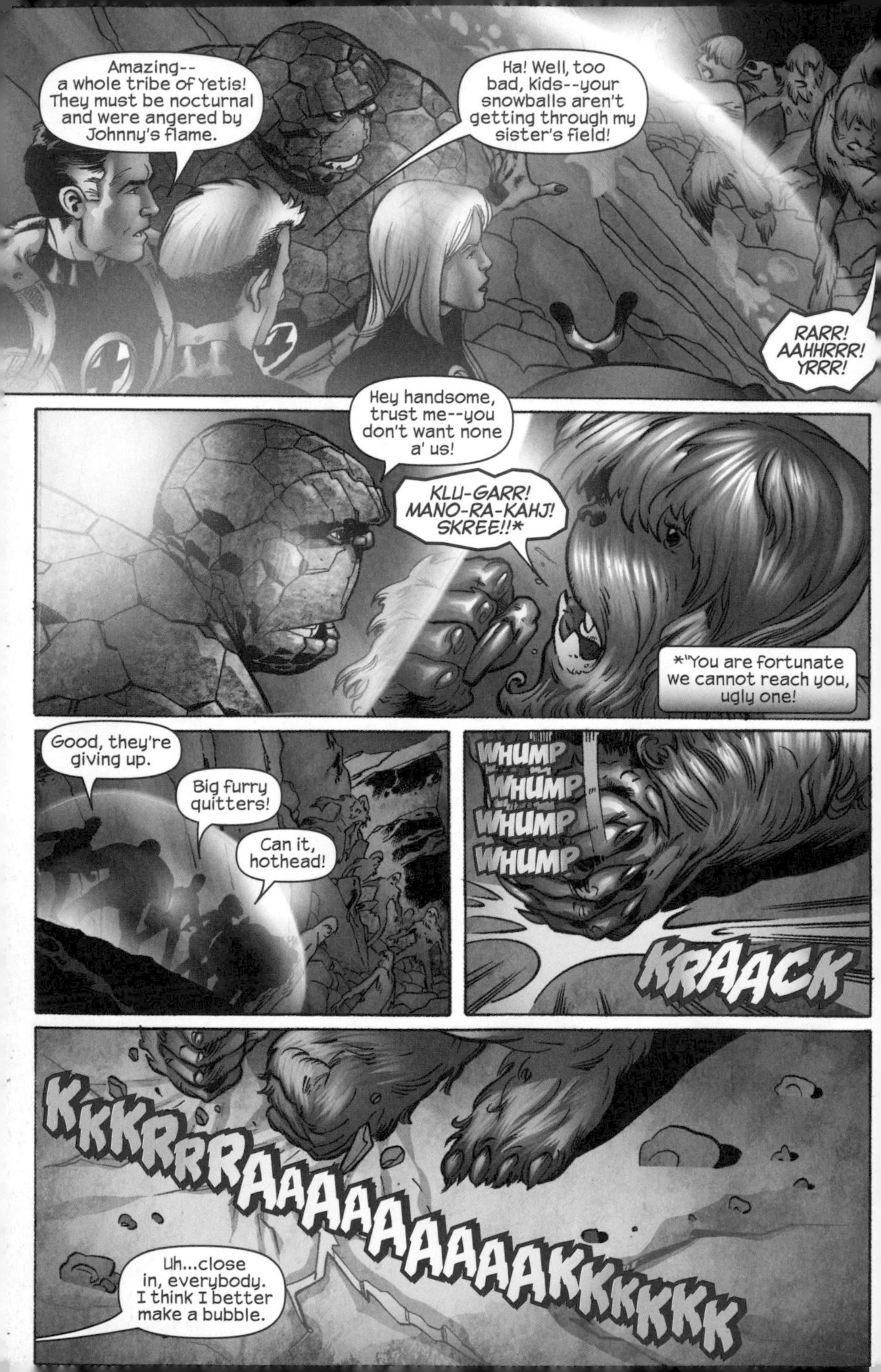
Amazing-- a whole tribe of Yetis! They must be nocturnal and were angered by Johnny's flame.
Ha! Well, too bad, kids--your snowballs aren't getting through my sister's field!
RARR! AAHHRRR! YRRR!
Hey handsome, trust me--you don't want none a' us!
KLU-GARR! MANO-RA-KAHJ! SKREE!!*
*"You are fortunate we cannot reach you, ugly one!
Good, they're giving up.
Big furry quitters!
Can it, hothead!
WHUMP
WHUMP
WHUMP
WHUMP
KRAACK
KKKRRRRAAAAAAAAAKKKKKKK
Uh...close in, everybody. I think I better make a bubble.

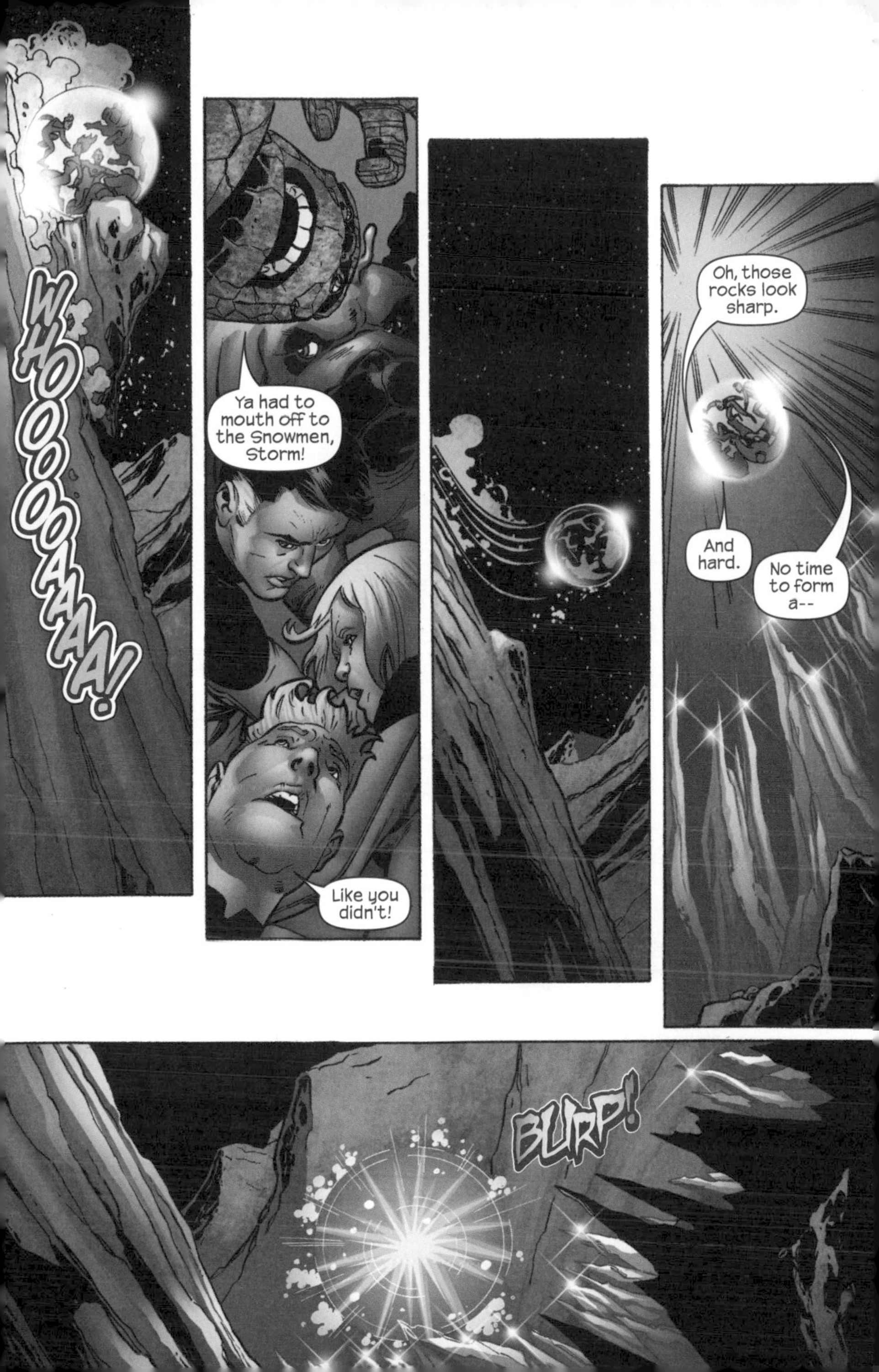
WHOOOOOOAAAAA!
Ya had to mouth off to the Snowmen, Storm!
Like you didn't!
Oh, those rocks look sharp.
And hard.
No time to form a--
BLURP!

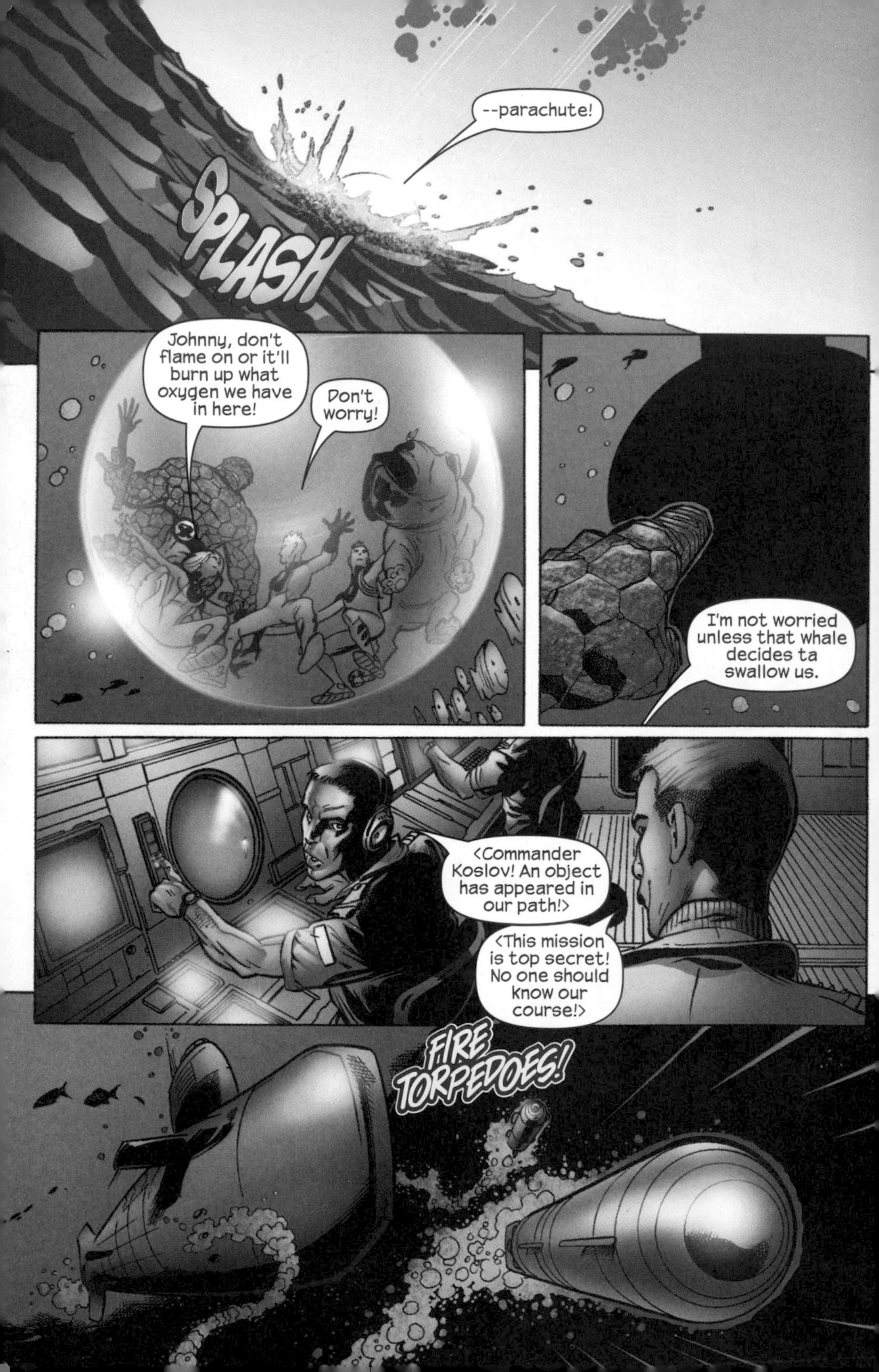
--parachute!
SPLASH
Johnny, don't flame on or it'll burn up what oxygen we have in here!
Don't worry!
I'm not worried unless that whale decides ta swallow us.
<Commander Koslov! An object has appeared in our path!>
<This mission is top secret! No one should know our course!>
FIRE TORPEDOES!

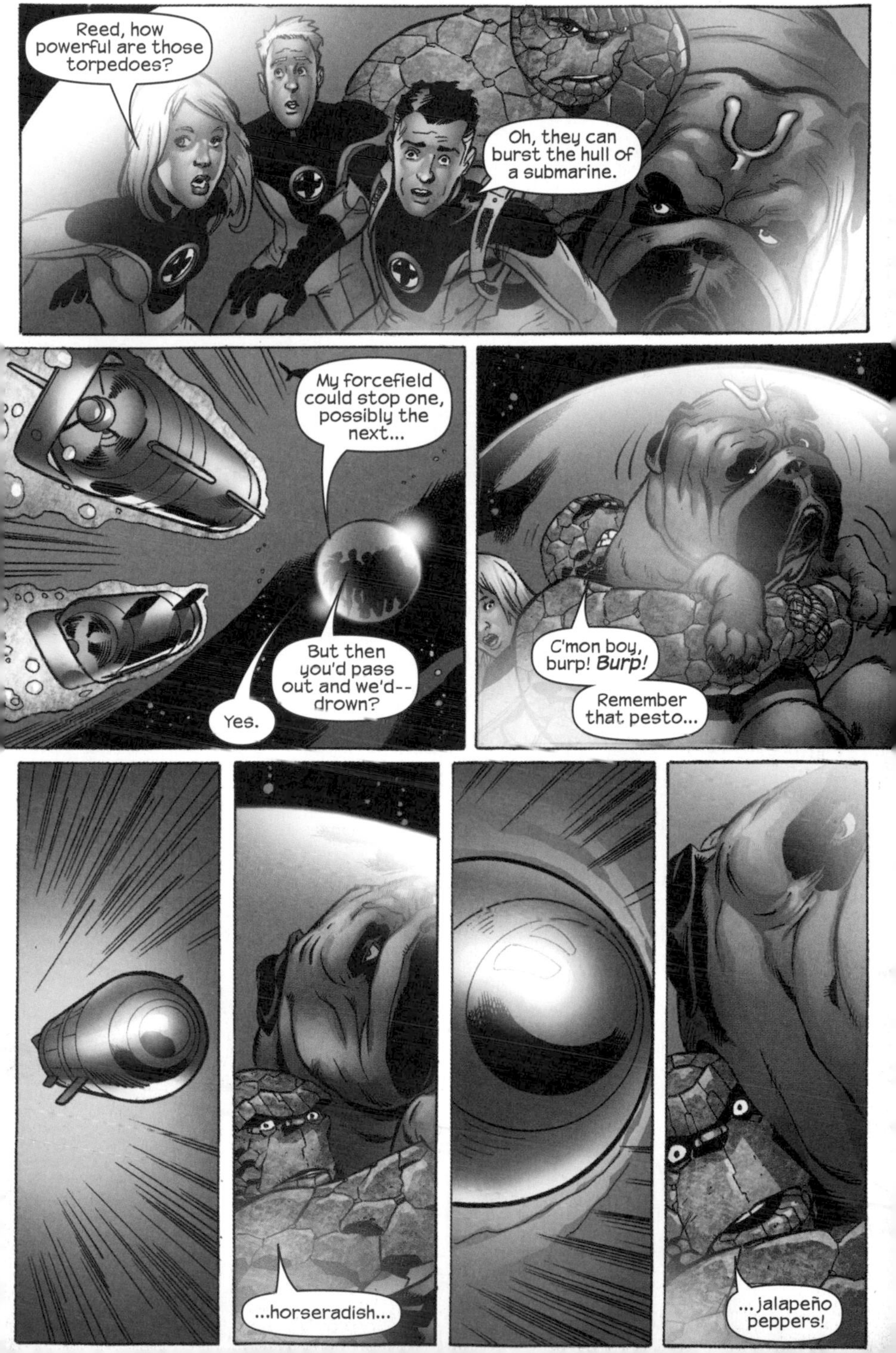
Reed, how powerful are those torpedoes?
Oh, they can burst the hull of a submarine.
My forcefield could stop one, possibly the next...
But then you'd pass out and we'd--drown?
Yes.
C'mon boy, burp! **Burp!**
Remember that pesto...
...horseradish...
...jalapeño peppers!

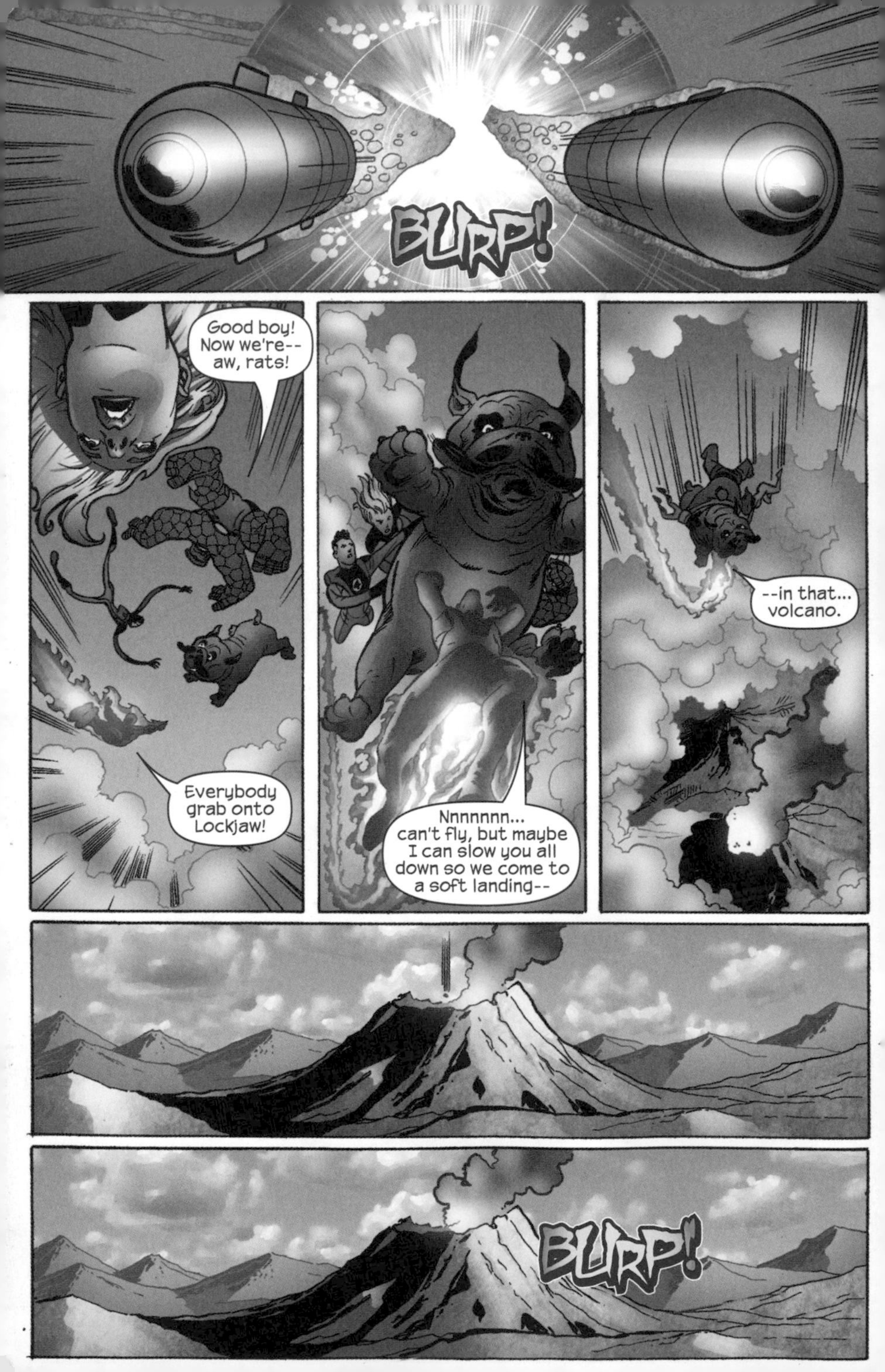
BURP!
Good boy! Now we're-- aw, rats!
Everybody grab onto Lockjaw!
Nnnnnnn... can't fly, but maybe I can slow you all down so we come to a soft landing--
--in that... volcano.
BURP!

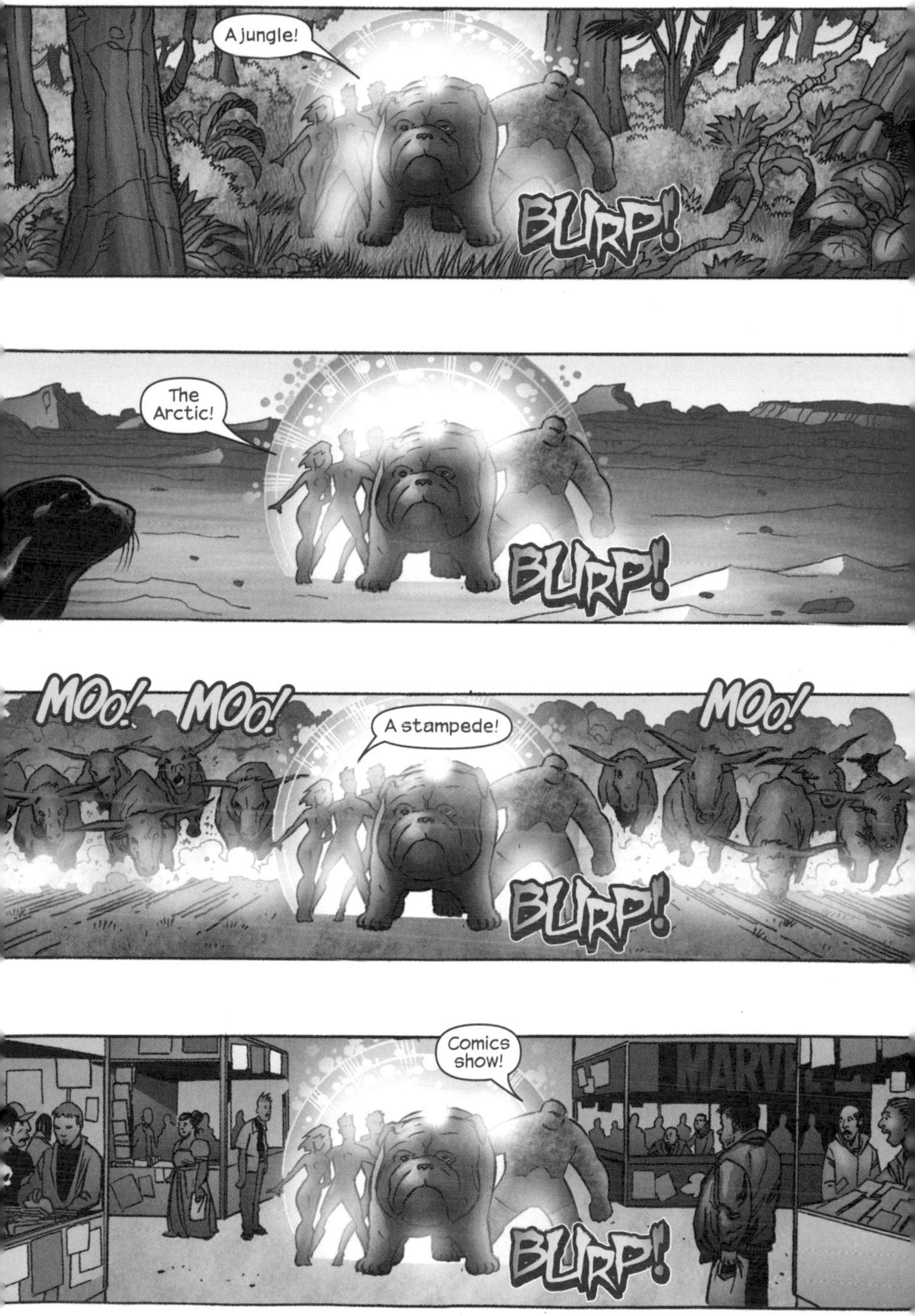
A jungle!
BURP!
The Arctic!
BURP!
MOo! MOo!
A stampede!
MOo!
BURP!
Comics show!
BURP!

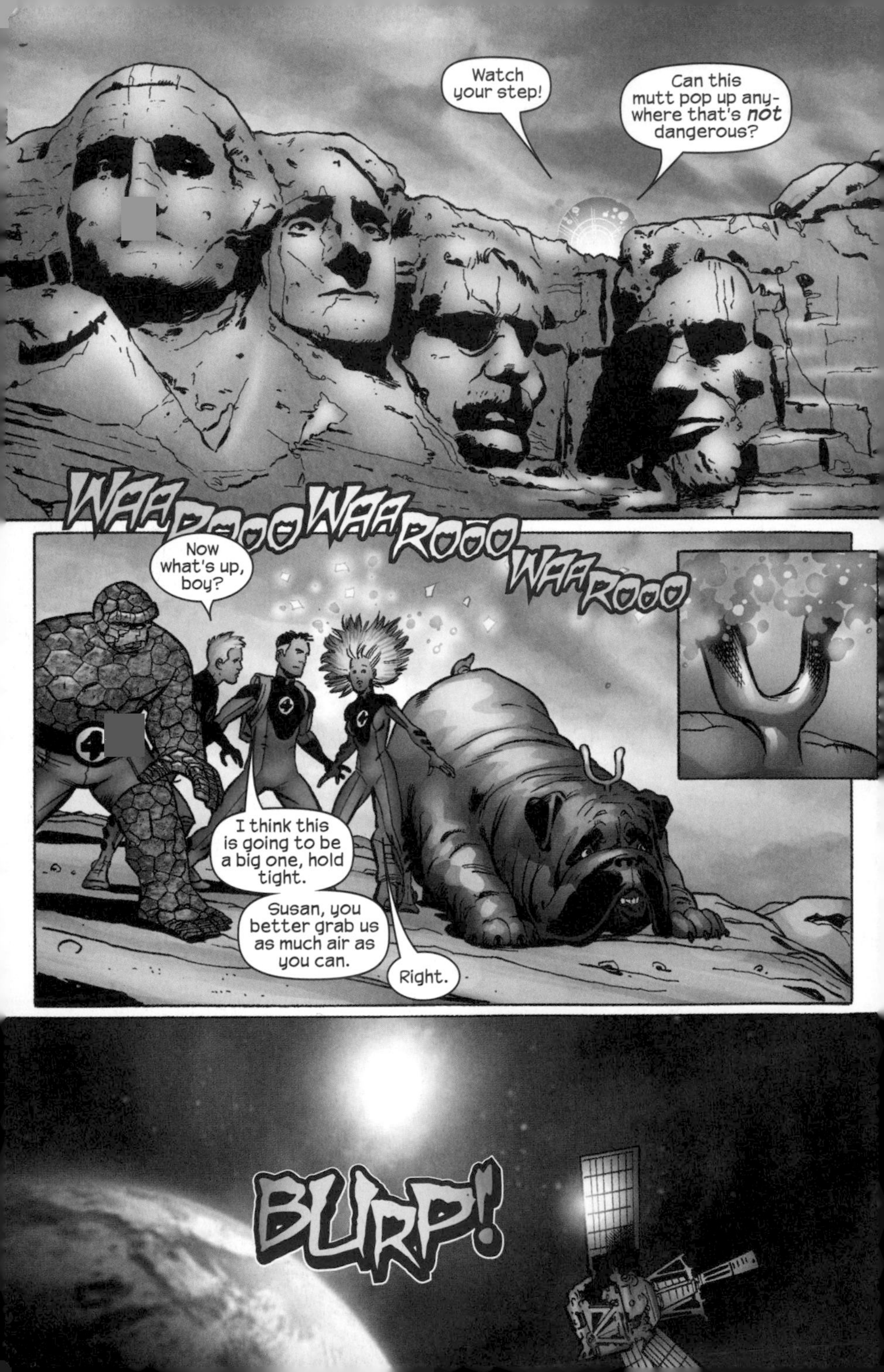
Watch your step!
Can this mutt pop up any-where that's *not* dangerous?
WAAROOO WAAROOO WAAROOO
Now what's up, boy?
I think this is going to be a big one, hold tight.
Susan, you better grab us as much air as you can.
Right.
BURP!

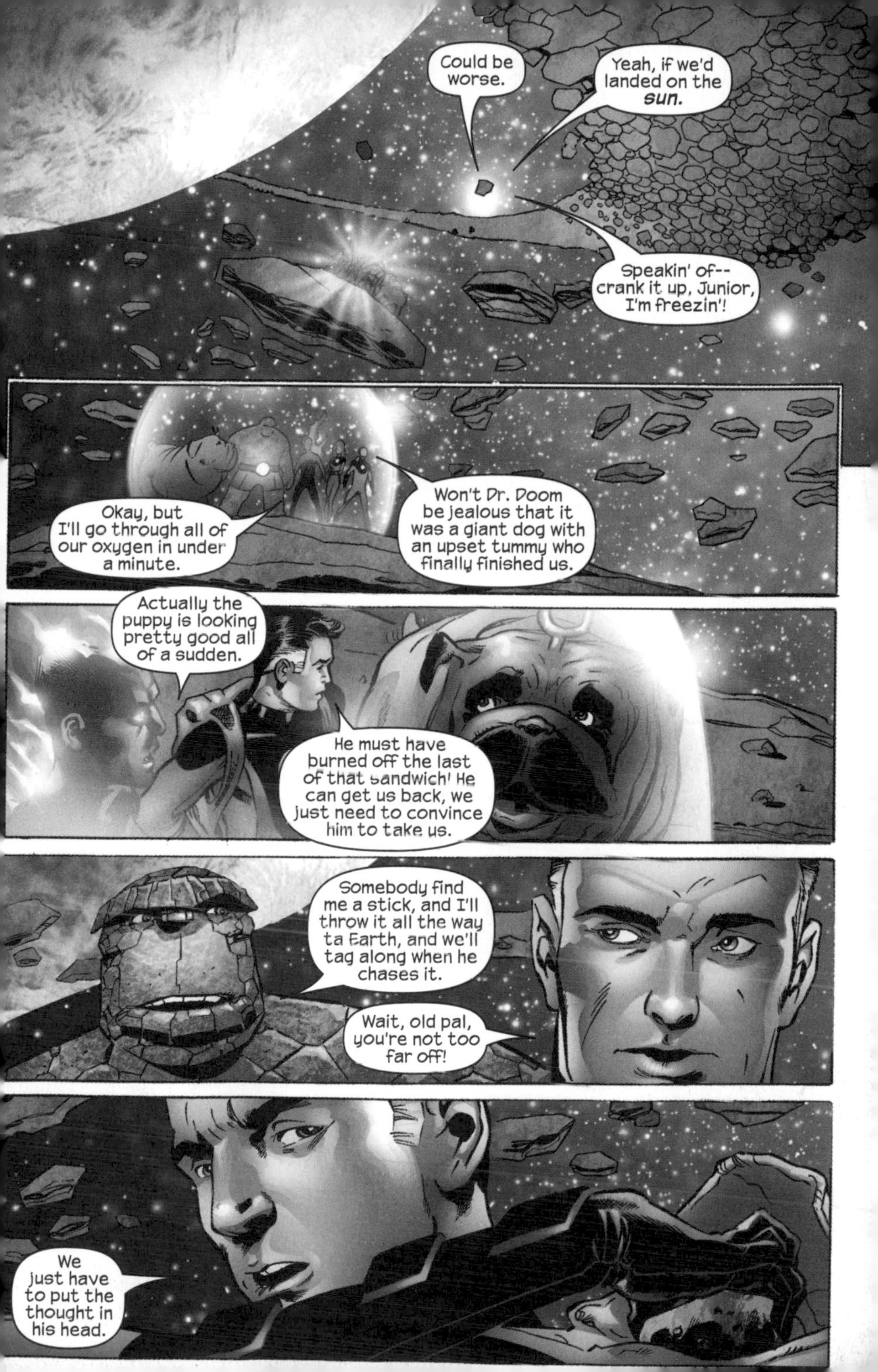

Could be worse.
Yeah, if we'd landed on the *sun.*
Speakin' of-- crank it up, Junior, I'm freezin'!
Okay, but I'll go through all of our oxygen in under a minute.
Won't Dr. Doom be jealous that it was a giant dog with an upset tummy who finally finished us.
Actually the puppy is looking pretty good all of a sudden.
He must have burned off the last of that sandwich! He can get us back, we just need to convince him to take us.
Somebody find me a stick, and I'll throw it all the way ta Earth, and we'll tag along when he chases it.
Wait, old pal, you're not too far off!
We just have to put the thought in his head.

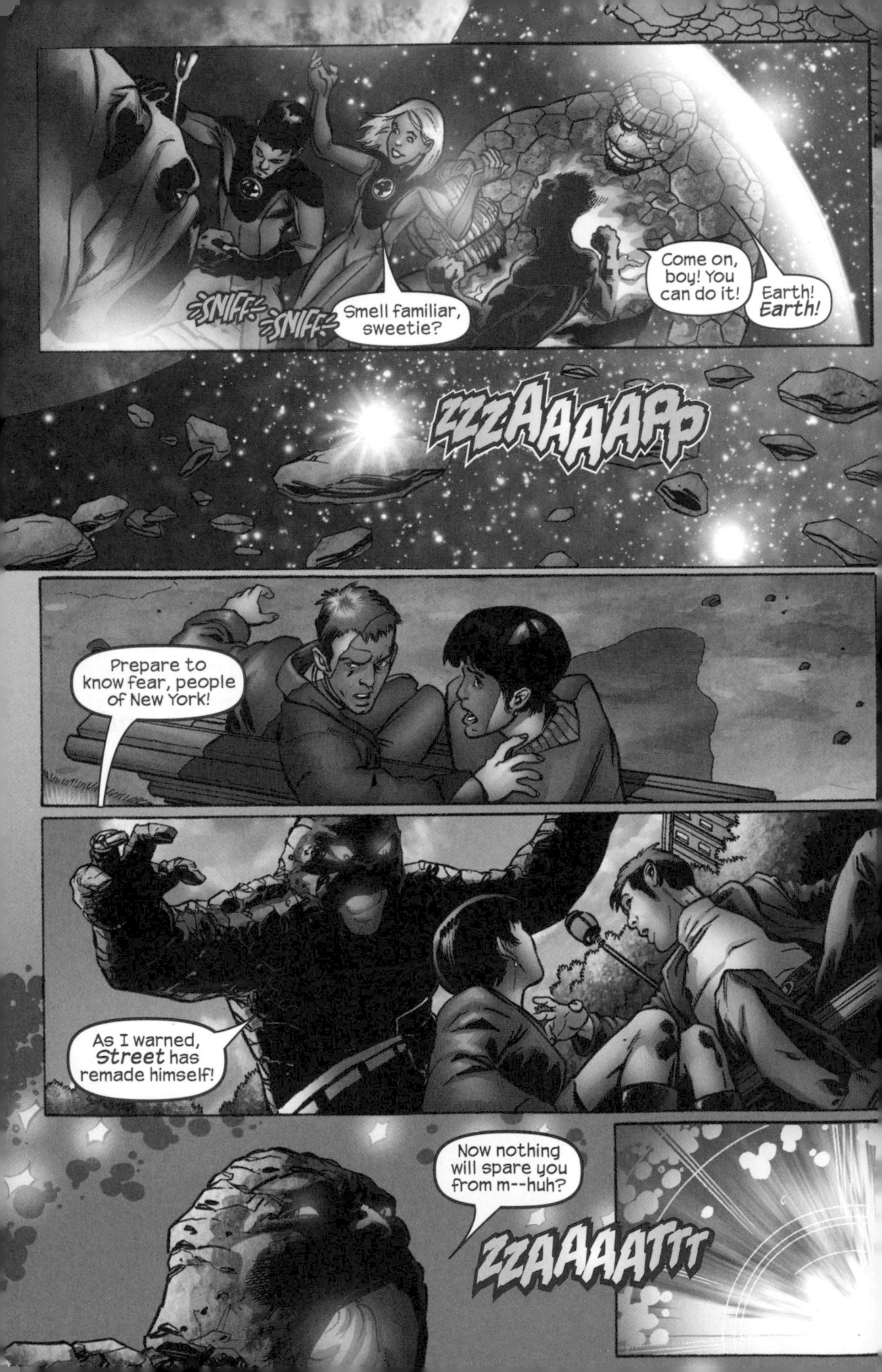

SNIFF SNIFF
Smell familiar, sweetie?
Come on, boy! You can do it!
Earth! Earth!
ZZZAAAAPP
Prepare to know fear, people of New York!
As I warned, Street has remade himself!
Now nothing will spare you from m--huh?
ZZAAAATTT

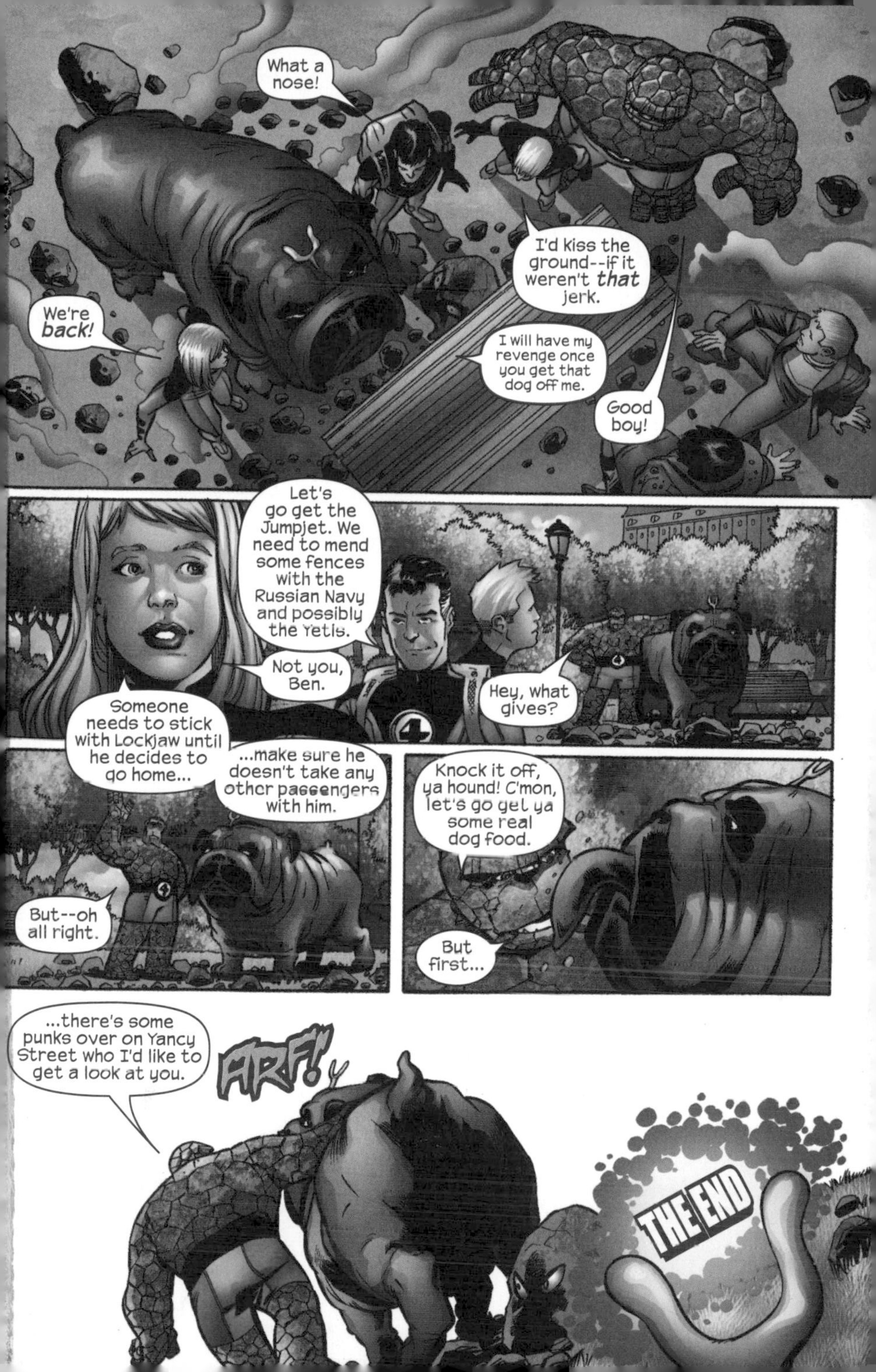
What a nose!
I'd kiss the ground--if it weren't *that* jerk.
We're *back!*
I will have my revenge once you get that dog off me.
Good boy!
Let's go get the Jumpjet. We need to mend some fences with the Russian Navy and possibly the Yetis.
Not you, Ben.
Hey, what gives?
Someone needs to stick with Lockjaw until he decides to go home...
...make sure he doesn't take any other passengers with him.
But--oh all right.
Knock it off, ya hound! C'mon, let's go get ya some real dog food.
But first...
...there's some punks over on Yancy Street who I'd like to get a look at you.
ARF!
THE END